GUTS & GLORY: WALKER

In the Shadows Security, Book 4

JEANNE ST. JAMES

Jeanne
ST. JAMES

———

Acknowledgements:

Photographer: FuriousFotog

Cover Artist: Golden Czermak at FuriousFotog

Cover Model: Brian Silvers

Editor: Proofreading by the Page

Beta readers: Whitley Cox, Andi Babcock, Sharon Abrams & Alexandra Swab

———

———

Keep an eye on her website at http://www.jeannestjames.com/or sign up for her newsletter to learn about her upcoming releases: http://www.jeannestjames.com/newslettersignup

Author Links: Instagram * Facebook * Goodreads Author Page * Newsletter * Jeanne's Review & Book Crew * BookBub * TikTok * YouTube

A Special Thanks

To Alexandra Swab for assisting me with Walker's blurb. Your help, as always, was invaluable!

Also, thank you to ALL my readers who belong to my readers' group:
https://www.facebook.com/groups/JeannesReviewCrew/
You all encourage me to keep writing! Love to you all!

Chapter One

WALKER STOOD outside the door and heard it.

He hated that apartment complex because the walls were so fucking thin. Anybody and everybody could hear what was going on behind them.

Which made it clear.

The woman he was banging was banging someone else.

He dropped his fist, deciding there was no reason to knock and instead turned, leaned back against the wall next to the door, cocked his leg and planted his boot on that wall. Then he crossed his arms over his chest and settled in to wait.

The Harley parked out front of Building C wasn't his, but that was his normal parking spot. Whoever was riding that bike was also riding the woman inside the apartment.

He wondered how long he'd have to wait.

Not too long, luckily.

Sami's familiar cries began to crescendo, a good indication she was about to come.

Or about to fake it.

She'd been known to do that, too. In fact, the second was more likely.

Sami was easy and convenient for when he needed to bust a nut. And it wasn't like they were exclusive or serious. They weren't. Or even that they cared about each other. They didn't.

Hell, they barely liked each other.

He'd come over, occasionally she'd feed his ass, they'd bang one out and when he was in the shitter getting rid of the condom, she'd steal a twenty from his wallet. Sometimes more.

Whatever.

Having his wallet lightened by a twenty was still fucking cheaper than having a wife or a girlfriend. They could financially break a man. He'd witnessed it and it was something he wanted to avoid.

What he couldn't avoid was hearing Sami's last high-pitched scream, which meant she was definitely faking it.

Walker twisted his wrist enough to see his watch and time the inevitable. He watched each minute tick by. He'd give it ten since that's how long it normally took him to bust and roll.

Ten...

Low voices were heard, though he couldn't make out words.

Nine...

The pipes in the walls squealed with the flush of the toilet.

Eight...

More low voices. One female. One male.

Seven...

A fake giggle. Typical Sami.

Six...

Walker rolled his eyes when he heard nothing, which meant Sami's guest was probably giving her a parting kiss and ready to split.

Five...

Footsteps heading his direction. *Yep.*

Four...

The pace getting quicker. Whoever it was wanted out of there.

Three...

More voices. The man throwing a last quick thanks over his shoulder and Sami inviting him to a "next time."

Walker snorted and shook his head.

Two...

The deadbolt being thrown. The door flying open.

One...

Game time.

"First time?"

The blond-haired man froze in the doorway, his eyes widening as he spotted Walker perched against the wall. The way the man was dressed and because his bike was still stock meant he wasn't a true biker, just a wannabe. Some weekend rider who wore a helmet and worked a nine-to-five. Got a bike to snag pussy. But he was a sucker and an easy mark for Sami.

"Check your wallet," he advised the wannabe, jerking up his chin.

As the man stared at him, his mouth opened and closed a couple of times, then he dug for his wallet in his... *yeah*... khakis.

"Fuck," Wannabe grumbled as he peered into his empty wallet. Walker doubted it was empty before the man walked through Sami's door. "She lifted a fifty."

Walker's lips curled at the corners. "Yep. Was she worth it?"

Wannabe's brow dropped low. "No. Maybe ten."

"Then I'd go back in there and get your change."

Wannabe glanced back over his shoulder. "Really?"

"Yeah," Walker said with a single nod. "Or go back in and get your money's worth."

3

Wannabe's eyebrows knitted together. "Are you her pimp?"

"Nope. Just passing through."

Sami appeared behind Wannabe in the open doorway. She finished tying the belt around her robe, then smoothed her hair down with her hand. She had sex hair and unless the sex sucked, it normally wasn't tamable with just combing her fingers through it. No, he liked to leave a woman's hair in knots.

Sami was able to straighten her hair with a few passes of her fingers, so the sex must have sucked.

Like he suspected, all that caterwauling had been fake. A way to get it over and done with quickly so she could slide into his wallet and out before the bathroom door was even shut.

"What are you doing here, Walker? I wasn't expecting you."

"Apparently," he murmured, letting his gaze roam over her from top to toe. He pushed off the wall. "You owe him some change. Or a real orgasm."

"What are you talking about?" Sami didn't bother to hide her outrage, as she pulled her robe belt tighter around her too narrow of a waist.

Walker wondered why his attention ever landed on her. She wasn't even his type. But then, he wasn't looking to put a ring on it. She was good for taking off the edge when he was still amped up over a job. Like tonight.

Ah, that's right. She had walked up to him at the local VFW, grabbed his dick, squeezed and whispered in his ear, "Want to fuck me?"

He'd turned on his stool at the bar, since his attention had been pulled from the Steelers game he'd been watching, took one look at her, and with a shrug, said, "Why the fuck not."

They went back to her apartment that night and fucked like rabbits.

Then she became a habit.

Now he was kicking that habit cold turkey.

He stepped closer to Wannabe, slapped him hard on the chest, almost knocking the guy back a step, and murmured a "good luck" before giving Sami a look over Wannabe's shoulder. "It's been real, honey."

He turned on his boot heel and strode down the hall to Sami screaming, "Walker! Walker! This didn't mean anything!"

No shit.

He ignored her and at the end of the hall, loped down the steps to the front door of the building, slammed the exit push bar and headed out into the late summer night.

———

WALKER LEANED his weight into one palm which was planted against the shower wall. His head tipped forward, the water from the shower soaking his hair and sliding down his back and chest.

He went through his Rolodex of women he used for jackoff material in his mind. Problem was, he always kept going back to one. An old memory. One he'd never forget. Not because he didn't want to, but because he couldn't. No matter how many women he'd been with for the past nineteen years, none could knock her off the top of the list.

Not one.

His fist tightened around the root of his cock, squeezed and he began to pump in earnest. Long steady strokes from root to tip.

The hot water continued to beat along his back, and he closed his eyes, his lips parting, inhaling the humid air from the shower, then releasing it.

He could've gone to the bar and found another woman to relieve his load since he wasn't in the mood for leftovers with Sami, but he didn't feel like making the effort of finding someone new.

The fake smiles, the fake laughs, the fake name and stories.

The questions. The made-up explanations.

Finding a woman to fuck for the night took work. He was tired, so his own hand would have to do.

He continued to stroke, closing his eyes, thinking back to soft thighs and soft sighs. A smile, a laugh. Green eyes sparkling. Auburn hair loose over the blanket he had spread out for them in the back of his truck.

Beautiful.

Nothing fake. All genuine.

What a lucky man he'd been.

His pace stuttered.

He hadn't been a man. He'd still been a boy.

Foolish.

But fucking in love.

Jesus fuck.

He needed to get out of the shower, find a porno with a little girl-on-girl action and just bang it out. This reliving history shit was fucking up his groove.

He shut the shower off with a curse and, balancing with one hand on the edge, leaned out of the stall to grab a towel. While he was wiping the water out of his eyes, he paused, tilted his head and listened.

His phone. Vibrating on the bathroom counter.

"Fuck," he muttered under his breath and wrapped the towel around his waist. He hopped out of the shower and made his way to the counter.

The vibrating stopped.

He shifted closer to the sink and snagged it.

UNKNOWN CALLER.

It was almost ten p.m.

He saw he'd missed several calls, but no voicemails had been left.

The phone started vibrating in his hand. Once again, an unknown caller. Something he normally didn't answer.

But it was late. And he wouldn't put it past one of his fellow Shadows to call him from a burner phone.

He swiped the screen and barked, "Yeah," into the phone.

"Trace?"

That name brought a head jerk and a frown. He had no idea why someone would be looking for Trace. The hairs on the back of his neck prickled.

"Trace?" A female voice. Quiet, but thick with worry.

He had no fucking clue who it was. "Got the wrong number."

A pause. A shaky intake of breath.

His spine stiffened and every muscle locked.

"I'm looking for Trace."

No shit. "There's nobody here by that name."

"Please, Trace, don't shut me out."

He glanced up from where he'd been staring at the water dripping onto the floor. He caught his reflection in the mirror. Walker stared at the man staring back at him.

He hadn't seen Trace in a long fucking time.

He also had no idea why someone would be looking for him.

There was no reason. None what-so-fucking-ever.

"How'd you get this number?"

"Your sister."

His blood ran cold when it hit him. Who it was. Why she was asking for Trace.

Nineteen years instantly disappeared. The object of his masturbation fodder was talking into his ear.

"I'm sorry. You're probably not happy about me doing that. But I had no choice."

"We all have choices, Ellie. You made a choice years ago."

"You're right, I did. And I made another difficult choice by contacting your sister, begging her to give me your number. I made an even more difficult one by calling you. But I had no choice," she repeated more firmly. Whatever was in her voice was no longer trepidation, but determination and a touch of stubbornness.

"I'm assuming you're between a rock and a hard place right now and you need me to be the crowbar. But if it wasn't for whatever you're involved in, you wouldn't have ever reached out."

"With... With everything that happened.... I assumed you didn't want me to."

"I didn't. Still don't. I should hang the fuck up." He should, but he wouldn't. He couldn't wait to find out why Ellie Cooke was calling him.

No, that wasn't right. It was Ellie McMaster since she married one of the rich motherfucking McMasters. A man who could give her way more than Walker ever could.

"No! Please... don't hang up. Please." The determination was now gone, replaced with desperation.

He set his jaw. "Why the fuck are you calling me, Ellie?"

"I hear you do... jobs."

Jobs.

"Whatever the *job* is, Ellie, have your husband handle it."

"I... I don't have a husband."

Walker stilled. "You leave him, too?"

"In a way, he left me," she whispered.

"Hurt, did it?"

"I—"

"Bye, Ellie." He pulled the phone from his ear and swiped his finger across the screen, cutting off her plea.

Chapter Two

HOPELESS.

Totally hopeless.

She didn't know what to do.

She had nowhere to turn. No one to help her.

George's family wanted nothing to do with her. Refused to help her, even though it was their son who caused the problem in the first place.

Ellie paced the small motel room. She had finally sold her wedding ring yesterday and only received fifteen hundred for it. But it was fifteen hundred more than what she had.

Unfortunately, that would only last so long. Then she'd be flat broke again with nothing but two suitcases full of clothes.

She didn't even have a car.

She'd had thirty days to pay the 1.3 million dollars. But now most of that time was gone. And if she didn't pay? She'd end up like George.

Not only dying but doing it horribly at the hands of some bad men. They said they tortured him. They didn't have to tell her. She knew.

They had texted her the pictures.

The proof.

The motivation to find a way. Any way to get them their money.

1.3 million was a lot to come up with in a lifetime, forget a month. She did her best, but it wasn't good enough.

And now that clock ticking was like a noose around her neck, getting tighter by the day.

She'd gone through all the scenarios in her head, how she could turn her last fifteen hundred into what she needed. Besides a lucky break with the lottery or at a casino, she had no way.

Her only hope had been Trace Walker.

Now, she was...

Hopeless.

Her desperation almost had her calling him back immediately. She wasn't above begging.

She'd never been one to simply give up. Though, he might think otherwise.

She had given up on him.

All those years ago.

The biggest mistake of her life. Next to marrying George.

She was surprised his sister Crissy had even given her Trace's phone number. But she did so reluctantly and then hung up on her, too.

Ellie stopped in front of the bed and stared at the phone in her hand.

She couldn't give up.

She closed her eyes, filled her lungs, then blew it all out until she was empty. Then she ate her pride. Her fingers flew over the tiny keyboard as she wrote Trace a text. *Do you know anyone who can help me disappear? I have $1500 to pay them.*

Her heart thumped in her chest as she waited.

And waited.

And after a while, she sank to the floor, pulled her knees to her chest and buried her face against them.

She could do this. She just needed to think of a solution.

Her phone rang, startling her. She looked at the screen.

BLOCKED CALLER.

It could be them. The men George owed money to.

"Shit," she whispered, her finger trembling as it hovered over the screen.

It stopped ringing and a text came through, making her jump. *It's Walker. Answer.*

The phone immediately rang again, the number coming up blocked once more. Weird.

She answered it but said nothing.

"Where are you?" came the low growl through the speaker.

"In a motel."

"Where?"

"Outside of Denver."

Nothing. Silence. Not even breathing.

Until... "Is that where you lived with him?"

Him. "Yes."

"You by yourself?"

She opened her mouth to answer but before she could, he barked into the phone, "You by yourself?"

She flinched. "Yes."

"Where are your kids?"

Ellie dropped her forehead back to her knees and took a shuddered breath. "I don't have any."

More silence. But even so, that silence was thick with tension.

She didn't want to admit that to him, but she had no choice.

She needed help.

She needed him.

He was her only lifeline at this point.

She had to give him what he asked for.

"Text me the info I'll need for your plane ticket, then get your ass to the Denver airport first thing tomorrow morning. I'll text you your boarding pass info. You get on that fucking plane, Ellie, and you get here. If you want help for whatever reason you need help, then you need to listen. Do you hear me?"

"Yes."

"Someone will pick you up when you arrive at the airport."

"Which airport?"

The call was cut off.

———

ELLIE STOOD by the luggage carousel watching the metal belt move in a continuous loop.

One by one, passengers from her connecting flight in Chicago to her destination in Pittsburgh, of all places, grabbed their bags and headed wherever they were heading to.

Ellie had no idea where she was heading besides where she was currently standing.

Until she felt a dark presence behind her.

She turned her head to glance over her shoulder and bit back a gasp. The man behind her was big. And intimidating. Scary, even.

The scariest part wasn't even the fact he had a long scar diagonally cutting his face in half.

Had those men tracked her down?

"Ellie McMaster." He wasn't asking a question.

Ellie's eyes slid to the side looking for the nearest airport security guard.

"You're Ellie McMaster."

Her eyes bounced back up to his face. His eyes were silver, cold. His face expressionless.

"Who are you?"

"Mercy."

Mercy?

"Walker sent me."

Some of her muscles loosened and she spotted her two bags circling again. Before she could grab them, Mercy did.

"Let's go." He turned and began to walk with long strides toward the exit, carrying her heavy bags instead of rolling them like a normal person.

Just outside the doors, he went to a huge beast of a vehicle that looked like something out of a dystopian movie. *Mad Max* or something.

He opened the back of the... whatever it was... and threw her bags inside, then moved around to the driver's door while she still stood just outside the revolving glass doors, unsure what to do.

"Let's go!" he yelled over the hood of his... beast.

That got her moving.

She opened the door, which was heavy as all get out, and scrambled into the passenger seat. Barely. Just as she was closing the passenger door, he took off.

"I need to put my seatbelt on," she insisted, searching for it as he took the curves around the airport faster than he should.

He said nothing.

"Do you know Trace?"

Silver eyes landed on her, something flashed behind them, then quickly disappeared. "Better fucking hope so, or you just got into a vehicle with someone you shouldn't have."

That still might be true.

They were out of the airport loop lickety-split. He

turned onto some highway heading... the compass in the vehicle said south.

A phone rang. He grabbed it from the dashboard and put it to his ear.

Ellie blinked in surprise as Mercy totally transformed into a warm-blooded man from an ice-crusted robot.

"Hey," he said softly.

Ellie raised a brow, but the man ignored her.

"Yeah... Warehouse," he continued in a voice which he had not used with Ellie. "Got it. Yeah. Same." Then he threw the phone back onto the dashboard.

"You should be using hands-free—"

The look he shot her made her swallow the rest of her words.

She stared straight out of the windshield for the next half hour or so until they pulled up behind a huge warehouse. The parking lot had an interesting mix of motorcycles and expensive-looking vehicles.

She glanced around. "Where are we?"

"Here."

Obviously.

She sighed as he got out and slammed the driver's door, striding toward the back door in the plain gray metal warehouse. It was nondescript. No sign. No windows. Nothing to indicate what it was.

She knew Trace worked for an outfit called In the Shadows Security and this business did a variety of jobs. That's why she contacted him directly.

Personal protection was one of them. Investigative work another.

But besides that, she didn't know much more about it. Could this be their headquarters?

"Let's go!" she heard bellowed from outside the vehicle.

So, she went.

WALKER LEANED back against the wall, his eyes closed, listening.

"Ain't a fuckin' charity," he heard his boss bellow. "Got fuckin' bills to pay an' kids to feed."

"Might wanna slow down on pumpin' out those kids, D," Walker heard Ryder bust their boss's balls.

Silence. Which, in Diesel's case, could be deadly.

"I've got fifteen hundred dollars," came a female voice. "I just need to disappear."

"Can make you go ghost for less than that. Just won't be breathin' afterward," Diesel grumbled.

That was Walker's cue to move into the room. He'd been avoiding it as long as possible, but D was getting crankier by the minute. He didn't like any of them doing jobs for free.

They all had skills he charged a fuck-ton of money for from his clients. Fifteen hundred wouldn't even begin to get his team scratching their balls.

Walker had a feeling, depending on what Ellie's malfunction was, he'd be taking this job up the ass.

Diesel wasn't the only one who had fucking bills to pay. Especially since Walker had a large rancher built in the DAMC compound recently.

No matter how grumpy the boss man was, working for him beat being in the military. Especially since he hadn't been shot at in a long fucking time. In fact, the last time was when Diesel got winged by that fucknut, the now dead biker Black Jack.

Walker smirked, thinking about his boss's minor "scratch."

His grin flattened when he heard Ellie ask, "Where's Trace?"

Fuck.

He pushed off the wall and strode the few steps down the hallway to the new "interrogation/meeting room" D had built since his office was now jammed with playpens, toys and girlie shit, and so they were unable to meet in there anymore.

He stopped short of the edge of the doorway, where he could see Ellie sitting at the end of the long table, but she couldn't see him in the dark hallway.

Something twisted deep inside him as he took her in.

It had been nineteen years.

Nineteen fucking years and she looked the fucking same.

Maybe a little more filled out from what he could see since she was sitting down. A little more mature in the face. But everything else...

Her long, deep reddish-brown hair, what she called auburn, was pulled into a messy ponytail, her bright green eyes were unmistakable even from where he stood. Her lips...

He had them. In a few different ways.

They had also parted with laughter, with sighs, with gasps, and groans. They had said his name. *Fuck*, had they said his name.

What came out of them had also broken his mother-fucking heart.

For fuck's sake, simply sitting there, even unaware he was watching her, she might as well have jammed a knife in his chest and turned it.

"Brother," Steel said quietly behind him.

Walker glanced over his shoulder and Steel jerked up his chin. "She yours?"

"Was," he admitted. "A long fucking time ago."

Walker waited for his fellow Shadow to say something smartass. Strangely, he didn't, instead just muttered, "Damn," under his breath. "Know why she's here?"

Walker simply shook his head.

Steel clapped his hand on his shoulder and said, "Let's go fucking find out."

His teammate pressed past him and Walker knew he couldn't put it off anymore. Like a lot of things in life, he just needed to push past the pain.

When he stepped into the room, he realized he was the last one to arrive.

Diesel was scowling as he stood to one side of the table with his legs spread, his heavily tattooed arms crossed over his massive chest. His ol' lady's nickname for him, The Beast, couldn't be more fitting.

Steel had jerked a seat out near where Diesel stood and had settled into it and was eyeing up Ellie as if determining if she was a threat.

Brick leaned back against one wall, pretending to be on his phone, when Walker knew he was also eyeballing Ellie, but not in the same way Steel was. Walker began to bristle, but he quickly tamped that shit back down.

Brick would fuck anything that walked, talked and didn't have a hairy set of balls hanging between its legs.

However, Ellie wasn't Walker's. She hadn't been his in a very long time. She'd been someone else's for almost that same amount of time.

Ryder sat in another seat, his eyes on Walker, almost as if he was waiting for a reaction. Because of that, Walker made sure to keep his expression neutral.

Hunter leaned against the wall behind Ellie, his eyes also glued to Walker as soon as he'd stepped into the room.

Walker dropped his gaze to Ellie from Hunter's smirk and slight chin lift.

His nostrils flared to temper the burn bubbling up from his gut.

"Trace," Ellie whispered, starting to rise to her feet.

"Sit down," he barked at her, keeping his voice cold. Unwelcoming.

Regret filled her face and she sank back into her chair, tucking her hands into her lap and turning her eyes downward to stare at the table.

He felt everyone's eyes on him, except for hers.

Yeah, he might have just screwed the pooch by not keeping his emotions on a short leash.

He ignored everyone else and looked at his boss. "She tell you why she's here?"

"Needs to go ghost," was his answer.

"Heard that part. Why?"

D lifted and dropped his heavy shoulders. "No fuckin' clue. Was waitin' on you."

"Well, I'm fucking here now." He reluctantly let his gaze land on Ellie again. "So, spill it."

Mercy lifted his hand, stopping Ellie from speaking, his silver eyes wary. The man, like Diesel, didn't miss a fucking thing. Two peas in a motherfucking pod. "You two got history?"

"Ancient," Walker answered.

"Want to do this on your own and catch us up after?" Mercy asked.

"Nope. Don't want to be alone with her."

Brick let out a long, low whistle, and shook his head with it still bent to his phone. Walker ignored him.

"Brother, you need to take a minute and think about that?" Ryder asked, his brow furrowed.

"Nothing to think about."

Ryder raised his eyebrows, glanced around the room and shrugged.

"Guess it's time for you to start talkin'," D told Ellie.

Ellie also let her gaze circle the room before it came back to Walker. Their eyes met and he pressed his lips flat and gritted his teeth.

She was here on business. That was it. He should've asked her what business before paying for her fucking plane ticket and having her show up in Shadow Valley. But then, he hadn't wanted to be on the phone with her long enough to find out.

Whatever it was, they'd see if they could deal with it and then he'd be shot of her ass.

Again.

Chapter Three

It wasn't a chill coming from Trace. It was the deep burning heat of anger. Maybe even hatred. So hot, it scorched Ellie's skin. It left her with no doubt how he felt about her. She didn't blame him, but she needed him to put that aside. If only temporarily.

Once they helped her find a solution, she'd be glad to leave him alone.

From what she'd heard, they were good... his team one of the best. And when she heard Trace Walker was part of that team...

She had pictured In the Shadows Security in an office building, with a crew of men who looked like security guards. She hadn't been prepared to be surrounded by men who looked... badass. Even dangerous.

None of them open, warm or friendly.

They were all business.

And her having "ancient history" with Trace made the room temperature drop a few degrees cooler when he mentioned it.

All except for the man who still stood by the door as if

ready to bolt, his gaze searing her, shredding her from the inside out.

"Maybe we should talk alone," she suggested softly to the table.

"No," was his curt answer.

She squeezed her eyes shut for a moment, opened them, put her palms flat on the table, her fingers spread wide and she nodded. That's when she noticed the indentation circling her left ring finger which remained from her wedding band. She quickly curled her hands into fists and put them back in her lap.

She took a deep breath, lifted her chin and began. "George—" A sharp noise interrupted her from the direction of the door. She took another deep breath and started again. "George owned an investment company."

"His family did," Trace muttered from across the room.

"Yes. His grandfather started it, his father continued the business and expanded it and eventually George opened a branch out in Denver."

"Long way from home," Trace said under his breath.

"I now know why," she confessed.

"Why?" the very handsome man leaning against the wall to her right asked. He'd been introduced as Brick. Weird name, but that wasn't her business.

"To be out from under his father's thumb. So he could do things in a way... He could do things his father wouldn't be aware of."

"He was crooked," the man sitting at the table and chewing on a toothpick, stated. Steel. Another odd name, though that one could conceivably be a last name.

"Not at first. At least, I don't think so. I think it started as bad deals and investments gone wrong. Then things began to avalanche."

"So, you're sayin' he was a good guy?" the man introduced as Ryder asked. She detected a very slight southern accent and he wore a baseball cap low over his eyes, hiding them.

"He was." Another sharp noise came from the doorway. Ellie ignored it and continued, "Or I thought he was. I'm not sure what happened. Why he changed."

Mercy stated in an icy tone, "Green and greed will do it to you."

And that was true.

"'But they that will be rich fall into temptation and a snare, and into many foolish and hurtful lusts, which drown men in destruction and perdition,'" the man called Hunter recited.

She wasn't a religious person, but she recognized the quote. "I can attest to that," Ellie whispered. "Just when you think you know someone well, you find out you don't know them at all."

"Ain't that the fucking truth."

Ellie lifted her eyes to Trace. Now his were trying to burn a hole right through her. Maybe contacting him was a bad idea. She should've found someone else.

But it was too late. She was here. And she was running out of time.

"I'm not sure why he kept getting into bad deal after bad deal." Apparently, George didn't have the same business sense as his father or grandfather.

Trace, who'd been leaning with one shoulder against the door frame, now straightened. "He had money."

"He did." Until he spent it all. On what? Ellie didn't know. He loved to live large, impress people. But even so...

"So, the family money dried up."

Ellie nodded at Trace's words. "Not only his trust fund, but everything dried up and became a bottomless pit he couldn't climb his way out of."

"But you stayed with him." Those words held a sharp

edge. And glancing around the room, she realized she wasn't the only one who heard it.

"He was good at covering it for a while. When I started getting suspicious, he began to blame me, saying I had expensive tastes. I didn't. I never cared about his money. I never cared about things like boats, jewelry or vacation homes. I wanted to settle down and raise a family."

A sharp intake of breath had her pause.

HER WORDS MADE Walker want to shake the shit out of her. *He* wanted to give her all of that. *She* didn't let him. "Then why were you with him?"

"Is that what you thought of me? I was only with him for his money? He was kind, handsome, well-spoken and I thought responsible. You knew him, Trace."

Fuck, she needed to stop calling him that.

And yes, for fuck's sake, he knew McMaster. They all grew up in the same town. Of course, he knew the fucker. Who the hell didn't know the goddamn McMasters? The McMasters who lived in the largest home in town, who drove the most expensive cars and sent their spoiled son to private school because the public school wasn't good enough.

"You didn't know he was broke?" Brick sounded suspicious of her. He wasn't the only one.

"No, not at first."

Walker needed to get her back on track so they could get the fuck out of that room. "How much does he owe? I assume that's why you're here. You're in a jam because your hubby owes a boatload of scratch. Am I right?"

"Yes."

Of course, he was.

"I don't know the true extent of how many people he

owes. But I gave the person who contacted me everything I could, and that debt still remains at 1.3 million."

The room froze, went dead silent. Not one person breathed until Diesel barked out a loud, "Fuck!"

D said what they were all thinking.

One.

Point.

Three.

Fucking.

Million.

Jesus fuck.

He covered his shock by asking, "And you need my... *our* help because..."

"They want the money."

No shit.

"I don't have it."

Apparently.

"I have nothing, Trace. I have absolutely nothing left."

"Get your fucking husband to pay it. He's the one who got himself in that fucking jam."

Her tone was flat when she admitted, "I can't."

"He disappear on you?" Steel asked.

"He's... He's dead. They killed him."

Ice slithered through Walker's veins. When she said that, Walker didn't miss everyone in that room go on high alert, every muscle tense.

"They gave me thirty days to pay the balance. But now time is running out and I only have fifteen hundred dollars to my name. This is even after I sold our home, the Lake Tahoe house, our cars, his boat..."

Lake Tahoe house. Boat. *For fuck's sake.* "Did you sell his fucking golf clubs, too?"

A flush rose up her neck into her cheeks. "Yes, I've sold everything. All I have left is my pride and I'm willing to sell that, too."

25

"By coming to me," Walker murmured.

"By coming to you."

"Go to his family." None of this was his problem. This was the McMasters' problem. Ellie had decided to tie her star to them, now she had to deal with the fallout.

"I did. But they disowned him. I found out his father had bailed him out a couple of times, but he eventually put his foot down. He wants... *wanted* nothing to do with George after that. Now, they want nothing to do with me."

Assholes. McMaster's son left Ellie spinning in the wind and the old bastard wouldn't even help her.

"Did they know you didn't have anything to do with it?"

"They didn't care. And I don't know what George told his father. But they never liked me, anyway. They only tolerated me to an extent."

That got Walker's attention. "Why?"

"Because I didn't come from the same 'caliber' of bloodlines as they did. I wasn't good enough for George, even though George loved me and told them that. And..."

Fuck, did he even want to know the rest? "And?"

"And I didn't give them grandchildren."

A sharp pain shot through Walker's temple. He pushed off the door frame and took a step deeper into the room. "You don't need me, Ellie. You need a bank."

Her wide green eyes hit him, and he felt that to his very toes. "No one will loan me that kind of money. No one would loan George that kind of money, that's what got him into this mess in the first place."

"No. Greed and living way above his means got him into that mess," Hunter said behind her.

If that's what it was. He might have been doing questionable business deals that Ellie didn't know about for a very long time. Deals like that, when they've gone wrong could go very wrong. And then a man can get desperate, making even sketchier deals to try to pull himself clear from the last one. And then it snowballed...

"Said they snuffed him. Who the fuck are 'they?'" Diesel finally spoke up, not looking any kind of happy about this whole situation. Not that he ever looked happy. Walker guessed the only time the man was happy was when he was holding his baby girls or fucking his ol' lady, making the next one.

Walker's gaze flicked from his boss back to Ellie as she answered, "I don't know."

"But they contacted you." Brick took the words right out of Walker's mouth.

"Yes. From a blocked number. They must have gotten mine from George's phone."

"They call or text?" Walker asked.

"Both. They called to demand payment, tell me how long I had before they did to me what they did to George if I couldn't pay them. They said they'd be in touch closer to the time, but now they're texting me every day with a countdown."

"What'd they do to your husband?"

Walker ground his molars at Steel calling McMaster Ellie's husband. And, fuck him, Steel's eyes were on him when he did it. He wore a slight smirk after seeing Walker's reaction.

But his smirk was quickly wiped away when Ellie took out her phone, pulled up a picture and slid it across the table to him.

"Fuck," Steel grumbled. He swiped through a few photos, his gaze slid around the room, then held the phone out. Diesel snagged it next, said nothing as he flipped through the photos, then handed it off to Ryder.

Ryder grimaced as he looked at the phone before handing it to Hunter.

Eventually it ended up in Walker's hands. He set his jaw and looked at it.

Jesus fucking Christ.

The photos were bad enough to bring bile up on any normal human being. And he wondered how Ellie could even stomach looking at them. Especially since she not only had been married to the man but loved him.

His eyes lifted from the phone and landed on her.

Right now, she was pretty fucking calm. She could be wailing, shaking, breaking down. She wasn't.

This shit was way more serious than Walker could have ever guessed. But she was holding herself together. She was a lot stronger than he remembered her being. Had she lost that softness he'd loved so much? Was the Ellie he knew all those years ago gone?

Walker went back to the pictures and pulled up the metadata on one of them. They were dated only a little over three weeks earlier.

She lost her husband less than a month ago. She should be more upset about it than she was.

"You don't seem to be the grieving widow, Ellie," Walker said, watching her carefully.

Her chin lifted. Just slightly. Enough for him to catch it. And he also caught the straightening of her spine.

Oh yeah. His soft, sweet Ellie was fucking gone.

That motherfucker McMaster did that to her. Stole that from him.

Too bad the bastard was already fucking dead.

"Once I got wind of the dark path he was traveling, how he was bleeding our accounts dry and wouldn't explain why, I left. He was not the man I knew. He was not the man I wanted to remain with."

His nostrils flared. *Hell,* Walker was no longer the man Ellie knew, either.

They had all changed.

Steel, his dark eyes glued to Walker, asked, "How long ago was that?"

"About a year and a half ago."

"Then how'd you sell all his shit to pay back some of the debt?" Mercy asked, his eyes narrowed.

"Our divorce wasn't final since he was fighting it. We were separated, but legally still married."

Mercy posed the next question, one probably all of them wanted an answer to. "How'd you sell shit so quickly?"

"George was already in the process of selling everything. And I had already signed off on anything owned jointly just to get myself free. He had brokers getting the paperwork ready for the houses and the boat. The cars I took to the nearest dealership."

"Where'd the money go?" Mercy asked.

"I had the brokers deposit it all into an account number they provided."

From behind her, Hunter asked, "An account in the Caymans?"

Ellie shook her head. "I have no idea. I was hoping they would extend the time I had to get the rest, but they didn't. Not that it mattered, I have no idea how to get the remainder, anyway."

"So, why the fuck you here? We're not a fuckin' bank or a fuckin' charity," Diesel barked.

"I don't know what to do and I was warned not to get the police involved," Ellie whispered, her bottom lip trembling. Proving his soft, sweet Ellie was in there somewhere. Maybe McMotherfucker hadn't destroyed her totally.

Fuck. That slight lip tremor would be the fucking death of him.

He shook off its effect. He needed to keep his head on straight.

Walker let his thoughts settle. He needed to get them off Ellie and onto her situation instead. This was serious shit.

These men, whoever they were, were no fucking joke. They wanted to do to Ellie what they did to McMaster. And what they did to McMaster was something Mercy could and would do.

It was that cold. That merciless.

"Where'd they find the body?" slipped from his lips before he could stop it.

Ellie, who'd been biting her lower lip, probably to keep it from trembling, released it. "I don't know."

"He hasn't been found?" Walker shouldn't be surprised. Whoever killed McMaster was a professional. Or at least hired professionals. This wasn't some street corner thug.

She shook her head. "Not that I'm aware of."

"No death certificate without a body," he murmured.

"No body, he'll be assumed missing, not dead," Mercy stated.

Steel added, "Won't be a widow until there's a body."

Mercy continued to no one in particular, "You saw those fucking pictures. There's not going to be a body."

Steel had his eyes on Walker when he said, "She's going to have to wait years to be clear of him."

"Most likely seven," Brick said next to him, his eyes also on Walker.

"That fuckin' sucks," Ryder said. "She was tryin' to get shot of him and now she can't."

They were talking as if Ellie wasn't even there. Her husband of however many years was now simply reduced to a "body." Probably not even that after they were done with him. Walker could only imagine.

"Once a-fuckin'-gain," Diesel growled, "ain't a fuckin' bank or charity."

Ellie turned her green eyes to D. "Can't you just help me disappear? Then none of this would matter."

"Going ghost would be the easiest solution," Brick agreed.

A solution that was suddenly bothering the fuck out of Walker.

Ellie Cooke walked out of his life after he joined the Army. Now nineteen years later she had walked back in as Ellie McMaster. Was he willing to let her disappear again?

He studied her.

"I know I have no right to ask anything from you, Trace—"

He cut her off. "You're right. You don't. The name's Walker, not Trace." Trace disappeared the same day Ellie Cooke did.

"Sorry."

That one word was heavy with more than just an apology about calling him the wrong name. It also held nineteen years' worth of apologies.

But fuck if he would tell her it was "okay." Because nothing was okay. Not what she did back then. Not her situation now.

And how he was feeling about her being there in Shadow Valley without a husband was definitely not fucking okay.

No, it was dangerous. For her. For him.

He couldn't let this whole thing rattle him. Especially in front of his brothers. Or his boss.

"Ghosting her might not be the solution. Neutralizing the threat would be," he said.

"This shit may be bigger than we can handle," Brick warned.

"An' the fuck if fifteen fucking hundred's gonna cover it," Diesel grumbled.

"We don't know if it's mafia, a cartel, or what... This could be a vast network of organized crime he got involved in. What they did to him was no amateur shit," Mercy said.

Mercy should know.

"Or it could be someone with deep pockets and a bit of clout who lent the fucker money," Walker threw out there.

"Sounds like a lotta motherfuckin' hours to find out," Diesel griped.

"Don't mind helping on my down time," Hunter offered.

"Me neither," Ryder added.

"Yeah," Brick said. "I need a good reason to blow the dust out of my MK-11."

"Oh, you didn't fuck it last night? Did you two have a spat?" Steel asked, then announced, "I'm in."

Walker's eyes hit Mercy's silver ones. The taller man jerked his chin up ever so slightly.

Yeah, his brothers had his six.

"Fuck you all," Diesel grunted.

That got grins all around the room. Until Walker asked Hunter, "What are we going to need to start the hunt?"

"You still got that account number?" Hunter asked Ellie.

She glanced back over her shoulder at him. "Yes, they texted it to me. It's the same number they want me to deposit the rest of the money."

"Will need that. Access to your husband's business records, his personal accounts and your joint accounts. The names of any brokers he was working with. Probably good you never got divorced. It'll make getting access easier."

"Did he gamble? Have a drug problem?" Ryder asked.

"Not that I'm aware of."

"Side bitches?"

Ellie's mouth dropped open at D's question.

Steel stepped in quickly. "How 'bout close friends, male or *female*, he'd confess his sins to?"

"I don't know."

"What the fuck *do* you know?" Diesel bellowed, making her wince.

Her head snapped up, her shoulders pulled back and her

eyes narrowed. "I know whatever George was into, he kept me out of it. I never expected my marriage to deteriorate like it did."

"Then why didn't you have kids with him?" Walker asked quietly. "When things were good."

Her green eyes widened when they landed on him, but she quickly hid her reaction.

"That's what you wanted. That's what you were chasing after. A family. Why didn't you have it with him?"

Ellie sat stiffly in her chair, her fingers curled into fists on top of the table. Her throat worked a couple of times, but she said nothing.

When she finally did, her voice was thick, raw and full of pain. "Just help me disappear. I don't need anything else from you."

"We need to get a good handle on what the fuck's going on before we make any plans," Mercy stepped in, his silver eyes sliding from Walker to Ellie. "That's gonna take a bit of time. When did the thirty days start?"

"Three weeks ago."

Mercy nodded. "Got over a week left, right? Plenty of time."

A week didn't feel like enough. Not when they had nothing to go on except some pictures of a dead man and an account number.

"Unless they get impatient," Steel murmured.

"They'd be stupid to rush it. They want their money, not bodies. Making bodies costs money. It's a lose-lose situation for them financially. If they think she can scrounge the cash, they're gonna give her that time," Mercy stated.

"We've dealt with some stupid fucks, Mercy," Brick reminded him.

"Those pictures and what I assume is an offshore account proves they know what the fuck they're doing."

Unfortunately, that was true.

"So, what do I do in the meantime? While you guys 'get a handle' on it? I've got nowhere to go. Only $1500 left. No vehicle. My life's been reduced to two suitcases."

Walker could hear the emotion welling up. He needed to shut that down. "Someone will get you to a motel 'til we figure this shit all out."

He did not miss Brick pursing his lips. He didn't miss Ryder dropping his head, suddenly finding his boots of interest. He certainly didn't miss Mercy raising his eyes to the ceiling. Or Hunter's snort. Or even Diesel's loud grunt-cough.

Nope, he didn't miss any of that.

And he absolutely couldn't miss Steel saying, "Got a couple extra rooms in your house, brother. No safer place for her to wait than the compound."

"Don't wanna bring trouble there, but agree with asshole. She don't got scratch to live for the next week since I'm takin' that fifteen," D concluded. "Better than fuckin' nothin'."

"But... I can't stay with you," she whispered, panic crossing her face.

Walker couldn't agree more, even so... "Got a credit card to charge your room, food, everything else?"

For fuck's sake, say yes.

Her face dropped. "No. Our credit was maxed out."

Fuck. Fuck. Fuck.

He'd be so fucked if he let her into his house. He gritted his teeth, then forced out, "Give D your fifteen hundred, Ellie."

"Fuck me," D grunted, shaking his head because once D took the cash, the deal was set, they were taking her case.

Walker glared at his boss across the room. "You want the fucking money?" he yelled at D.

D shot him a scowl. "Yeah."

"Give it to him," Walker ordered Ellie.

34

With one last look at him, she leaned over, grabbed the purse sitting on the floor by her feet, put it on the table and dug out her wallet.

Walker noticed the purse and the wallet were some fancy brand name. Probably cost a small fortune.

He never took her for that type of woman. She'd always been down-to-earth. Happy with the basic necessities in life. Like he had been. Things had certainly changed.

She pulled fifteen crisp Benjamins out of that brown leather wallet and placed them on the table. She stared at the small, neat pile for a few seconds, then slid it toward where Diesel stood. Steel snagged the money and handed it over his shoulder to their boss.

"Fuck me," Diesel grunted again. He grabbed the cash in his fist and lumbered out of the room, not showing any kind of pleased, even though he just took her last dollar.

That amount of money was nothing to D. Not for what this job would entail. Walker knew he'd be doing most of it *pro bono*. And so would his brothers since they were willing to help and didn't mind not getting compensated for their time. But they had their limits.

They all did.

Once D was out of the room, Ellie said softly, "Now, I have nothing."

Fucking goddamn it.

Walker sucked in a breath at the worry in her voice. He mentally kicked himself as the words left his mouth, "You've got me."

Chapter Four

ELLIE'S STOMACH churned the whole ten-minute ride from the warehouse to Trace's house.

Walker.

Whatever.

She didn't know what to think, what to say to his last declaration, "You've got me."

Instead, she said nothing during the short trip, in which he drove insanely fast. As if he couldn't wait for it to be over. Like he couldn't stand being in such close quarters with her.

When they'd stepped out into the parking lot of the warehouse, her bags were sitting next to a matte black Dodge that looked and sounded "growly." That was the only way she could describe it. When he opened the trunk and threw her bags in there, she noticed it said Charger SRT on the back. The Pennsylvania license plate was also personalized with "HELLCAT." Whatever that meant.

It had black wheels, smoked windows, black trim. It oozed "badass." Like Trace.

Shit, Walker.

He'd been the bad boy in the little town they grew up in outside of Ithaca, New York and every girl panted over him.

Even though she was younger than him, it was Ellie who got him.

Then she gave him up.

Probably the biggest mistake of her life. One she lived with for years. One she still lived with.

Trace hit a button on the bottom of his rearview mirror and a long metal gate split in two when it opened. The gate had a big emblem in the center. The same emblem she noticed on the back of Diesel's black leather vest.

Trace drove through, hit the button again and stopped, waiting for the gate to close behind them. After it did, he jammed his foot on the accelerator again, throwing her back into her seat.

Whatever "compound" he lived in was surrounded by concrete walls and looked, for the most part, secure. The houses appeared newer and large; the lots even larger. From what she saw of the neighborhood, there was still a lot of space to grow. Some streets had more houses than others.

He took a few turns and entered a very large cul-de-sac with three sprawling ranchers that took up most of their pie-shaped lots. They were gorgeous with large windows, stone fronts, three car garages, well landscaped and maintained.

Plenty big enough, unlike the mini-mansion George insisted they buy in Denver, which was way too large for the two of them. It had been too much for her to clean, so he had hired help. And eventually hired more. To clean, to cook, to landscape, to maintain the pool and hot tub. To mow the expansive, unneeded lawn to look like a golf green.

Money. It all took way too much money. Money she thought they had. She had complained about spending it and George would just kiss her on the forehead and tell her not to worry.

Well, she should've worried.

She should have complained louder, should have looked

at their accounts. She should've done something instead of just living life thinking everything was perfect.

Okay, maybe not perfect. But great.

Not great. Good.

No, not good, either. It started out great, slid slowly into good but, by the end, it had sped past okay into "off."

As in something was off with George, but she couldn't pinpoint what and he wouldn't talk about it with her. He ended up shutting her out of everything. He stopped talking about work, the business, their friends.

When she expressed concern, he'd wave it away, stating everything was fine.

It wasn't.

Not even close.

One of the three garage doors went up automatically when Trace pushed another button on his mirror. And then he pulled his badass car inside next to a really cool, just as badass motorcycle.

It looked old but restored to perfection. The gas tank claimed it was a Harley Davidson. It was a beautiful bike decked out in chrome and painted brown, tan and maroon.

Again, beautiful but still badass like its owner.

He shut off the car and sat staring out of the windshield for way too long. She studied his profile, which showed he was not happy at all. Just like his boss.

Well, she wasn't happy to have to rely on others, either. She thought she was breaking free of George and his issues. Until a month ago when shit hit the fan.

She didn't ask for any of it, but here she was, sitting in a garage south of Pittsburgh with a pissed off Trace Walker, because even if she didn't want it, that garbage had been handed to her and she had no choice but to do something about it.

"We're gonna set some rules."

Rules.

That sounded fun, just like all the rules George had for her to be the perfect wife. Dress a certain way, talk a certain way, entertain a certain way.

"Soon as we get your shit sorted, you're gone. I don't like the fact you're here in Shadow Valley. I don't like the fact you're here in my fucking house. I don't like that you're sitting in my fucking car. And I certainly don't like that you're back in my fucking life."

The longer he went, the louder he became, but it was the harshness of his words that made Ellie wince. His jaw was set, his fingers gripping the steering wheel like he was strangling it, his eyes still pointed straight ahead.

"You said I've got you." Had she misheard him? Or was it a slip of the tongue?

"Yeah. For however long this shit takes."

"Honestly, Trace, I just want to disappear. Help me do that and you don't have to deal with me ever again."

He turned his head and his blue eyes pinned her to the seat.

She used to love his eyes. The blue shade varied depending on what light they were in. Whether in the sun while swimming in the lake, or in the shadows when they made love.

They also used to hold adoration in them when he looked at her. Now they just held contempt.

"That was one rule," she said, wanting this list of rules over with. She'd listen and agree to every one of them just to get this over with.

"The second one is, you let us do what we need to do without interfering. No exception."

"Okay."

"Third one is, you respect my privacy. This house is mine. It was built specifically for me. You'll see things you'll want to ask questions about. Don't. If I choose to talk about those things, that's on me. Not you. You don't ask me personal questions. I won't ask you any, either. I'll only ask you what we need to know to do this job. That's it. I'm warning you now, you're going to see things in this house you're going to want to ask about. It's none of your fucking business. You gave up the right to know my business a long time ago."

Ellie couldn't breathe. His words were cold, business-like. But she detected something deeper. A hurt he was trying to hide.

"Okay," she whispered, wanting to absorb the hurt she caused. "I'll mind my own business and keep to myself."

"The house is big, but it's not McMaster big. Which means we'll run into each other and often. Roommates. That's what we are. Roommates 'til this is over. Nothing more."

"Okay," she said again.

"I'd dump your ass at Shadow Valley Motel if Steel wasn't right. You're safest here. And if whoever is behind this whole mess calls or texts you, I'll know right away. Unfortunately, your being here is for the best."

"Okay," she repeated, unsure what else to say. It probably wouldn't matter if she did have more to say. He most likely wouldn't want to hear it.

"Now, get out of my car."

She got out of his car.

He popped the trunk and unloaded her two suitcases. It wouldn't have surprised her if he left them sitting next to his Dodge and went inside, leaving them for her to deal with. But he didn't, he rolled them across the garage, and she followed him, not only past the vintage Harley but an older blue and white pickup truck. Normal. Nothing badass about it. Something he would have driven when they were teens.

He had an old Ford truck back then, too, one his father had handed down to him. Plus, a dirt bike. She rode in that pickup and on the back of that bike more times than she could remember.

He had actually taken her virginity in the bed of that Ford the night she turned eighteen. They had waited for two long years. And they counted down every minute until that night.

It was the best birthday—no, best night—of her life. Especially since they spent it under the stars out in a field next to the lake, music playing, crickets chirping, owls hooting and, best of all, she was in Trace's arms.

She had given him her virginity, but they were giving each other a future.

She closed her eyes. A future that didn't pan out because of their choices.

"Ellie..."

She opened her eyes and found she still stood in front of the Ford pickup. Then with shock she realized it was the one he had back then. He still had it. He didn't get rid of it.

He. Kept. It.

It looked better now than it did back then. It was restored, the paint fresh, the chrome shiny, like the Harley. But this vehicle had meaning. The bed of that truck was where they promised to love each other forever.

They were young and foolish. And, at the time, they didn't realize life never turned out as planned.

She learned that the hard way.

So did Trace.

"Trace," she whispered, still staring at the truck. Memories sweeping through her, almost crippling her.

"Ellie," he repeated sharply. Her name wasn't said with any kind of softness. It was hard. Unbending. And held a warning.

She wasn't supposed to ask questions. So, she only nodded and followed him inside.

———

WALKER STOOD off to the side, just inside the rear French doors. The lights were off in the large kitchen, so he had no problem seeing outside. Ellie sat in one of the deck chairs he'd purchased recently, her legs pulled up, her chin resting on her knees, her arms wrapped around her shins.

She looked like she had when she was a teen.

They began dating when she just turned sixteen and he was eighteen. He should've walked away from her then. He didn't. He couldn't. He knew the minute he noticed her she was his.

He'd been impatient but he had dug deep and waited. He also promised her mother he wouldn't fuck up. Mrs. Cooke trusted him and that meant a lot to him. So, he kept that promise.

They had the rest of their lives to be together, so there was no rush. He could wait. She would be worth the wait.

That fucking night... he found out how right he was. She was more than worth the wait. They had fooled around for two years, so they knew each other well. He knew how to get her blood pumping. She knew how to do the same to him.

But they always held back. It was torture, but sweet torture at that. It was then he learned how much he liked the anticipation. The tease without the reward.

Much later he learned what that denial of pleasure was called.

He'd take them both to the edge time and time again, but never let them go over. He'd push her toward the cliff, but never let her go. So, when that time finally came, it had been the best night of his fucking life. He waited for two years to make her completely his.

That moment he took her, that moment she finally was his in all ways, it was the sweetest, most satisfying gift anyone could give him.

He never experienced anything like that again.

He dropped his head, ran a hand over his hair, and stared at his boots. It was soon time to reveal something he wouldn't be able to hide with her staying in his house.

Something he hid from most people. His brothers knew, Diesel knew. Very few others.

He kept it that way for a reason.

He'd lived that way for so long, he didn't remember how to live it otherwise.

He inhaled air through his nostrils, filling his lungs to capacity, then slowly released it.

She was going to ask questions even though he told her not to. And he may have to make an exception and answer them.

Tonight, his past was slamming him from two directions.

He lifted his head and stared at her for another long minute. Wondering if he'd be in this house, in Shadow Valley, doing what he did, being who he was, dealing with what he had, if that phone call she made nineteen years ago had turned out differently.

Either way, it was too late to change any of that now.

It was getting late and they hadn't eaten yet. They needed food. But he wasn't sure he was ready to sit down at a table across from her to do that. He wasn't ready to look into her green eyes and relive all the memories now hovering below the surface.

That day so many years ago, after that phone call, he'd done his best to put her out of his mind.

His best wasn't good enough. She was back. She was in his house. In his life.

How the fuck did that happen? And why the fuck did he let it?

He let it because he had no choice. Last night when she contacted him, he heard in her voice something was wrong and when he was hardly grown, he vowed to himself and to her to only give her "right."

"Fuck," he whispered. The need to make things right for her, whether she deserved it or not, remained deep within him.

He opened one of the French doors and when he did, her head turned until her cheek pressed against her knees instead of her chin. It was getting dark, so he couldn't see the green of her eyes. But he knew too well what they looked like.

"You have a nice place."

He ignored that and asked, "You cook?"

She nodded without lifting her head.

"Hungry?"

She shook her head.

"Need to eat anyway," he told her. "Need to make us something. Even if it's just grilled cheese sandwiches with ham and tomato slices." He winced. He had no idea why he suggested that.

"You always loved when I made those for you."

Right. Memories were too fucking close to the surface.

"It was the only thing I knew how to make back then."

"And now?"

"I do all right," she said softly, lifting her head.

A home-cooked "all right" meal was better than his own cooking or take-out. "Since you don't have enough money to pay for the job, expect you to do all the cooking while you're here."

"It's the least I can do."

Yeah, it was the least she could do.

"I can clean, too. It'll keep me busy."

"Not asking for that. I have a housekeeper who comes once a week, cleans, brings groceries. Make a list of what you need, I'll send it to her."

"Okay."

Ellie had never been a person who simply answered with an "okay." She'd always had something to say and a lot of it.

It was one reason for his rules. He wasn't sure he could handle having in depth conversations with her. Not like they used to have. Walker used to love watching her talk animatedly about subjects she was passionate about. Sometimes he'd pretend his view was different from hers, just so she'd want to debate him. He'd fight back his smile and his urge to kiss her until she realized what he was doing, then he'd laugh.

So would she.

Neither of them was laughing right now.

She also hadn't moved from her chair.

"Ellie, come inside." It came out softer than he meant it to.

She nodded, unfolded her legs and stood. She was petite in all ways. A good eleven inches shorter than his six-foot-one. And he wouldn't be surprised if his hands could still encompass her waist.

Her tits had filled out, so had her hips, but she wasn't nearly as curvy as the women who belonged to his teammates. Or at least the three Shadows who had been hobbled by pussy.

He stepped back from the doorway and let her pass just inches from him to catch her scent. It was light, probably a lotion. Ellie had never been one for makeup, clothes and perfumes. She had loved being barefoot, her coloring came from the sun, and she always smelled like the outdoors. That's why he couldn't understand her leaving him for McMaster.

Fuck. This shit had to stop.

He couldn't spend the next how many days, possibly over a week, with her and keep getting pulled back in time.

It wasn't healthy for him. And it might pull other shit, long buried, to the surface.

When she hit the center of the well-equipped kitchen he barely used, she stopped, turned and looked at him with her head tilted, her hands on her hips. "Do you have the stuff to make them?"

His eyes slowly slid up from her hips, paused on her tits, then he met her eyes. "Your tits fake? I don't remember them being that big." It wouldn't have surprised him if McMaster wanted her to look like the Barbie doll she wasn't.

Her whole body jerked and she frowned. "I don't weigh the same, either. When you put on some pounds, they tend to land in a couple places first. I guess I was lucky where they landed."

He agreed.

"So?" she asked.

"So, yeah, you're lucky."

Her eyebrows rose. "I meant the stuff for grilled cheese."

"Don't have tomatoes but have the rest. Plus, bacon. Want bacon on mine with the ham. I need more than a sandwich, so check the cabinets and the fridge to find something to go along with it. Whatever you can find, you can use."

"Okay."

There it was again.

"I'm gonna go take a shower. Yell when it's ready."

"Okay."

He gritted his teeth. He hated her submissive like that. But he'd also told her to mind her own business. So, maybe it was for the best.

"Gotta shower," he muttered and stalked off.

Chapter Five

ELLIE WATCHED him turn and bolt from the kitchen. She waited for the slam of a door at the other end of the house, but it never came.

He didn't remember her "tits" being that big. She didn't remember him ever calling her breasts "tits." But then...

Things had changed and she needed to resign herself to that fact.

While he was as tall as she remembered and towered over her, his shoulders seemed much broader than when he was twenty. His muscles were not nearly as developed back then, either. His face also held lines that could probably tell stories.

And most likely, not all good ones.

His body moved differently now, too. Gone was the youthful swagger he had, the looseness of hips and shoulders. He appeared to be as tight as a stretched rubber band. And as he walked away, she might have even picked up on a slight hitch. For only a step, no longer.

She sighed, glanced around the kitchen and then began her search for what she needed.

Within a half hour, the sandwiches were crispy and

brown on both sides, the cheese perfectly melted and gooey. She'd found a can of creamy tomato soup in his pantry, which now simmered in a pot, one hardly used, on the stove, also hardly used.

Her stomach had been growling the whole time. She hadn't eaten all day besides a tiny bag of peanuts and a Sprite on the plane. While she hadn't had much of an appetite then, she also wanted to save every penny she had by avoiding buying a meal.

She had plates out, found the silverware, napkins, everything they'd need, but no Trace.

He hadn't come back into the kitchen. In fact, she'd heard nothing from the other side of the house at all.

"Trace!" she called out and winced at her *faux pas*. "Walker! It's ready."

No answer. Nothing.

She turned off the burners under the soup and grill pan, leaned back, tilted her head toward the hallway where he'd disappeared and called out his name again.

The right name. Walker.

She didn't like calling him that but would try to remember to do it.

Still nothing. No footsteps. No answer. Silence.

Men like Trace didn't take a half hour to shower. Not unless they used a lot of product on their hair and body. Like George did. His side of their master bathroom had been packed with product.

In truth, Ellie had always been satisfied with a quality shampoo, conditioner and a functioning hairdryer. She only put on makeup and fancy clothes when it was expected of her, while entertaining, dinner at the club, meeting "friends" or potential business clients for drinks.

She didn't mind doing it. She actually enjoyed dressing up on occasion, but she was glad she didn't have to do it every day.

"Walker," she called one more time, then padded barefoot down the hall. She had kicked off her shoes when they first got to his house because she'd always preferred going barefoot.

I'm gonna keep you barefoot, pregnant and in the kitchen, Trace had teased more than once.

George didn't like her working in the kitchen, which was why he paid a cook. He always worried about her running around barefoot. She wasn't sure why since it wasn't like she was doing it on the streets of New York City. And the pregnancy part....

She passed by an empty but large guest bathroom, and two spare bedrooms. Trace had put her luggage in the one farthest from the master.

The door at the end of the hallway was open, a light on and in the master bedroom, on the opposite side of the king bed from where she paused, sat Trace. He perched on the edge, his back in full view, only a cream-colored towel covering him from his waist down. His blond hair was cropped short but even so, she could tell it was still damp. As short as it was, it wouldn't take long to dry.

He was bent over doing something. A plastic tub of cloudy liquid set nearby on the nightstand.

He straightened as she took another tentative step into the room.

Now she could see the large back tattoo he had a little better.

At first she thought it was Pegasus or a Centaur inked into his skin. But it wasn't. It was a combination of the two. The creature had the upper body of a man, the lower body of a horse with wings. The man held a raised sword. And a crescent moon was tattooed on the upper portion of his right shoulder. The "horse" was rearing up as the man pointed to the sky with one hand held flat and holding a raised sword with the other.

But this wasn't a typical horse. The front left leg of this "horse" was missing from the knee joint down.

A mythical three-legged winged man-horse.

Strange. She had never seen a creature like that anywhere before. She wondered what the meaning was behind it.

She raised her eyes from his tattoo to see him looking at her over his shoulder.

She had expected him to jump up and yell at her to leave, since he didn't want her to know anything personal about him. And here she was, standing in his bedroom, seeing his tattoo, seeing him only wrapped in a towel. She couldn't get any more personal than that.

"You shouldn't be in here," his voice was low, but held no anger, surprisingly.

"I called you several times. Dinner's ready."

"Just got out of the shower," he grumbled. "I didn't hear you."

That was a hell of a long shower, then. What does a man do in a shower for that long?

She closed her eyes as heat bloomed in her face.

Shit.

In those two years they had waited, Trace had joked with her that he was always squeaky clean and had pruned fingers constantly from all the time he spent in the shower. What he did in there was one way to keep himself locked down tight and under control.

She had teased him back, telling him that one day she wanted to watch. They never got that chance.

Now that vision was burned into her brain. Not of an eighteen or nineteen-year-old Trace, but of the one currently sitting on the bed. All mature thirty-nine years of him.

Her knees wobbled a bit, but she locked them in place. She also turned her face away to hide the blush and the fact she had to squeeze her thighs together when everything inside her clenched.

As she went to backtrack and leave his room, her attention got caught on something else. Not just one thing. A few things lining the floor of his large walk-in closet, which had not only the door wide open, but the light on.

She blinked, unsure of what she was seeing. "What..." escaped from her on a hitched breath.

She stared at those items in that closet, unable to wrap her head around what they were. Unsure why Trace, of all people, would have them. Why he needed them. She threw a glance over her shoulder at him, then turned back, taking a hesitant step toward his closet.

A muttered "fuck" came from the direction of the bed. "Trace..."

HIS NAME CAME out on a pained whisper. One that held a hint of a tremble. "Trace," she whispered again. "Are those yours?"

"Ellie," he said, making it clear his saying her name was a warning. Her breaking down and getting emotional about something that couldn't be changed wouldn't help either of them.

She spun on her heels, stared at him, her eyes shiny, and let her gaze slowly wander down until it hit his lap. Where he sat, she couldn't see the rest of him.

"I want to see."

His head jerked back, and his heart began to thump in his chest.

He wanted her to mind her own business, but this was one area he knew couldn't be avoided if they were going to live in the same house for potentially the next week or so. He thought he could at least delay it, but apparently not. "Ellie..."

"Trace, I need to see."

He lifted his chin toward the closet and his line-up of prostheses. "You saw."

She shook her head and murmured, "No."

"I set rules—"

Her head snapped up. "Fuck your rules!" she shouted and moved around the bed.

She stopped short, her eyes focused below the bottom edge of the towel.

Trace gritted his teeth, his fingers gripping the bedding in an effort not to hide what she was seeing. To cover himself up.

None of this was any of her fucking business.

None.

He waited for a look of horror to cross her face. Or even a look of sympathy. Something to fuel his anger so he could snap out at her, chase her from his room.

Her face showed neither.

She raised her gaze to his and asked, "What happened?"

"No, Ellie. I told you no questions."

"I'm going to ask it anyway."

Of course she would. He knew this would be one area she'd have a hard time biting her tongue. Not simply responding with a meek "okay."

Ellie had never been meek.

Even at sixteen. *Especially* at sixteen.

He swept his hand toward the open closet and then his bare legs. "Now, I gave you this. That's all you're gonna get. We're done talking about it and can move on."

"You didn't give me anything, Trace. I want to know how, why... When."

"You don't get that, Ellie. That's not yours to have. Now, I need to get dressed." He cocked an eyebrow at her. "You sticking around for that?"

"I need to hear it, Trace."

54

Fuck, she was determined.

"Guess you're sticking around for that." He unknotted the towel, letting it fall open, not caring she was only inches from him. He reached behind him to snag the long shorts he'd thrown there earlier, then pulled them on, working them up his hips.

She was now leaning back against the wall where she'd been watching how he maneuvered them on. Then he pushed from the bed and held out an arm. "I need my crutches."

Ellie followed his eyes to where they were propped in the corner. Her gaze slid to the closet. "You don't need one of those?"

Those.

"No, I normally use crutches in the house when I'm done for the day."

Fuck, he was giving her more than he wanted to. But him using crutches around the house would be a bit obvious. He just needed to ignore her questions.

He planned on only taking off his prosthesis in his bedroom at night, holding off on this whole conversation as long as he could.

Now that she knew, there was no point in not going about his normal routine.

"If you're gonna continue to stand there and gawk, at least hand me my fucking crutches."

She sprang into action, grabbing them and bringing them over.

But she didn't let them go when he took them from her. Instead, she held on tightly, her green eyes locked with his. Now, he was seeing something in them he *definitely* did not want to see.

Concern. Caring.

Maybe something more. But he didn't want to look any deeper.

"Ellie, I'm used to it." He hoped that would put an end to it there.

Of course, it didn't.

"How can you get used to a piece of your body missing?"

The same way you get used to a piece of your soul missing.

You just do.

"You have no choice. You adapt. You can lie down and give up or you can rise and keep going. You look at the negatives and find a positive and that's what you hang onto. That's where you draw your strength."

He said too much. Enough to spur more questions, demand more answers, explanations.

He couldn't do it.

He was done.

If she had stayed, she would have known all the answers to all the questions swirling in her head.

And that was a good reminder, this conversation needed to be over.

He jerked the crutches from her grip and moved past her. On his way out of the room, he paused, turning off the closet light and closing the door so she could no longer see the evidence of what had been taken from him because of the choices he made.

Chapter Six

SITTING at the table with her was worse than he imagined. He shoveled his grilled cheese sandwich into his gullet, picked up the bowl of soup and drank it, not giving a fuck about manners. And as soon as he was done, he grabbed his crutches, rose from the chair, made his way over to the fridge and snagged a beer.

"Need help?"

"Been doing this myself a long time, Ellie. I managed before you got here, will manage after you leave."

"But I'm here now, I can help."

Walker kept his eyes to the fridge as he squeezed them shut. They opened when he heard her get out of her chair and move in his direction. "I'm good," he muttered. With his crutches and beer, he pushed past her and went to the French doors, opened one and went outside. Not to enjoy the late summer weather, but to escape her.

Even so, he didn't bother to close the door because he expected her to follow him. To hover.

Once he settled in a chair and cracked open the bottle of lager, he was surprised she hadn't.

It had been a long fucking day. He didn't think one

beer was going to cut it. A fucking six-pack wasn't going to cut it. However, there was no way in hell he was getting blitzed with Ellie in the house. His guard could go down and...

Hell, things could become more fucked than they already were.

Nope, best to keep sober. He was meeting Hunter at the warehouse early in the morning, anyway, so they could start what they were both good at. Hunting and tracking.

They needed to find out who McMotherfucker owed money to. And why. Then decide where to go from there.

They might even have to fly out to Denver and put boots on the ground. Do face to face visits with McMaster's brokers, his banker and whoever else might have some clues.

They'd figure that out tomorrow once they dug as deep as they could electronically.

He lifted the bottle to his lips and let the cold beer slide down his throat and into his gut, which was still tense. The grilled cheese sitting in it like a brick didn't help.

He guzzled half of the bottle down and then looked at it.

One definitively wouldn't be enough.

"Trace, we talked about starting a family soon."

"We can have a family."

"With me here and you there? That's not us raising a family, that's me raising a family. And what if you don't come back just like—"

He had cut her off not wanting to hear the rest of it. He understood her fear, but still... *"Doing this to provide for us, sweetheart."*

He finished off the beer in one swig.

"Ellie."

"Yes?" He could hear the tears in her voice but steeled himself against them. This was her doing. She wanted this to end. Not him. *"You do this, I'm done. No changing your mind. I won't be back."*

With a grunt, he whipped the bottle across the deck, his aim accurate when it hit a nearby tree and exploded.

He dropped his head, scrubbed his palms over his face and bit back a scream.

I won't be back.

No, it was she who was back. And only because she needed something from him. Not because she wanted him. Not to beg his forgiveness.

No. She was desperate.

And he was someone who could help her.

A fucking tool.

He felt her presence behind him to his left. Her breathing came slightly ragged which meant his outburst had upset her.

Good.

He grabbed his crutches and prepared to stand, muttering, "Need a fucking beer."

"I'll get it." Then she was gone.

She was back quickly, offering an open bottle over his shoulder, but stayed behind him. Out of his view.

All he'd have to do was turn his head.

She was right there.

So close.

Within reach.

"Can I join you?"

He gripped the bottle tighter and took a long swig. When he dropped it back to his lap, he said, "You already have."

"I can go inside if you'd like. It's pretty out here. Peaceful. I could see why you'd want a house here."

"That's not why I built it."

She didn't say anything for a long time. After a few more pulls on his beer, he continued. He didn't know why he did, but he did. "Mercy lives to your left. Ryder to your right. Hunter's building a house on another street near his son's uncle. Expect the rest to move in here eventually. The invitation's there, they just haven't jumped on it. No need when you're a single man, unless you're a man who needs to accommodate his disability."

Silence. One heartbeat. Two.

"You previously lived somewhere that didn't."

"In a lot of places that didn't. You learn to adapt." Why was he giving her this? Why was he even opening the line of communication?

It was dangerous.

"Walker," she began.

It was the first time he heard her use the name he demanded she use. A less personal name than Trace.

But he didn't like it on her lips.

"If you're gonna stand out here talking when I told you I wanted to avoid that shit, you might as well sit the fuck down where I can see you instead of hovering behind me."

She moved, but not to grab another chair. No, fuck him, she moved in front of his, to stand at the railing just feet away and leaned back against it. She planted both hands on the top rail, pushing her tits out as she did so.

She probably didn't realize she was doing it, but Walker couldn't miss it.

He was glad he was wrong about the boob job. Because the top she changed into gave him no doubt those tits were real.

With living next door to both Mercy and Ryder and their women, he'd seen something similar on Rissa and Kelsea both. Snug tops that clung to their curves and tits. Camisoles they called them. Thin shoulder straps that made him wonder how they didn't snap from the weight. Especially when it came to Rissa, who had the biggest tits out of all the women.

And all the men had told Mercy he was a lucky motherfucker. But not out loud. They were envious, but they weren't stupid.

Ellie wasn't nearly as big as Rissa but still... he was right.

They were fuller now than they'd been the last time he saw them.

She had aged well.

At almost thirty-seven, she could pass for twenty-seven. Especially with her long, auburn hair now sweeping past her shoulders. Hair he had a sudden urge to fist, to yank her head back, scrape his teeth down her delicate neck and then fuck the shit out of her while he bent her over the railing.

He wondered if she'd made all the little noises she used to make with him—the night he took her virginity and all those nights afterward—with McMotherfucker.

He closed his eyes and turned his head away, picturing George McMaster lying between her thighs, fucking Ellie all those years it should have been him.

That shit just stuck in his fucking craw.

His jaw tight, he kept his head turned away and his eyes shut. But even so, words slipped out. "You were supposed to be mine. No one else's."

He counted the seconds waiting for her answer. Six. Six long seconds.

"Yes, that was the plan," she whispered. "You changed our plan."

"Ellie, someone else had you."

"Someone else had you, too, Trace. Probably a lot of someones." This time her words were louder, holding a different kind of hurt. Was she imagining him laying between some other woman's legs the same as he had imagined with her?

He opened his eyes and met hers. "None of them meant anything to me. Can you say the same?"

Her fingers tightened on the top railing as the color drained from her face. "Since I married the man, no."

His breathing stopped for a moment as that knife twisted deep. She not only gave herself to someone else, but loved him, too. He wasn't sure which was worse.

Starting at the top of her head, he raked his gaze down her body, not hiding what he was doing. And he didn't miss when her whole body went tight. But she said nothing. She didn't move away. She allowed him this.

He paused on her lips when they parted, and her tongue darted out to swipe across the bottom one. He slid his eyes over her neck, wondering how hard her pulse was beating just beneath her smooth skin. He hesitated at the hollow of her throat. A delicate, vulnerable area he had sucked, licked and kissed too many times to count. He continued over her bare shoulders, which were currently pulled back stiffly.

He dropped his gaze to the round, creamy flesh pushing out of the top of that black camisole and the shadowed crease of her cleavage. He was tempted to nuzzle her there. Her nipples were noticeably hard, pressing against the soft fabric. His thumbs ached to brush across them.

He made his way lower over her slender stomach, her still narrow waist until he reached the flare of her hips. He was right. They were curvier. Fuller. And even though he couldn't see it now, he knew her ass was, too.

He closed his eyes for a moment, remembering those nights in the back of his pickup, with him on his back on a blanket and Ellie straddling him, riding him hard and fast, tossing her hair, his fingers digging deeply into the flesh of that ass, encouraging her to take what she wanted from him.

Because he would've given her whatever she wanted. All she had to do was ask and he would have broken his back to get it for her.

The tan shorts she had pulled on earlier looked soft and worn and extremely comfortable. They only came mid-thigh, so it left a lot of her smooth skin exposed. And he took his time exploring every inch. All the way down to her pink painted toenails.

He worked his way back up until he landed on her face. Her expression was sad, haunted, filled with regret.

He was sure it mirrored his.

"So damn beautiful, Ellie. So fucking beautiful. When I looked at you, I saw everything that was right in the world." The fingers around the bottle clenched. The one on his thigh curled tight. "You stole that from me."

Her chin rose and from where she stood, she looked down at him. "You might have thought my decision was self-ish, but so was yours. You left me first, Trace."

He did, but not in the way she was making it out to be. "You didn't miss me."

She pulled in a ragged breath, then breathed out, "I missed you."

"You didn't love me."

Her eyebrows knitted together, and her expression and words became harsh. "How can you say that? It was the hardest thing I ever had to do in my life."

"Then why d'you do it? Why did you destroy us?"

Her head snapped back and then her face crumpled. Surging forward, she fell to her knees next to his chair, her hands gripping his. "Trace, your soul was restless. You enlisted. You needed something I couldn't give you."

He shook his head. "No."

"Yes. I saw it. I recognized it. I was hoping it would go away. It didn't."

"You knew that I wanted you. I wanted us. But you took that away."

"You enlisted without talking to me first!" she screamed. She dropped her head, her hair covering her face. Her chest rose and fell a few times before she lifted her head again.

He had no doubt what she was feeling, it was easy to read it on her face.

Devastation.

He knew exactly what that felt like.

He stared at their hands, hers squeezing his tightly as she continued, "I messed up big. I got it. I hear you loud and clear, but you have to let the past go, Trace. You can't torture yourself like this. You can't keep torturing me like this. If I could go back and do it all over again, I would. I wish I could, but I can't. I can't change it. I can only accept my mistake, learn from it and move on. But you have to accept yours, too."

His breath burned his lungs. She was on her knees, pressing her stomach against his legs.

"You volunteered to leave *me*. To get shot at. To put yourself in danger. I was afraid to lose you, Trace. You were my everything. My world. Then you left. You went over there. *There*. Where people go and never come back or if they do, they're never the same. I couldn't watch or wait for that. Someone knocking on my door to tell me the worst news of my life, just like what happened to my mother when my father was killed over there. I watched her try to cope, to put on a brave face when dealing with me. But she couldn't hide it. It utterly devastated her, Trace. It took her years to recover from losing the love of her life. Years and I'm still not sure she's fully recovered. The possibility of that happening again crippled me, paralyzed me to my very core. It was easier to give you up than watch you come back destroyed. Or in a casket covered in a fucking American flag. Because that's all my mother has to show for my father's need to serve. A fucking flag."

Every word struck a blow, cut him deep. Seared his heart.

But she didn't stop. She kept going and he didn't even try to stop her. Because she needed to say it and he needed to hear it.

"For what? You would have sacrificed for what? How would have losing your life changed anything? Was what I did selfish? Yes. You enlisting without discussing it with me first was also selfish, Trace. Especially when you knew what happened to my father, how I'd feel if history repeated itself.

When you told me, I was crushed. It told me that I wasn't enough for you. You didn't love me enough to stay, to find another way."

Yeah, he needed to hear everything she said but she also needed to hear him. Something that should've been done all those years ago instead. Like adults. But they had been young and immature. Trying to figure out life and what it might hold for them.

"I loved you more than life itself, Ellie. That's why I did what I did. I wanted to be the best husband, the best father. I wanted to give you the world. But I only had a high school diploma. I had no money. I had nothing but me to offer you. That's it. I knew the military would make me a better man, a disciplined one, give me skills, build my career. Give me the tools to be the best man I could be. For you. For us. I only planned on doing four years, then becoming a cop. The military was a step into that world. I was told when you came home a vet, doors opened. I was only going to do my time and get out."

"Not everyone gets out," she whispered.

Once she was done with him, he didn't leave after his obligated service, he stayed. He did what he needed to do to make the Army his career since he had nothing to come home to. He successfully made it through, not only airborne training, but all the requirements for the 160th Special Operations Aviation Regiment.

He became a Night Stalker. And he was damn proud of it. He was proud of every drop of blood, sweat and tears he shed to attain that.

But that was all he had.

Until he didn't even have that.

"I didn't die over there, Ellie."

She leaned back and her eyes flicked down to his left leg where his stump was exposed. His weakness exposed. "You could have. You almost did."

"I was too fucking stubborn to die. And, Ellie, you know the saying, what doesn't kill you makes you stronger."

She lifted her green eyes from what remained of his left leg, her voice thick, "You used to call me sweetheart."

He jerked his hands from her grip. "And after that I called you a lot of other things." He grabbed his beer and downed the rest of it before telling her the truth. "You shutting me out ripped out my heart, crushed my soul. I had nothing left but a dark empty cavity in my chest. So, sorry if I'm not in the mood to call you *sweetheart* anymore."

Her sadness hit him in the gut. "We both messed up."

He knew they both messed up. But it was easier to blame anyone but himself for fucking up the best thing he'd ever had.

She was right. He should have sat down and had a discussion with her about enlisting. Especially after she told him about that day the Marines came and knocked on their door. About how much her life changed after losing her father. After listening to her cry when she mentioned how much she missed him.

But he didn't. He had walked into the recruitment office just to talk to them, check out his options, see what the military offered. But when he'd walked out, he'd already signed up. At the time he was proud to do his "patriotic duty," be able to provide for his future wife, his future kids.

Being older than her and "the man" in the relationship, he had this fucked-up notion stuck in his head that he'd make all the decisions for them both. That he knew best.

He didn't.

That decision back then had been stupid because he didn't realize how it would affect her. While he saw it as doing something good for the two of them, setting up their future, she saw it as something bad, where it would destroy it.

But even so, she didn't have to end up with McMaster,

the only guy in town who could give her everything he couldn't. More than what he could ever hope to provide for her.

When he'd called home and his father told him that news, he'd gone on a violent, alcohol-induced bender.

It was far from pretty. And if it wasn't for some of the members of his platoon covering for his destructive ass, he would've been thrown out of the Army.

If that had happened, he definitely would've been left with nothing. Only holding his own fucking dick in his hand.

"Do you want another beer?" she asked softly, bringing his attention back to her.

"No." Because if he had another one, it still wouldn't be enough. He'd need another and another until he'd have no control over his urges.

And the urge to touch Ellie was eating at him, burning his gut, the pressure in his chest stifling.

He planted his palms onto his thighs, pressing them down, holding them there, so he wouldn't reach out to her where she still knelt at the front of his chair. Close enough he could pick up her scent as the light late summer breeze swirled between them.

"How long do you think I'll be here?"

"I don't know. Until we figure out what the fuck is going on."

"Days?"

"Hopefully." In truth, they only had about eight days to find a solution.

"A week?"

Hopefully not. Having Ellie sleeping two doors down from his master bedroom for even a few days would be difficult enough. "I don't know."

"It's good we got things settled between us, then," she said, rising to her feet.

His hand snaked out and snagged her wrist, holding her in place. He looked up at her, tilting her head. "Have we?"

She lifted her eyebrows in question.

"Have we got things settled between us, Ellie? You think those words we just spilled, confessions we just made, *settled* things between us?"

Her mouth opened and nothing but a breath escaped.

"Are you feeling settled?" he asked her. "Because the fuck if I am."

Chapter Seven

ELLIE'S GAZE lifted from his firm grip on her wrist to Trace's face. His expression sent a shiver down her spine and caused a simmer in her belly. He looked hungry. Like she was his prey and he wouldn't be *settled* until he hunted her down and consumed her.

She blinked slowly at her thoughts, then dug her teeth into her bottom lip.

She wasn't sure what to do, where they would go from here.

He'd said roommates for the time it would take to help her. But he was not looking at her right now as if she was a roommate.

She saw this look before. She recognized it. He wore the same expression when they were at a pep rally at school and the seniors were on one side of the gym, the sophomores on the other. His blue eyes had landed on her and remained there for the whole thirty minutes. Even when his friends were talking to him and joking around, vying for his attention. She knew he answered them because his mouth had moved, but he kept her in his sights. Afraid she might disappear into thin air, if he even glanced away for a moment.

She had never seen him before that fall day. It was her first year attending that high school, since they had only moved to town late that summer after her mother married her stepfather.

When she first noticed him staring at her, heat filled her cheeks and she'd ducked her head. As the rally went on, she became braver, sneaking peeks, and eventually not hiding her own interest. Even going so far as giving him a smile and meeting his eyes across the large room.

She had no idea why a senior would be interested in her when all the senior girls were so much prettier, had nicer clothes and dressed so much more maturely than she did.

Those blue eyes were intense then, but, as she learned later, that was nothing. His interest in her only sparked that day. Eventually it became a roaring bonfire which engulfed her.

Engulfed them both.

His words brought her back to the present. To their current situation.

"My Ellie."

Warmth swirled through her at him calling her that.

His.

"You were always mine. Not his..." He reached up and, using his thumb, pulled her bottom lip from between her teeth. The metallic taste of blood hit the tip of her tongue.

Still gripping her wrist and holding her in place, he shifted forward in his chair, brushing his fingertips lightly over her cheek, down her jawline. Over the pounding pulse along her throat. "And when you gave yourself to him... That was a goddamn betrayal. You willingly gave him what was mine, what *I* had claimed."

She pushed words past the lump in her throat. "You were mine, too, Trace, and you gave yourself to the government. You gave them what was mine, what *I* had claimed."

He dropped his gaze to her lips, his thumb still sweeping back and forth. It stilled when she pressed the tip of her tongue to it.

He abruptly dropped his hand, released her captured wrist, and reached for his crutches, using them to pull himself to a stand. "We don't need to complicate things. And we don't know each other anymore."

No, they didn't. So many things had happened since the last time they spoke. A lifetime of things. Things that changed them both.

But deep down inside—though, she wouldn't tell him— she knew him. Even now. Whatever connection they had long ago still remained. He didn't want to acknowledge it, but it was hard to ignore. The second she heard his voice on the phone, the second he'd walked into that room at the warehouse, she knew.

The piece of her which had been missing was found.

However, she wasn't sure if it would ever fit neatly back into place again. The edges were now damaged. Maybe permanently so.

And the tension between them was still tight.

He was right. Nothing had been settled.

She'd only been in his house a few hours and it was already wearing on her. She couldn't imagine what it would be like after days of this.

She might lose her mind.

"Trace, you need to stop this. I can't do this. We need to move past this."

"How are we supposed to do that, Ellie?"

She took her time whispering each word to underscore how important they were, "You just... let... it... go."

RIGHT. He just needed to let it go. *Move past this.*

His whole life had changed the moment he spotted her across the gymnasium during a pep rally. And then it changed again after she gave him the boot.

And now... Now, she was back, changing it one more time.

Unless he stopped it.

He had set rules so that wouldn't happen. Remain roommates while she was there. She was out the second the job was completed.

Simple.

Just as simple as "letting it go."

Which meant it wasn't and he wouldn't. And basically, he was fucked.

You used to call me sweetheart.

Why did she even bring that up? To drive home the fact something still existed between them?

He could deny it all he wanted, but it was there. It had always been there.

She was deeply rooted inside him.

Which was why he could never find another woman to take her place. There wasn't one. That woman did not exist.

And now, the only woman he ever felt a connection with stood on the deck of his house inches from him.

She belonged to no one.

She could be his again.

Did he even want her?

For fuck's sake, there was nothing, no one, he wanted more.

He needed to reclaim her. Fill that deep, gaping hole.

"You're right. We need to move on," he finally murmured, doing his best to convince himself that was what needed to be done.

Relief filled her face and she nodded, then turned to go inside.

He stopped her with only her name. "Ellie."

She paused in the open doorway and glanced back at him over her shoulder.

And, *fuck*, if that sight didn't steal his breath and get his heart pumping furiously.

He shook his head. "Nothing."

She hesitated, nodded and went inside. He followed her, closing the door behind them.

"I'm exhausted... with the flight and... everything. I'm going to turn in." She kept moving, heading down the hallway.

He didn't answer her. Instead, he grabbed another beer from the fridge and moved into the living room, which was situated off the kitchen, not bothering to turn on the lights.

It was too early for him to sleep. And he wasn't sure he could, even if he tried. Maybe some mindless television would drown out the thoughts and urges he had. Especially since his jerk-off in the shower earlier hadn't tempered any of them. It only made things worse.

He settled into the recliner and leaned his crutches against the table next to it. After taking another guzzle of beer, he put it aside and grabbed the remote, trying to find the most boring thing on television. With all the reality TV out there, it wasn't hard to find.

He used the lever to kick the recliner back and his legs up as he settled in.

———

"*TRACE.*"

The voice calling him sounded familiar.

"*Trace.*"

He should know who it was, he just couldn't see her.

"*Help me.*"

Then he did. He stood in a room and saw her bound to a chair, surrounded by men who didn't care whether she lived or died. They only wanted one thing.

Their money.

Cash was a commodity worth more than life to them.

Her eyes, the color of that money, were turned to him and what they held froze him from the inside out.

Fear.

And that debilitating fear seeped into his own bones.

Three men stood around her. He couldn't make out their faces since they were blurred, but what he could see clearly were the weapons in their hands.

One held a bloody hatchet. The second one, a knife. The third, a handgun down at his side.

His gaze ran over her to see where the blood on the knife and hatchet had come from. His own voice screamed in his head as he saw her hands had been hacked off. Her throat slit.

But somehow, she once again called out to him. *"Trace. Help me."*

"Do you have the money?" One of the men asked him.

Fuck. *"No."*

"Then you're too late." The man holding the pistol raised it, put it to the back of Ellie's head and pulled the trigger.

Walker's head jerked back as his face was splattered in warm spray of blood and brain matter.

As she slumped forward in the chair, he collapsed to his knees, not even realizing in his nightmare, he had both of his legs.

Walker gasped for breath, his eyes popping open. He'd been clutching the recliner's arms so hard, his fingers had locked.

He slammed the recliner upright, his heart racing, his breathing ragged, sweat beading on his brow.

Darkness surrounded him, except for the eerie glow of the TV.

He turned his head and glanced at the nearby couch. Empty.

The room was empty.

He shut the TV down, grabbed his crutches and stood. His weight-bearing knee almost gave way and, for once, he was glad for the support of his crutches.

He headed past the kitchen and down the hallway, stopping in front of the spare bedroom door. Leaning on one crutch, he opened the door a crack.

He was surprised to find the light on, even though Ellie was under the covers, her back turned toward the door.

He closed his eyes and couldn't wipe that picture of her from his nightmare out of his mind.

She wasn't dead. She was alive. In that bed. Sleeping.

He'd seen her, he'd assured himself of that fact, now he needed to climb into his own bed and get some solid sleep. Otherwise, he'd be useless in the morning to help Hunter. He needed his mind sharp to make sure what happened in his nightmare didn't materialize in real life.

Adjusting his crutches, he pushed the door open wider and moved farther into the room to turn off the lamp on the nightstand.

As he reached to switch it off, her hand snaked out from under the sheet and grabbed his arm. "Don't."

Stupid but true, he was glad to see her hands still attached, the skin on her throat still smooth and her green eyes looking up at him in surprise.

He cleared the rough from his throat to ask, "You can sleep with the light on?"

"I can't sleep with the light on or off right now. At least keeping the light on..." She took a deep, audible inhale. "The truth? I'm spooked."

After that fucking nightmare, she wasn't the only one.

"I don't know who these men are. I don't know what they're capable of." She sat up and shook her head. "I'm wrong, I do. They're capable of killing. But the death would be the easy part. It's what comes before that final breath that would be unbearable."

He was sure she couldn't get the pictures of her husband, the man she married and supposedly loved, tortured and killed out of her mind. Especially when she still had them on her phone.

He should transfer them off hers to his, in case they needed them in the morning.

Her cell phone was within reach, so he handed it to her. "Unlock your phone and then give it back to me. I'll forward those pictures to mine so you can delete them."

As soon as it was unlocked, she handed it back to him. He saw that as a sign of trust. He'd never hand anyone his cell. A burner, yes. His personal phone? No.

She only had two strings of text. His and from the man or men who had killed McMaster.

He quickly forwarded all those texts, along with screenshots of each picture's metadata, to his phone and then locked hers again, placing it on the nightstand. "I won't let them do that to you."

"I know you won't."

He dropped his crutches to the floor and sat on the edge of the bed. He twisted his head to face her. "Do you trust me?"

"Absolutely."

That one whispered word hit him hard. "Why?"

"Because you're you, Trace. I wouldn't have come to you if I didn't."

He followed her hand as it rose from the bed to his face. Her fingers lightly touched his cheek and a small, sad smile played along her lips. "You can grow a beard."

He closed his eyes, cupped a hand over hers and rubbed his stubbled cheek into her soft palm. "Yeah."

He tried to grow a beard his senior year in high school. It ended up looking like a moth-eaten shag carpet. Ellie hated it, so he shaved it back off.

Over the years it had thickened and filled in, but he usually kept it shaved now. But even so, by the end of the day the growth was back.

"Back then I thought you were a man. Even at eighteen. But I know better now. You have grown into a man, Trace. And I'm sorry I missed that journey."

Fuck.

He pulled her hand off his cheek and pressed her fingers to his lips. Then dropped his head and pulled their hands into his lap. "Gotta be honest with you, maybe you shouldn't be trusting me to be in your room right now."

Her fingers twitched within his. "Earlier you asked me if I missed you back then and I told you yes. I wasn't lying. You also asked me if I had loved you. I have to be honest with you, too. I still do. I never stopped."

He opened his eyes and met her green ones brimming with regret again. And, again, he was sure his mirrored hers.

They had lost so much time.

"We're different people now, Ellie. Life changes us."

She nodded slightly and he could see her throat bob when she swallowed. She probably had just as big of a lump in her throat as he did his.

He continued when she stayed quiet. "You love who I used to be. I'm not him anymore. I haven't been him for a long time."

She lifted their hands from his lap and placed them against his chest over his heart. "I'm sure you are."

"Fuck, El," he groaned, twisting the hand she had a hold of, grabbing hers and yanking her to him.

He cupped both sides of her face and crushed his mouth

to hers, swallowing her gasp along with her groan as their lips meshed, their tongues clashed. Her hand fisted in his shirt and twisted, pulling him closer.

He tilted his head, pressed their mouths together harder and took control of the kiss, blocking her tongue from his mouth so he could explore hers instead.

With one hand still gripping his shirt, she wrapped the other around the back of his head and pulled him off balance until he landed on an angle over her. With his chest pressing against hers, he wasn't sure if it was his heartbeat thundering or hers.

Her hand slid down the back of his head to nab the collar of his T-shirt and she began to yank it up.

This needed to end. He couldn't do this. They couldn't do this. He couldn't let himself fall again only to end up falling apart.

He ended the kiss and raised his head. "We can't do this." Every one of those words had to be painfully pulled from him like a jagged splinter.

"The hell we can't." She lifted her hips so the thigh he was leaning over brushed against his hard-on.

For fuck's sake, that wasn't helping. "I'll rephrase. We *shouldn't* do this."

He wasn't sure he'd survive doing this. He had survived the first time. Barely. He wasn't sure he could survive a second.

She shifted her thigh against his erection again just enough to make him bite back a groan. "Are you worried about things getting complicated?"

Fuck yes. "Aren't you?"

In a throaty voice, she said with all seriousness, "I feel it's worth the risk."

Fuck yes.

He stared into her hooded green eyes, dropped a quick

kiss on her lips and then murmured against them, "My bed is bigger." He sat up, leaned over, snagged his crutches from the floor and rose. "I'd throw you over my shoulder and carry you to my bed like a fucking caveman, but those days are over."

Her lips, swollen from their kiss, curled just slightly at the ends. "I'll manage to find my way there."

He backed up and waited for her to get up. She wore a cream-colored pair of panties and as she climbed out of bed, an unmistakable dark line caught his eye.

His cock began to throb. "You wet?"

She hesitated. "Yes."

"I'll race you to the end of the hallway."

"That's not funny," she scolded him with a frown.

"I'm not being funny. Even with these," he tipped his chin to his crutches, "for that?" He tipped it again toward her wet panties. "I'm gonna win that fucking race."

Her wrinkled brow smoothed out. "If you leave me in the dust, what's your reward?"

"Watching you walk into my fucking room wearing a camisole and those damp panties, knowing you'll soon be riding my cock."

A flush rose up her chest into her cheeks.

"Not used to anyone talking to you like that?"

"No."

"It bother you?"

Her lips parted, a short breath escaped, and she whispered, "No."

He didn't bother to hide his grin. "Good. I used to talk dirty to you and you liked it. I was hoping that was one thing that hadn't changed."

"It's been a long time."

"Pity for you. Not so much for me." He was glad it was one thing he'd given her no one else had.

All those late nights on the phone, with Ellie in her bed, he in his, he had perfected the art of dirty talk. He'd taken them both to climax many, many times during those two years they waited impatiently.

Was it wrong? Maybe. But it was one way to be intimate with her and keep both her virginity safe and him out of trouble.

He adjusted his crutches more securely under his arms and hauled ass down the hallway. When he got to his bed, he dropped his crutches to the floor, ripped his shirt over his head, and twisted as he toppled so he landed on his ass onto the mattress. He ripped his shorts down his thighs and let them fall to the floor as well.

His cock was so fucking hard it ached. His balls were tight, his heart racing and his mind was on who was slowly coming down the hallway.

Coming to him.

After all this time.

She was coming back to him.

He only hoped this wasn't some sick dream he would wake up from and find Ellie Cooke wasn't walking from his bedroom door toward his bed looking a million times better than his memories.

She was goddamn beautiful. So fucking beautiful it hurt to look at her.

"Stop," he yelled.

Her step stuttered in surprise and she stopped just feet from him.

"You trust me, right?"

"Yes," she breathed. Her chest rising and falling, her tits swelling above the tight stretchy fabric of her top.

"Then you'll do what I say?"

She didn't answer verbally, her lips parting and her ragged breathing was answer enough.

"Take your top off." He had one hand planted in the bed behind him and one wrapped around his leaking cock. He swirled a drop of precum around the tip and stroked the length slowly as she began to tug the camisole up over her belly. It got caught on her tits, but she freed them and pulled the black fabric over her head and dropped it to the floor.

Fuck yes. Things had changed. Her breasts had been perfect before but now...

They hung a little heavier, the pink flesh puckered around the tightly beaded tips. He couldn't wait to taste them, sink his teeth into them, suck them until she cried out.

"Trace..."

"Circle the tips with your thumbs. Just the tips. Nothing else."

The movement was slight, but he caught it. She had pressed her thighs together. That meant where she was wet before would soon be soaked.

And he couldn't wait to run his nose along that slick line and inhale her scent, savor her taste.

Reclaim her inside and out.

"Twist one nipple and touch your clit."

"Trace," she said more firmly, her brow scrunching up.

"Trust me."

A few seconds later she did what he demanded, sliding her hand into her panties and touching herself. Her eyelids got heavy, her breathing even more uneven.

"Stop."

Her eyelids lifted, but her movement stilled.

He widened his thighs and demanded, "Panties off. Then come here."

She shimmied out of her underwear and his eyes followed them as they dropped to the floor at her feet.

Absolutely soaked.

"Come here," he murmured again, his fist tightening

around his cock, hoping he didn't blow his load before he even got a chance to play.

He frowned when she covered her breasts before stepping between his thighs. "Don't cover yourself from me."

"It's been a long time, honey."

The "honey" was so soft and sweet, he could taste it. "Yeah and I want to see every inch of you. Every fucking inch." He grabbed her wrists and pressed them to her side, moving her back just a half-step so he could see all of her.

Fucking gorgeous. Better than he ever remembered. No, his memories hadn't held what was before him.

Perfection.

Starting at the top of her head, with his eyes following every move, he brushed his fingers over her hair, down her forehead, her nose, her cheekbones, over her lips and chin. He circled his fingers around her throat to feel her breath, her pulse, the smallest noise that bubbled up. He swept both hands over her shoulders and down her arms all the way to her fingertips, then returned on the same path back up. The pads of his fingers traced her collarbones, then slipped to her sides, over her ribs to the dip of her waist, over the softness of her lower belly and the outer curves of her hips. He let his fingers travel from both hip bones to meet in the center and hover on her warm skin right above her patch of damp, dark, curly hair.

He could smell her. That feminine scent which brought back memories, too. She was ready for him. Slick with need, but she remained still as he continued to explore, his hands sliding down her thighs, around her knees to the tops of her calves until he couldn't reach anymore.

"Turn around," he murmured.

Goosebumps broke out over her skin. An uncontrollable reaction he liked to see.

She wanted this. She wanted more.

He would give it all to her.

"Turn around." Even though it wasn't a suggestion, he kept his voice soft but firm.

She turned as he kept his hands on her hips, her soft skin sliding along his palms. When she was facing away from him, he started at the top again. Combing his fingers through her hair, then gathering it into his fist.

"Hold it on top of your head."

She took it from him, her fingers brushing against his as she did so. She pulled her hair up, exposing the back of her neck. That delicate line. Years ago, when he'd bite or suck her skin hard enough to leave a mark, he'd do it back there. Where he knew she wore his claim but no one else could see it.

When his fingertips swept over that spot, she shivered.

She remembered, too.

He pressed his fingers hard there, right below her hairline. Her low groan, one it sounded like she was fighting, made his cock flex against his stomach.

Before the night was over, he planned on marking her there again.

He slid his hands down to the top of her back, spread his fingers wide and with both thumbs at the center, he traveled her spine. Her muscles shifted slightly under his fingers as they moved lower, stopping at the small of her back. Two indentations marked her back above both hips. Divots, in the past, he couldn't resist tasting each time he saw them.

He wanted to taste them now, but he waited.

His hands whispered over her skin until he cupped the bottom curves of her ass, but he didn't linger, he kept going. Down her thighs, the creases at the backs of her knees and around until his fingers curled around her calves, the tips sliding along her shins.

He was done.

Lost. But found.

The beauty of the woman before him almost blinding.

"Turn around," he told her again and she did it more quickly this time.

After the last shiver, she had begun to tremble. He understood it, he was having a hard time keeping the tremor from his own hands.

"My turn?" she asked with unfocused eyes, parted lips, and flushed cheeks. Her hair once again falling in waves around her slender shoulders.

Beautiful.

He wasn't sure if he could wait for her to do the same thing to him as he did to her, but if he could...

This was more than a reintroduction to each other. What he just did to her, his exploration, was something he enjoyed. Taking his time and learning every inch of a woman's body. He viewed the curves and planes of a woman like art. But he hadn't done it in a long time. He didn't waste time doing things like that with women like Sami.

She'd been a means to an end.

Ellie was anything but that.

That also meant he was anything but that to her.

If she wanted to take the time to rediscover him, what she'd missed in the last almost two decades, he wouldn't deny her.

In fact, he'd encourage it.

He released her hips and shifted back on the bed. "How do you want me?"

Her green eyes flashed as she said in a husky voice, "On your belly first."

His cock twitched, a string of precum stretched like a bridge from the crown to his hip.

He gathered it onto his thumb and before he could do anything with it, she grabbed his hand in both of hers and lifted it to her mouth. Her lips closed around his digit as she sucked it clean, her eyes drifting shut for a moment, a groan coming from deep within her chest.

Fuck. If he had been standing on two good legs, that right there would've taken him to his knees. The look of ecstasy on her face as she tasted him pulled his balls so tight, he thought they would explode.

The second she released his hand, he stretched out in the center of the mattress and rolled over, giving her what she wanted. His only issue was he couldn't watch her as he'd like.

Soon.

Waiting was a good thing. Could be a great thing in the right situations.

This was one of those. It would be all worth the wait.

After climbing onto the bed and straddling his thighs, all he could think about was how her thighs were stretched apart and her pussy ripe for his taking.

But he endured.

Through every touch, light brush of her lips, scrape of her teeth, touch of her tongue. In places a woman hadn't touched him in a long time. If ever.

They spent many hours exploring each other when they were young, but after a point, he would lose his patience and would settle her on his cock, or he would settle between her thighs. Or both.

He could control his urges better now. He'd taught himself to do so. To prolong the pleasure so it was more intense when he finally let himself have it. Or when he decided it was time to give it.

And as much as he wanted to flip over, put Ellie on her back and drive himself home, to a place where he belonged, he also told himself he could wait. For that very reason. The intensity of the pleasure would be worth the delaying of the release.

He jerked when she nipped his right ass cheek and then tensed when she did the same to the left.

He smiled into the pillow. He could watch her over his shoulder if he needed, but he was enjoying the tactile pleasure she was giving him and the unknown of what she'd do next.

What he didn't expect was where she went from there. As she moved lower, her fingers brushed along the back of his right leg, while her mouth trailed down his left.

Every muscle locked and he held his breath as she didn't stop or reverse her path. She kept going.

Lower.

Her mouth and fingers touching the back of both his knees.

Lower.

To where his legs were no longer symmetrical. One still whole. One not.

He squeezed his eyes shut and forced himself to take a shuddered breath as she explored the area, the scar, what remained of his leg just below his knee, lightly with her lips and her fingertips.

And just when he thought he couldn't take anymore, she was gone. As she moved away, both the bed and the air around him shifted.

So, he stayed still where he was.

Looking forward to what was to come.

What came next was her straddling his waist, her leaning over until her diamond tipped nipples skimmed the skin of his back and she whispered, "Turn over," near his ear.

Fuck.

He wouldn't be surprised if there was a wet spot on the covers where his dick had been planted.

She rose to her knees and he took his time turning over and when he was finally on his back, he took her in. When she settled back down, her damp curls pressed to his skin, the heat of her pussy searing him, tempting him.

He kept his hands to his sides, wanting to touch, but also wanting to wait.

Her auburn hair fell around her face as she tipped her chin to stare down at him. "I didn't think you could get any better with age, but you proved me wrong. I never imagined in a million years that the boy I fell in love with would turn into the man you are, Trace."

"You don't know me anymore, sweetheart."

Her body jerked and she quickly hid the surprise that crossed her face. Whether she was reacting to his statement or his endearment, or both, he wasn't sure.

But what he said was true. Who and what he was at twenty when he enlisted was not the same person who left the Army on a disability discharge. What he'd done in those years as a Night Stalker and what he'd done since as a Shadow...

If she knew, the pride he heard in her words might not be there. She might rethink what she just said.

No. If she knew some of the things he'd done and might do in the future, she'd most likely be appalled.

But she didn't know, and she'd never know the secrets that he—and all his fellow Shadows—kept. It remained that way to protect themselves, as well as the select few who surrounded them.

She hadn't responded to his comment, instead she'd studied his face, her head tilted just slightly.

Did he fuck up the moment?

He wouldn't be surprised if he did.

He took action to reverse that by popping his hip up, throwing her off balance, grabbing her arms and flipping her to her back, a loud *oof* escaping her.

He caged her in. His hands planted on each side of her head, his thighs squeezing her hips, as he gave her some of his weight. Not all, just enough to pin her to the bed.

It was his turn once again. To hold the power. Take the control.

To show Ellie how much he not only wanted her now, but how much he had missed her.

And to steal back the piece of himself she had taken from him.

Chapter Eight

A simple kiss became so much more as Trace sealed their lips together once again, his tongue, sweeping through her mouth, teased hers.

She'd never forgotten what a great kisser he was. But then, they'd had lots of practice.

Hours. Days. Months. Even years.

How he made a kiss so satisfying was beyond her comprehension. She had kissed other boys before him. And none of them could hold a candle to Trace.

And George couldn't even begin to compare, either. While his kisses were pleasant, they were hardly toe-curling.

No, Trace's kisses made every part of her clench, every molecule of her body sigh. They stole her breath. They made her moan. They made her want... so much more.

She wanted everything from him.

He pulled away slightly, his breathing as ragged as hers, his erection pressing hard against her thigh, the crown slippery against her skin. The tip of his tongue swept along her bottom lip before he gently snagged it between his teeth and pulled.

After a brush of his rough cheek against hers, he slid his

lips down her jaw, tucking his face into her neck. His warm breath swept over her throat as his tongue traced her pulse, dipped into the hollow of her neck.

Ellie threw her head back and air rushed from her lungs as Trace traveled lower.

He pressed kisses across her chest, around the outer curves of her breasts. And like with his fingers earlier, he avoided what she wanted him to touch most. Her breasts swelled and ached for him, her nipples pebbled painfully. He blew lightly across each tip.

"Please," she groaned.

He said nothing, only making her want to beg more when he lightly touched the tip of his tongue to the very tip of her nipple. One. The other. She arched her back, her body screaming for more. But he didn't give it to her. He denied her.

He continued lower, scraping his rough cheek down her belly, dipping his tongue into her navel and went even further. His warm breath battered her skin, raising goosebumps along her flesh in his path. Only stopping when he reached the top of her curls. He buried his nose there, inhaling deeply.

She lifted her head, seeing his arms curled over the tops of her thighs, his eyes tipped to hers. A slight smile on his face, a wicked gleam in his eyes. His tongue came out and he parted the curls in a downward line, only stopping right at the very top of her pussy, right above her clit, which was swollen and throbbing and *oh so ready* for his touch.

"Trace," she whispered, her voice catching.

He nuzzled his nose above her pussy, his hot breath beating against her slick folds and with his hands he spread her thighs even wider.

But he waited.

And she was going out of her mind.

Did he want her to beg? Because she wasn't above begging.

"Trace," she moaned.

A quick touch of the tip of his tongue at the top of her folds and he was gone. He brushed his hands, his lips, his warm skin down her thighs, over and around her knees, her calves and shins. He pressed his lips to the tops of her feet. And he pulled her big toe into his mouth and swirled his tongue around it.

Her pussy clenched and she fisted the sheets at something she never expected to drive her crazy. She never expected having a toe in his mouth would be so sensuous. An almost forbidden pleasure.

He released her toe and worked his way back up, tasting her skin as he went, tracing her flesh with his fingers.

She gasped when he threw her legs over his shoulders and buried his face between her thighs.

Finally, whispered through her mind and maybe even over her lips.

The tip of his tongue circled her clit, flicked it. Then he put his lips on her and sucked hard.

Her hips shot off the bed and she slammed her palms against the mattress, almost tearing the sheets within her fingers.

She released them and grabbed his head, her fingers digging in hard. He grabbed her wrists and pulled them away, pinning them to the bed on either side of her hips.

And during all that he didn't stop what he was doing, which was making her crawl out of her skin. His mouth, his tongue, his teeth. All wreaking havoc on her sanity.

Her heels dug into his back as she drove herself up and into his mouth. He sucked harder, both her clit and swollen folds, and she cried out his name.

He released her wrists and she groaned when he spread

her and slid two fingers inside her, fucking her hard, sucking her even harder.

His words vibrated against her sensitive clit. "Tell me when you're gonna come."

He nibbled along her folds, down one, up the other, scraping his teeth over her clit until her hips twitched uncontrollably.

"Tell me."

"Soon," she forced out.

He lifted his head, his fingers stilling, and she hissed out a breath.

She frowned. "I was about to—"

"Tell me," he ordered before dropping his head back down and started his routine all over again. Circling, flicking, sucking. Biting.

It wasn't long before she was almost there again. Just at that point where... "I'm—"

He lifted his head again, his fingers slipping from her.

What the hell! "Trace," she growled.

He chuckled.

Chuckled!

"Really?"

He buried his head again between her thighs, making her melt back into the mattress once more, letting the pleasure he was giving her crescendo again.

This time she didn't warn him.

Hell no.

She locked her jaws together, twisted her fingers into the sheets and let the most intense orgasm she ever had roll through her.

Holy shit.

Now she got what he was doing and why. And she wanted more.

"You didn't warn me," came his growl against her pussy.

She lifted her head off the pillow and looked down her

body at him. "How did you know?"

He tilted his face up to meet her eyes, his lips shiny, his eyes intense. "Because I know."

"Do you want to explain that?"

"You gonna get bent if I do?"

Would she? "Maybe." He probably had a lot of women in nineteen years. "I was only with you and—"

He surged from between her legs, letting them drop to the mattress, and moved up her body until he braced his weight in his palms, one on each side of her head. He dropped his head again until they were almost nose to nose, this time to lock their gazes. "That conversation ends here. When you're in my bed, you don't mention another man. Especially him. Hear me?" When she didn't answer fast enough, he continued. "And I won't tell you where I learned that. But I can tell you it started with us."

It started with us.

With those years of waiting. Of only allowing themselves to go so far before stopping.

Until finally... That night.

Their first time was better than she'd ever dreamed. She had heard from her friends losing her virginity could be painful and awkward. They were all thankful it was over quickly.

But that wasn't how it was with her and Trace.

Not even close.

The waiting might have been torture, but in the end? It was perfect and special and unforgettable.

They finally gave each other the most precious gift that they could give each other. A gift they could only give someone once.

But age and experience only made things better. And the orgasm he just gave her was the most intense one she ever had.

And she couldn't wait for the next one.

He dropped his lips to hers, making sure she got a good taste of what he had. Then he shifted enough to latch onto one of her nipples, sucking it hard and deep, just to the point where it could turn painful, but he knew how far to take it. To take it to that very edge.

He rolled her other nipple between his fingers and slid his cock along her thigh. It was hot and hard, the tip slick, making her pussy pulsate in anticipation.

She scraped her nails down his back, grabbed two handfuls of his ass and squeezed. "Trace."

It was just his name, but it was enough to let him know she was ready. To encourage him.

But he suddenly became still.

Was this another one of his waiting games?

He groaned and moved up, pressing his forehead to hers. "I have no condoms in the house. I've never brought a woman here before and never planned to."

She bit back a whimper. No condoms? How could a single man have no condoms?

I've never brought a woman here before and never planned to.

While she found that surprising and interesting, she had a more pressing matter to deal with at the moment. "Not in your wallet?"

"In my car and under the seat of my bike. Do you want me to go and grab them?"

That meant he'd need to pull on at least his boxers, find his crutches, and work his way through the sprawling house and come back.

Her fingers flexed against his back. "No, I don't want you to go. I'm covered."

He lifted his head. "The pill?"

"An IUD." Pregnancy wasn't the only worry when it came to sex, but she'd only been with two men in her life. And Trace was one of them. The other she was married to for over sixteen years.

94

So, while he didn't have to worry about her history, she had to worry about his.

"Do you trust me?" he whispered.

She nodded. "Yes."

"Then know I've never once had unprotected sex." He hesitated. "Can I trust you?"

She nodded again. "Yes. I—"

"No. Don't say it."

Right, he didn't want her mentioning another man in his bed. Well, she didn't want to think about any other man while in his bed, either.

She grabbed his face and pulled him down, capturing his lips, this time taking control of the kiss. Showing him how much she wanted him.

And she was tired of waiting.

As she kissed him, he dug his fingers into her hair, holding on, and settled between her thighs. With his other hand between them, he slid the head of his cock through her wetness, from her clit all the way through the crease of her ass and back up until it caught.

He stopped right where she wanted him.

Then it hit her. There was no going back from this.

Seeing each other had ripped open old wounds, but maybe, just maybe, this would heal them.

Or maybe it would make them worse.

Because in the end, things were still raw between them. And her future was still up in the air.

If she ended up having to disappear, she'd never see him again.

If she was smart, she wouldn't let herself fall because it was going to be even harder this time to pick herself back up.

Even so, it was too late to be changing her mind. She could, and she was sure Trace would accept her decision, but, in truth, she wanted him to continue.

Consequences be damned.

She realized she had stopped kissing him and his mouth hovered right over hers. She focused on him and he was looking at her with concern.

"You sure about this?"

She wiggled her hips, but he managed to only give her the tip and no more. "Yes."

He pulled her arms straight over her head, ran his hands from her armpits up, and when he got to her wrists, he not only drove them into the bed, he drove his cock inside her with a grunt.

The air rushed from her lungs as he did so, then stilled. Her body stretched around him, accepting him. Squeezing him.

He pressed his forehead to hers and he began to move, his breath puffing with each thrust, his eyes locked with hers, even though they were too close to focus, his fingers circling her wrists tightly.

"You fit me like a glove, El. A perfect fucking glove."

El. Funny enough, no man had ever called her that but him. Just like sweetheart.

He glided in and out of her with each tilt of his hips.

"Fuck," he whispered and closed his eyes. "Fuck."

Yes, she agreed, it felt that good, that right.

She had missed him, missed this.

Missed *them.*

She expected him to go slow, to tease her, like he did when his mouth was on her, but he didn't.

He ground deep at the end of each long, full stroke. And his pace quickened.

"Legs around me."

She pressed her thighs to his hips, and held onto him with her calves, doing her best not to dig her heels into his thighs.

He drove harder and deeper and faster, with a power she had forgotten.

"Ellie." Her name was a ragged whisper that made her nipples ache as they pressed against his chest.

His weight on her should be too much, smothering, but it wasn't. It was perfect.

She wanted more of it. She wanted him to absorb her, protect her. Keep her safe.

Then she was rising, climbing, her climax building.

His pace became more fevered. "Ellie." He released her wrists, gripped both sides of her face, driving his fingers into her hair and he took her mouth as hard as he took her pussy.

Claiming her.

He drove the air from her lungs with each thrust, then gave it back to her. Until finally she felt the peak. Right there. She was there.

But she said nothing because she didn't want him to pull back. Not this time. This time she just wanted to let go. To set them free.

She struggled to keep her mouth on his when the orgasm ripped through her like a tornado. She swore it swept through her from her head to the tips of her toes.

She knew he felt it because he groaned into her mouth but didn't let up. He continued to pound her, taking what he wanted, giving her what she needed.

She gasped as another orgasm came from nowhere, curling her toes, forcing her to rip herself from his mouth to gulp air.

But he didn't move away, he held her head in place and stared down into her eyes.

"Sweetheart," he breathed, then he tensed, curled over her one more time, driving deep, holding even deeper, never losing her eyes as he let go, filling her, marking her.

Then she saw it. The slight flinch.

Reality had suddenly reared its ugly head.

Whether that flinch was from discomfort because of his leg or from the realization of what they just did, she didn't know.

She just knew she didn't want it to be either.

"I've added another rule."

She lifted an eyebrow but waited.

"You're in my bed while you're here."

Ellie finally breathed.

———

WALKER LAY on his side in bed, waiting.

Ellie had gone to the bathroom to clean up, and dropped a wet washcloth off for him on her way out the door to the kitchen.

All of this while naked.

Maybe he needed to set another rule. When she was in his house, she was forbidden to wear clothes.

Yes, her body had changed, but, *fuck*, he loved every single one of those changes. She had grown from a girl into a woman.

And just like she was sorry she missed him turning into a man, he was sorry he hadn't been around to watch her mature and get comfortable within her own skin. Which apparently, she was, since she stepped right over his shirt she could've thrown on in her travels.

A few minutes later, she was back, her face soft, her lips holding a slight curve and two glasses of water in her hands. She set one down on his side, then rounded the bed to put the other on the far nightstand.

Her side of the bed.

He kept his back toward her as the mattress shifted as she climbed on. "You sure you want me to stay in here with you? I'm afraid I might kick you during the night."

"It'll be fine," he murmured, grabbing the glass and taking a few gulps.

He had just put the water down when she fitted herself to his back, her arm snaking around his waist.

He flattened his lips to keep from smiling like a fucking fool.

She pressed a few kisses over his shoulder and the top of his back, and he was disappointed when she pulled away just slightly. "Tell me about the tattoo."

One of his rules had been that she not ask questions or get personal.

But with what they just shared, he was ready to throw that rule out the window. However, he'd keep it in place just in case she wanted to know things he couldn't give her.

Especially about his job. Or his time in the service.

Or how he coped after she gave him the boot.

Those were things he'd keep to himself.

But the tattoo? Not off limits.

"It's the insignia of the Night Stalkers."

"What are the Night Stalkers?"

"Soldiers who specialize in nighttime operations. We flew choppers."

"You were one."

"Yeah."

"I had heard you became Airborne, right?"

"I did. That was the first step."

"Was it difficult?"

Walker rolled to his back, taking her with him and pulling her into his side. Her thigh curled around his right leg—his good leg—and he liked the weight of it. He also liked the feel of her cheek pressed to his chest, her breath sweeping over his skin, her soft tits pushed into his ribs. He liked his fingers in her hair.

He fucking liked all of it.

He had missed this. Missed her.

He never thought life would come full circle.

No, not full circle. Not quite. Some things would never go back to being the same.

"After I finished basic training and you..."

Her fingers drifted up his stomach to his chest. He tucked his chin into his neck to glance down at her. She was avoiding his gaze.

"After that, I completed my Green Platoon, and moved on eventually joining the 160th."

"160th?"

"A unit that specializes in nighttime operations by air."

She lifted her head just slightly, her soft hair sliding along his chest and side. He curled his fingers into the long reddish-brown strands, rubbing them back and forth between his fingers.

"Like Black Hawks?"

"And others."

"You were a pilot?"

"I'm still a pilot," he murmured. That was one thing they couldn't take from him. He earned it, he was keeping it. Whether he ever flew a chopper again or not.

"Is that how you lost your leg?"

He'd been expecting it, but he also wasn't ready to have that conversation. It was time to shut it down for the night, anyway.

"Not tonight."

"When?"

"Not tonight, El. I need sleep so I can work on your case first thing in the morning."

He needed sleep, whether he'd get any was questionable.

Bringing Ellie into his house wasn't smart. Bringing her into his bed even less.

But keeping her there...

That might just destroy him.

Chapter Nine

WITH A HUGE COFFEE mug in one hand and his cell phone in the other, he strode down the narrow hallway in the warehouse. Hunter was going to meet him in "Badass Central," their electronics room in which their boss's ol' lady dubbed it so. She had even painted a little sign and tacked it over the door, saying she could get pregnant just walking into that room with all the testosterone that filled it when the whole team was present.

As if his thoughts conjured up the boss's ol' lady, Jewel came waddling down the hallway from the opposite direction. He could pretty much guess where she was coming from. The bathroom.

At this late in the game, her pregnancy had her in and out of there so many times she said she should just set up a desk in there.

Jewel's belly was huge and leading the way since she was due to give birth to Diesel's third child any day now.

Diesel.

Third child.

Walker snorted.

Not one of them—not one—could've guessed he'd even get tied down to a woman, forget producing babies.

But he had. And if anyone was perfect for their grump of a boss, it was Jewel, who took no shit from D and knew how to shovel it right back when he tried.

And this was why she was about to pop again for the third time. Because she frustrated Diesel so much, he was always "teaching her a lesson." In turn, those "lessons" knocked her up.

Her hands were under her protruding belly like she was afraid the baby was just going to split her open and walk the fuck out.

She stopped toe to toe with him—more like belly to waist—and gave him a frown. "Last one."

Since that had been her mantra for the last few months, he knew what the hell she was talking about.

"That's what you said last time." He snorted again, then took a sip of his coffee to hide his grin.

She shook her head, her dark brown hair pulled back into a ponytail flipping around as she did so. "No. This is it. My vagina can't take anymore."

Walker opened his mouth, then shut it. He quickly took another sip of coffee. There was no way in hell he was commenting on his boss's ol' lady's snatch. Even in jest.

No fucking way. There could be hidden microphones. And then he might die.

So, no.

He tried to switch gears with, "Did you guys ever find out the sex?" If they had, he'd heard nothing. As long as the baby was healthy and his boss didn't drop over dead from worrying about Jewel suffering through another labor, he couldn't care less what they had.

"He wants it to be a surprise."

Walker raised his eyebrows. Just like the three pregnancies. "Afraid it's not gonna be a boy." That was his best guess.

"He wants a boy."

After two baby girls, Walker would want a boy, too. In the past, females had always only been a sexual outlet for D. Until Jewel. Then his household went from one female to three. And if they had another girl? That would mean four.

And once they were all the age where their cycles synchronized?

Fuck. Poor bastard.

Walker bet D was also rethinking all the things he did to women and *where* he did them for all those years. Now he had daughters and he bet it drove D nuts to think one of his own daughters could be getting fucked against the wall in a bathroom somewhere in the future.

Oh yeah. Walker was pretty fucking sure D was wishing he'd done things differently.

"He's gonna need help kicking the asses of teenage boys when Violet and Indie get to that age."

"I'm already signing him up for blood pressure meds, even if I have to crush them up and hide them in cheese."

Walker laughed. "This being the last one, he gonna get snipped?"

"You'd think that would be the easiest solution, right? But fuck no. The way he acts, a vasectomy would be the same as a sex change operation. Thinks his voice will get girly and he'd have to start wearing a bra."

"He probably should wear a bra," Walker teased. "And a thong."

Jewel laughed then her eyes went wide.

Oh shit. "What? Baby coming?"

She shook her head. "No, I just fucking peed a little again. Fuck my life." She turned carefully in the narrow hallway, trying not to bump her belly and waddled back toward the bathroom. "Last one!" she screamed.

"Should I remind you of that next time?" he asked, following more slowly.

Jewel flipped him the bird over her shoulder.

He chuckled and stepped into "Badass Central," closing the door behind him.

Hunter was leaning back against one of the desks, his own travel mug full of caffeine in his hand. "Should I ask?"

Walker moved around the desk, set his coffee down and settled into one of the leather desk chairs. They were fitting for "Badass Central" since they were designed for gamers.

"You can ask, doesn't mean I'll answer."

Hunter sat at the computer next to him. Both consoles had three screens that were set up in a curve around the user.

"You start digging yet?" Walker asked.

He shook his head. "Just got here a few minutes ago."

Walker cocked a brow at him. Hunter was normally up before first light.

He shrugged. "Got a woman at home now. Gotta take care of business before taking care of business."

"Jesus," Walker muttered. "Didn't need that image in my head."

Hunter grinned. "Gotta make son number two before I get to be old like you and it's too late."

"I'm only like a year or so older than you, asshole." He turned his head to study Hunter. "How's son number one holding up?"

Hunter sobered. "Okay."

"No nightmares?" Leo, Frankie's son, who Hunter was in the midst of adopting, had been kidnapped and traumatized by his real father before Hunter's woman took the man out with a Louisville Slugger to the melon.

"Nothing out of the ordinary. Doesn't mean we're not watching."

"Yeah," Walker said softly. "He's a good kid. I hope it doesn't fuck him up."

"Agreed. There are enough of us fucked up around here." Hunter logged into the computer and began to type. "So, you guys work out your shit?"

Walker was typing in his own password when he paused. "You guys?"

"You and Ellie."

"Why would you think that?"

"Expected you to walk in here this morning ready to snap everyone's head off. You didn't. You came in here like you had a taste of the sweetest pussy on the planet. Though, I know that ain't right since I've claimed it already, so maybe the second sweetest."

"I have a hard time believing Frankie doesn't care about you talking about her pussy."

Hunter chuckled. "You gonna tell her?"

Walker grinned. "Fuck no. I've seen the damage she can do with a baseball bat. Not only on Taz's head but your Range Rover."

Hunter's chuckle died. "Yeah. I almost cried over my Rover. Anyway, seriously, how'd it go?"

"It went."

Hunter's fingers flew over the keyboard. "She know about your leg?"

Walker sat back in his chair and ran a hand down his cheek which was back to being smooth after shaving this morning. "No."

"She know now?"

"Yeah."

"You showed her your ugly-assed stump?" he asked in surprise.

"Ain't as ugly as Mercy's face."

"Or Steel's and he doesn't even have an excuse."

"Yeah. He was just born ugly."

Both of them swallowed their snorts when the door opened and Steel walked in.

"What are you doing here?" Walker asked him.

Steel stopped, took a good look around the room and said, "Last I checked, I work here."

"Don't you have a job?"

"To annoy the fuck out of you two." His eyes landed on their mugs. "Jewelee make coffee?"

"Frankie made mine."

"Ellie made mine," Walker announced, then waited.

Steel moved closer and perched his ass on the corner of the desk. "Yeah? She's sweet."

"Don't get any ideas," Walker stated.

Hunter chuckled and told Steel, "He showed her his stump."

Steel's toothpick went from one side of his mouth to the other. "Damn. Were you looking for a sympathy fuck?"

"Works every time," Walker answered, feeling the tightening of his jaw, even though he knew Steel was just busting his balls.

"Are you glad I pressured you into taking her home?"

"No."

"Shame, then. Thought you guys would've fucked for old time's sake."

"If we did, I wouldn't tell you."

"I'll tell you," Hunter cut in. "They did. He walked in here with a 'just laid' swagger."

"Didn't know Peg Leg could swagger."

Hunter raised his hand. "I witnessed it. Swear to fuck."

Walker dropped his head and shook it. After a second, he lifted it and shot a frown at Steel. "You here to work or just be a dick?"

"Work, I guess. D doesn't have a job for me. Meeting Slade at the gym later to spar. May even teach Diamond's kick-boxing class this afternoon since the women in there are..." He whistled low. "The shit they wear. I keep them kicking and punching the whole time and I get to watch tits and ass bouncing everywhere. Enough to cause an earthquake."

"Good thing you have a micro-dick and they can't see your boner, or they'd have you arrested for being such a fucking perv," Hunter warned him. "And now I'm telling Frankie not to take that class if you're filling in."

"You're gonna deny me the pleasure of your woman's luscious tits and ass causing a tsunami?"

"Yeah, since they're mine and I don't share. So, remember that."

"Need to sign up Rissa so—"

"Fuck," Walker barked, his eyes sliding toward the door Steel left open. "You know better than to let those fucking thoughts come out of your mouth. Jesus, you wanna die?"

Steel quickly looked toward the door. "He ain't here."

"You don't know that," Hunter whispered, dropping his head and typing even faster.

"He's a fucking ghost," Walker whispered, then raised his voice. "Now get the fuck out or sit the fuck down and help us dig."

"Will you tell us what Ellie did with your stump?" Steel asked with a grin.

"How about if I shove it up your ass? You helping or not, Steel?"

"Helping."

"Then sit the fuck down and shut the fuck up."

For the next few hours, the only words spoken were about what they were finding online. Even though he could see both Hunter and Steel bursting at the seams to find out what happened between him and Ellie.

Walker hacked into McMotherfucker's business bank accounts and found nothing out of the ordinary other than the man being in debt. Their joint personal bank accounts were financially anemic, too, only holding the minimum to keep them open.

They didn't have to hack into their credit card accounts since they were still held jointly, and Ellie texted him the info when he asked. However, all five were maxed out. Worse, none of them had a small limit. In fact, just in credit cards alone, McMaster had stuck Ellie with over two hundred thousand in debt. And since they were never divorced, she would be held liable.

Any real estate McMaster had invested in had been sold. Some at a loss. The mini mansion they'd lived at—and Ellie sold—barely covered what was still owed in a mortgage. However, she did pull some equity, which was what she had the brokers hand over to the men who'd killed her husband.

Her husband.

Walker set his jaw. McMaster had had what Walker had last night. He'd had Ellie *for years,* over sixteen to be exact, while Walker only had her completely for less than one before he enlisted.

He forced his wandering thoughts back to the business at hand, since his blood pressure was rising.

With no large chunks of cash coming or going from his business or personal accounts, McMaster probably had more accounts Ellie didn't know about. Possibly offshore. Or in some shell corporation's name.

The more they dug, the more Walker discovered what a shitty businessman McMaster was, a complete opposite from the two elder McMasters. The apple not only fell far from the tree, it rolled away and fell into a ditch.

McMaster had been in the middle of filing for bankruptcy, too. Ellie hadn't mentioned that, so maybe she didn't know. Doing that, the asshole would destroy her credit, too. Not that her credit was great now, since still being legally tied to him had sunk her financially. She would be hard-pressed to get any kind of loan in the near future, even a small one. She had no collateral and was drowning in debt she might not even be aware of.

And that was all before the 1.3 million dollars she owed whoever the mystery men were who killed McMaster.

Unfortunately, they hadn't dug up one piece of good news that would give Ellie some hope. Not one.

Hunter tried to find out who held the account Ellie had wired money into. It came back to a AAA Acme Corporation, which made it a shell, obviously. They needed to find out who was behind that dummy company and why McMaster owed them so much.

They had seven days left until the deadline. He and Hunter both agreed, they needed to fly to Denver, talk to the office manager and any employees who might give them some clues during the day and then break into McMaster's office at night to search for anything that might help them.

They needed to find out who was behind all of this. If they had that, they could form a plan from there.

But nothing in the records they dug up today gave them anything solid to work with.

And time was ticking...

———

AFTER STEEL LEFT to meet Slade at Shadow Valley Fitness, Hunter went to go pick Leo up from daycare since his woman, Frankie, had to work until five at Shadow Valley Body Works. Slade, Leo's uncle, had gotten Frankie a job in the Dirty Angels MC run business after she moved from Manning Grove to Shadow Valley to be with Hunter.

Walker had a headache from staring at computer screens for hours.

He should head over to the gym, too. Or he could go home and get cardio another way...

Like putting on his blade and going for a run.

Or... taking Ellie to bed and working up a sweat.

The third option was sounding the best, even though he needed to get a real workout in.

Maybe he'd go home, do a warm-up with Ellie, go for a run, then fuck her again afterward.

His cock seemed to like that idea and so did he.

Before Hunter left, they'd decided to spend another day in front of the computers, make some calls and then hop on a plane and shoot to Denver for a couple days.

After that, he was tempted to head to Delaware, where McMotherfucker's father now lived, to pay the man a little visit. Maybe encourage him to pay his son's debts. Especially the one hanging over his daughter-in-law's head.

If he couldn't be convinced, then Walker might have to take further action.

Instead of turning left out of the warehouse lot to head to the gym, he turned right toward the DAMC compound. Normally when he rode his bike, he took the long way home to put in a few extra miles to enjoy the restored machine that sat between his legs.

Today, the urge to ride directly home was strong. He didn't fool himself with denying why that was.

He'd been tempted to fuck her this morning before he'd left but she'd already slipped from the bed, made coffee and was sitting out on the back deck.

He didn't bug her. Instead he showered, got dressed and headed out with a mug of that coffee. He had only stuck his head out the door and told her he was leaving and wasn't sure when he'd be back.

He also told her to text him a list of groceries and anything else she needed so Jesse, his weekly housekeeper/sometimes cook, could pick those items up for her.

Ellie had only nodded and gave him a small smile.

And because of that, he wondered all fucking day if she regretted climbing into his bed. He didn't want to keep her there if she only felt obligated. Especially when he'd made it one of his rules.

You're in my bed while you're here.

He didn't ask. He told her.

Just like the day he met her at the lake for a swim and told her he'd enlisted.

She'd been shocked and hadn't said much. Probably because she'd been in disbelief. And it wasn't until he'd been gone for months, when he called home to tell her he was headed overseas, that she said it was over between them.

Even now, if she didn't want to be with him, he wasn't going to force her. And Steel's earlier words hit him. He didn't want her fucking him out of pity, either.

He pulled his Harley into the garage between his truck and his Charger Hellcat. On his way into the house, he paused and stared at his Ford.

He shouldn't have kept it in storage all those years. But he had a hard time getting rid of something that meant so much to him. After being discharged from the Army, he hadn't had much. In fact, he came home with less than that, since he was missing the lower portion of his left leg.

But he had his pride, his dignity, and his memories.

One of his best being all those nights in the back of his old Ford with Ellie.

So, after he met Ryder for the first time in a small town in Kentucky outside of Fort Campbell, the man convinced him to join D's crew. At the time, he couldn't understand why any "security" team would want a cripple to be a part of it. But as he learned to live without his leg, learned to walk again with the use of prostheses, eventually learned to be able to live with the way he was and stop feeling sorry for himself, he realized he needed a new venture. He went home to New York, took the truck out of storage, drove the rust bucket to Shadow Valley and never looked back.

Eventually he had Crash, the DAMC member who ran

Shadow Valley Body Works, restore it for him and it was the first thing he moved into his new house. He rarely drove it because, every time he had, he imagined Ellie snuggled up against him, his arm around her, her head on his shoulder as he drove to "their spot."

Then he'd remember what they did at their spot.

Now, that old memory took him right back to his newest one, last night's.

He needed to rectify that fuck up and set things straight with her.

As he opened the door from the garage into his laundry room, the smell hit him. He knew right then and there, it sure as hell wasn't grilled cheese sandwiches with tomatoes and ham slices.

No, the fuck it wasn't.

Whatever it was smelled goddamn delicious and made his stomach growl. Apparently, a day full of two protein bars, ten cups of coffee and three slices of cold pizza weren't enough to satisfy him.

But the smell of her food wasn't the only thing that made his mouth water. He paused at the doorway of the laundry room, which led into the eating area off the kitchen and leaned his shoulder against the jamb to take it all in.

Ellie was wearing black clingy leggings of some sort, similar to what a woman would wear to yoga, and another one of those camisoles, this time in teal. What she had on left not one thing to the imagination, it clung to every single one of her curves.

She must not have heard him come in since she kept her back to him, and he saw she had a wire running behind her neck from ear to ear and her cell phone was tucked into the waistband of her leggings.

He wasn't sure whether to be amused or worried, since anyone could have breached his house and kidnapped or killed her before she was even aware someone was there.

His attention was drawn back to her ass when she grabbed a set of hot pads, opened the oven and bent over to pull something out.

At that sight, he was ready to pull something out and it wasn't a casserole.

He reached down and adjusted himself but stayed where he was. He liked watching. And waiting... Even though he was very ready to eat.

But now it had nothing to do with food.

She continued to fuss with something on the stove, but then she froze.

Was he busted?

No, she reached out, planted her hand on the counter, tipped her head back and shuddered.

What the fuck?

Her eyes were now squeezed shut, her bottom lip tucked between her teeth before her head fell forward, her hair covering her face. A second later it snapped back up and she went about doing what she'd been doing, like nothing had happened.

He had no idea what that maneuver was about. And as she turned toward the fridge, he could even see a flush running from her chest up into her cheeks and a soft smile on her lips.

One would have guessed she just had a spontaneous orgasm.

But that couldn't be right.

After closing the fridge door, she turned and froze once again. Her whole body jolted when she spotted him, and she slapped a hand to her chest so hard that it had to hurt. "Oh! You scared me."

He pushed off the door jamb and sauntered over to her. Reaching up, he plucked one of the earbuds from her ear. "What're you listening to?"

"A... an audiobook."

His eyes dropped to her hard nipples. "Must be a good one."

The flush in her cheeks darkened. "It is." She pulled the other earbud out and fiddled with her phone.

His soft, sweet Ellie could still get embarrassed. "You need to stay more aware, El. I could've disabled you, raped you, and killed you because you weren't paying attention."

Her pink cheeks quickly turned pale. "What?"

"You couldn't hear me. You were... distracted. Anyone could have walked in. You have people who want you dead, Ellie, take that seriously."

"I am. And they don't *want* me dead, they want their money."

He leaned in until they were almost nose to nose. "You got 1.3 million, sweetheart?"

She only hesitated for a second. "No."

"Right." He slid his eyes from her back to the stove area. "What are you making?"

"Um... Dinner?"

Walker raised a brow at her. "Since it's about that time of day, I could've guessed that. I'm talking specifics."

"I'm making roasted chicken with lemon and garlic with a side of cheesy garlic mashed potatoes and green beans."

At first, all he heard was two dishes with garlic. He hoped he had mouthwash. But once the rest of the meal sunk into his brain, it all sounded great.

He hadn't had a good home-cooked meal like that in ages. "Will it keep?"

"Do you need to..." Her eyes tipped down to his leg.

"No. I want to go for a run."

Her eyebrows knitted together. "A run?"

"Yeah, you know, like jogging but only faster."

Her pretty green eyes widened. "You can run?"

"I can do a lot of things, El."

"I... I..." The breath hissed out of her and the color was back in her cheeks. "Shit. Sorry."

His soft, sweet Ellie.

He ran a thumb over her heated cheek. "Baby, it's okay. You learn to adapt, remember?" He ran it over her bottom lip next. "Dinner will keep?"

"Yes. I can keep it warm. I wasn't sure when you were getting back, anyway."

"Give me about forty-five, then we can eat. I assume Jesse dropped off everything you asked for?"

"She did. She said she was on her way to Z's house. I had no idea who she was talking about."

"He's the president of the Dirty Angels MC, the club which owns this compound."

"A motorcycle club built this neighborhood?"

"Yeah, well, we all built our own houses, but the land was obtained by them and then sold for cheap to anyone in the club who was ready to build."

"But... But you're not a part of the club?"

"No. I just work for their enforcer, Diesel. So, we're separate but, in reality, not completely."

"We? As in all of the Shadows you work with?"

"Yeah."

He stared down at her and she stared back at him. Her lips parted as he dropped his head down closer.

He wanted to kiss her. *Hell*, he wanted to do more than that, but he needed to get one thing straight first....

"El, made a rule last night I maybe shouldn't have made."

"Which one?" she whispered.

"The one where I said you were going to be in my bed."

"You don't want me in your bed?"

The corners of her lips had turned down while his twitched. "I do. But I don't want you to feel obligated. I only want you there because you want to be there, so I'm going to let you break that rule if you want to."

"I don't want to." She lifted to her tiptoes and pressed her lips to his. "I don't want to. I think you need to go run now so we can..."

"Eat," he finished for her with a grin.

Heat flickered in her eyes. "Yes, eat."

Now he was tempted to push back dinner for an hour and a half. Before he decided to do that, he said, "Forty-five minutes," more to get himself in motion than to remind her.

Fuck.

If he wasn't going to work out at the gym, he at least needed to run to keep his leg muscles in condition.

He forced himself to turn and walk away from Ellie and go for a fucking run.

Chapter Ten

His RUNNING blade was made from carbon fiber. That's what he had said while she stood in the kitchen staring at him.

He had walked in the front door and headed to the kitchen first thing to grab a glass of ice water.

Ellie had pretty much lost her tongue and her breath as he stood by the sink downing the water so quickly that some of it didn't make it into his mouth but instead dripped off his chin onto his chest. Which was also shirtless and glistening with sweat.

Seeing him standing there, his head back, gulping cold water, his throat undulating as he swallowed, she just took in everything that was right in the world when it came to Trace.

If it wasn't for his carbon fiber running blade prosthesis that made up his left leg below the knee, he'd be perfect.

No.

That wasn't right.

Even with that, he was perfect. From the damp blond hair on his head, his intense blue eyes, his handsome face, his body...

Oh yes, his body.

All muscle goodness wrapped in a tight tan package. The man even had a six-pack.

Who had the kind of six-pack that didn't belong in a fridge?

Not George. No, George wanted to live the easy life. Socializing and making money. He only did the minimum not to get fat by playing a lot of golf and tennis. That was it.

His body certainly hadn't been honed like Trace's was. She'd never complained because true attraction and love were never only about someone's appearance. With Trace...

He had it all.

And when he finally put the glass down on the counter, he was looking at her with concern.

Probably because she hadn't said a damn word since he walked into the kitchen and started explaining about his running blade, though she hadn't asked.

It wasn't like she wasn't interested, she was. And she was glad he told her, but right now, it wasn't about the running blade.

No, it was all about the goodness that was Trace.

Especially since he was standing in the kitchen looking sexy as hell in silky olive green *short* running shorts that clung perfectly to everything that *was* Trace.

Everything.

Even though she knew what he looked like without those shorts, something about them emphasized his assets.

She swallowed hard, then raised her gaze from those assets to see an amused expression and a grin on his face.

"I'm assuming by the look on your face, you like what you see." His low voice rumbling made her insides clench.

She finally found her tongue. "I can't complain about the view."

"You've seen me naked."

"Yeeessss," she drew out, "but it's not the same."

"Want to explain that?"

"You're not a woman, so I can't explain it. Just trust me, it's not the same."

He grinned and shrugged. "Gotta shower, then we can eat."

She raised a brow. "Is it going to be a long one?"

His grin widened. "No."

She nodded and turned toward the stove where she'd been keeping dinner warm. "Okay, I'll get stuff ready."

He said nothing, nor did he move toward his bedroom.

She lifted the lid of the mashed potatoes to give them a quick stir, then gathered some dirty cooking utensils to put in the sink.

Only Trace was still blocking it.

And watching her.

Once again, he had a look in his eyes that reminded her of a hungry predator with his eyes on his prey. That made her nipples bead instantly but she ignored it, saying, "Excuse me," so he'd get out of the way.

He only moved enough so she could put the items in the sink to wash later but before she could step back, he had her trapped. His chest pressed against the top of her back and his hands were on either side of her, planted on the edge of the sink.

He pressed those damp silky shorts and the hard package beneath them against her. Her being so much shorter meant that it pressed mid-back.

"Ellie," he whispered into her ear. A shiver ran through her at how he said her name and the fact that his warm breath swept over her skin. "Did you come when you were listening to that book?"

Shit. She'd hoped he'd forgotten that. Of course he didn't. She hadn't but it was very close with a few involuntary twitches and a splash of wetness.

"No," she sort of fibbed.

"But it got you wet?"

That she didn't mind admitting to. "Yes," hissed softly out of her.

"Are you still wet?"

"Not from the book."

"From what?"

She tipped her head back slightly to give him better access. "From you."

He traced the tip of his tongue around her ear, his long fingers wrapping around her waist, as if he was trying to see if he could circle it with his hands.

He used to be able to do that. He no longer could. A few inches separated the tips of his left fingers and the tips of his right.

He said nothing, instead sliding them up her ribs and around to cup the undersides of her breasts. Both thumbs brushed back and forth over her hard nipples.

"Hold your hair up, El," he murmured.

Oh, God. She knew what was coming next.

She reached behind her, gathered her hair and pulled it to the top of her head, exposing her neck. With his thumbs still lightly caressing the tips of her nipples, he ran his tongue up her neck from the top of her back to her hairline. Then his warm breath caught on the wet he left behind.

He used to mark her there. Where she could hide it under her hair. A place where they both knew it was there, that they belonged to each other. Forever and always.

Though, forever and always turned out to not be true.

She wasn't his for always. He wasn't hers forever.

Dreams and reality were two different things.

She was quickly brought back to reality when she bit back a whimper as one of his hands slid down her belly and into the waistband of her yoga pants. Since she wore nothing beneath them, his palm brushed along her skin until he reached the top of her pussy. Then a finger separated her slick folds and caught on her clit.

She shuddered and her hips twitched. The touch so light, it drove her insane since it wasn't enough.

"More," she moaned.

"When I give it to you," was all he said. He cupped her mound and squeezed. With his middle finger, he breached her folds, sliding through her wetness from back to front and on the return, he slipped it inside her.

Her breath caught and her head tipped back. Still not enough.

"Head up, sweetheart. You know what I want."

Yes. Yes, she did. She wanted that, too.

"So fucking wet. Fuck." His thumb pressed on her clit while his middle finger glided in and out of her slowly. "Ready for another one?"

This time she could only answer with a soft whimper.

He slipped another of his long fingers inside of her and curled them.

Yes. Perfect.

"Close your eyes. Whatever scene in that book was getting you off, picture us doing that. Me and you. Take us there."

She closed her eyes and took herself back to the sexy part she was listening to in the book which had scorching hot scenes. It wasn't a struggle to imagine the two of them taking the place of those characters because it was what she had done while listening. Imagined Trace doing the same things to her the hero did to the heroine in that romance novel had caused her reaction. And she also imagined it was Trace talking into her ear instead of the male narrator, just like he was doing now.

Not only had his body matured over the years, his voice had deepened. And it was perfect for the storyteller of an erotic dream.

So, she replayed that scenario in her head as his thumb strummed her clit, his fingers slid in and out of her, now faster, no longer as gentle as when he'd first started. With his other hand, he slipped inside her cami and captured her nipple, at first tweaking it, then twisting. Again, not so gently.

His breath was coming as quickly as hers, his cock rock hard against her back. And when he placed his lips at the top of her neck, her head fell forward making sure he had unencumbered access.

The suction against her heated skin made everything inside her quiver and her knees buckle, but he managed to keep her on her feet without stopping his sensual onslaught.

Short puffs of breath escaped her as he sucked her flesh into his mouth with the intent on leaving his mark on her.

His claim.

She whimpered again and squeezed his fingers deep inside her when his teeth made contact.

Yes, that would definitely leave a mark. A mark she wouldn't have to hide like she did when they were teenagers.

Heat rushed through her at the thought of someone else seeing that mark, that claim, and knowing who gave it to her.

Whoever would see it would know she belonged to Trace Walker. Though, in truth, she didn't. Not anymore.

But still... It made her heart skip, her stomach flip and a few seconds later, her slight tremor grew to an intense climax.

She ground into his fingers, riding out the ripples of orgasm as he kept his mouth to her skin, his teeth in her flesh.

And when those waves ebbed, every part of her quivered like jelly.

His hand stilled and with a last brush against her now overly sensitive clit, a tweak of her nipple and kiss to the mark he left behind, he slipped his fingers from her, wrapped his arms around her and held her tightly against him.

His breathing was ragged, his cock throbbing so hard she could feel it against her. But he held her there. Not moving. Not doing anything to take his own pleasure.

As soon as her breathing slowed enough, she asked, "What about you?"

"I'll wait."

He'd wait? He had to be suffering. "Trace..."

"Gotta shower."

"Yes, but—"

"I'll wait, El."

Her eyebrows pinned together as he released her, turned and walked away. Holding onto the counter so she wouldn't collapse into a pile of jelly, she watched him.

When he hit the edge of the kitchen right before the hallway, he stopped and glanced back over his shoulder. "Back then you had said you wanted to watch how I dealt with not fucking you until you were eighteen. Give me a few minutes then come watch."

Heat rushed through Ellie at not only his rougher than normal voice, but the anticipation of watching him in the shower as he made himself come.

"Okay," she whispered.

With a single nod and a slight grin, he turned and headed down the hallway.

She gave him the few minutes he needed, then, with her heart thumping in her throat and her legs still weak, she followed him.

———

ELLIE COULDN'T THINK of anything more beautiful in the world than Trace with water running over every inch of his body, with his muscles flexing and his long fingers sliding back and forth over his hard cock.

Pure beauty.

So hot and sexy, it made her struggle to breathe as she watched him. He had removed his running blade before getting in and had one hand planted against the shower wall for balance, his ass and hips flexing as he pumped into his own fist.

The acoustics in the bathroom amplified his low grunts that accompanied each thrust.

She thought she was wet in the kitchen. Now the crotch of her yoga pants was soaked.

As much as she wanted to join him in that shower, she forced herself to remain where she was. She would join him in another way.

She did so by pulling her yoga pants off and perching on the bathroom's vanity, spreading her knees and stroking the outside of her pussy with her fingers. She knew it wouldn't take much for her to come, so she only touched herself enough to take her to the point of no return but not past it.

She wanted to go at the same time as Trace.

Deep in his own head, she wasn't sure if he was aware of what she was doing right outside the shower stall.

If he was, he gave no indication.

She watched as every muscle in his body locked and his mouth parted. He was ready.

So was she.

She kept her eyes focused on him as he threw his head back and grimaced. And at that very moment, she only had to circle her throbbing clit twice to make herself come when he did. Long spurts of his cum shot out, mingled with the spray of water and quickly disappeared.

After a few seconds, he dropped his head forward, his chest heaving, his spent cock still in his hand.

Then he turned his head, his blue eyes pinning on her. Once again in predator mode.

His gaze dropped to where she stroked herself lightly, enjoying the occasional aftershock of her orgasm.

His eyes, as intense as her orgasm, rose again and met hers. "On the bed, back to the headboard, knees cocked and wide. Wait for me."

Every part of her body tingled, every nerve ending popped. From her toes to the roots of her hair. The spot on the back of her neck where he marked her began to pulsate.

"Ellie, now," he growled.

She nodded, pushed off the vanity, leaving her yoga pants behind, and rushed into his room to do what he demanded.

Then she waited.

WALKER TOOK his time shutting down the shower, getting out, toweling off, even knowing Ellie waited for him in his bed. *Especially* knowing she waited for him.

He didn't rush because he wanted her in there by herself, wondering what he would do next.

Whether she knew it or not, he didn't miss what she had done while he did the same in the shower.

It was hot as fuck.

She had come at the same time he did, but he wasn't done with her yet.

No, he was going to eat her. Then they would eat dinner.

After that, he was taking her to bed and fucking her until they both had nothing left to give each other. Until they were both ready to pass out and sleep.

She would sleep next to him tonight, wrapped around him like last night. Something they never had a chance to do in the past because they had both lived at home. Her with her mother and stepfather. Him with his parents until he left for boot camp. Because of that, they never had a chance to spend a whole night together. At the time, he hadn't worried about it since he thought they'd have a lifetime of nights together.

He was wrong.

So, he missed out on years of waking up with his Ellie next to him.

That ended last night.

Tonight and every night until this job was complete, she would be in his bed. She wanted to be there, he wanted that, too.

He stared at himself in the mirror seeing a man who hadn't been whole in a long time. Her being in his house, in his bed, made him feel whole again. It shouldn't and it bothered him that it did.

He would do what was needed to be done to help her, to get her out of the jam she was in, but once he achieved that, he had no idea what would happen from there.

Would he remain whole or would he go back to being a man with missing pieces?

He couldn't think about that. They had tonight. Then they had tomorrow and the next week to figure things out.

Right now, Ellie waited for him in his bed.

He had no doubt she had set herself up exactly as he ordered. And after grabbing his nearby crutches, he left the bathroom to find exactly that.

His Ellie. Her back against his headboard, pink filling her cheeks, her eyes dark and hooded, her sweet lips parted.

As he moved closer to the bed, he could see everything. Her knees were bent, and her thighs spread. She was completely exposed.

He caressed her with his gaze as he stopped at the end of the bed and dropped his crutches to the floor. Her pussy lips were plump, swollen, and a dark pink, the hair above it now trimmed to a small patch. She had to have done that when he was working earlier. It wasn't that neat last night.

Not that he complained. Bushy, trimmed or shaved bald, he wanted her no matter how she came to him.

Her hands were pressed to her knees, holding herself open for him.

An offering he'd accept.

"Did you touch yourself?"

"No."

"Why not?"

"I wanted to wait."

He hid his grin as he climbed onto the bed and walked on his hands and knees until he was between her feet.

"You remind me of a lion."

He paused. "How's that?"

"You remind me of a strong predator. Powerful, but graceful."

Graceful. He never thought of himself as that. Especially after the accident.

"A protector. But also a leader. Full of courage."

"Sharp teeth," he added, nipping playfully along her inner thigh.

"That, too."

"And a skilled tongue."

"Do lions have skilled tongues?"

"You tell me..." He pushed her legs even wider and ran his tongue from her knee to the apex of her thighs. He hovered above that small patch of hair and the scent from her orgasm in the kitchen and the second one in the bathroom made his mouth water.

Fuck yes, he was hungry. But for her.

He would normally tease her almost to the point of orgasm and pull back, wait for it to wane before starting again. Then once she was completely out of her mind, he would let her come.

But most likely, she was already at the point after two orgasms—one by his fingers, one by her own—that it wouldn't take much to draw a third from her.

He could wait until later to play as he liked to.

Maybe she would even let him bind her so he could play as long as he'd like to, also.

He would leave that decision in her hands. They hadn't done anything like that when they were young. And he was sure McMaster...

He gritted his teeth. Not now, he reminded himself.

Not when his face was between Ellie's thighs. Not when she was giving herself to him to do with what he wanted.

No. It was just him and her in this room. No one else.

Everybody else could wait until the light of day tomorrow.

Sliding his tongue between her folds, he drew the tip from the bottom to the top, flicked her clit, then ran it back down. Her hips jumped, so he lifted his head to say, "Hands on your knees and keep them spread wide."

She adjusted her feet and knees, opening herself up even more to him. Her pussy was perfect. A deep shiny pink, inside and out.

He had never doubted she'd been put on this Earth for him. She was made for him.

That was one reason why he never settled for anyone else. Because that was what it would have been, settling. And that wouldn't be fair to the woman he would only accept because he couldn't have the one he was meant to be with.

Using his fingers in a V, he alternated fucking her with his tongue and sucking her clit.

He lifted his gaze to see her face and her head had fallen back with her eyes closed, soft pants and mews rising from her lips.

"Eyes on me, El," he demanded and stopped until she obeyed.

As soon as she did, he continued. Tasting, sucking, licking, fucking. With his tongue, his lips, his teeth. He would take her there with just his mouth. Nothing else.

Her hips began to rock, and he watched to make sure she kept her eyes open and on him. He could see her struggle with it. She wanted to close her eyes again, submit to the sensations, let them take her away.

But he didn't want that. He wanted her to remain there. With him. Knowing it was him between her legs making her feel this way. Him taking her there.

He almost stopped and pulled away when her hands wrapped around the back of his head, holding him to her.

With each lick of his tongue, scrape of his teeth, suck of his lips, her fingers convulsed against his scalp, her nails digging in to the point of pain. She was wanting to let go in one way, refusing to in another.

Her hips rocked and lifted as she ground her pussy into his face, his name crossing her lips on a moans, sighs and cries.

She repeated his name until only bits and pieces of it remained along with her shuddered breath.

But her fingers dug harder, encouraging him to devour her until there was nothing left. Except her release.

Her hips shot up as she cried out his name one more time, everything about her quivering and clenching against him. Her legs, her pussy, her fingers trembled.

When her hips slowly lowered, her hold softened, her knees fell open once again, he pressed one last kiss to the top of her mound.

Her cheeks were no longer pink but held a deeper color. Her green eyes were dark, unfocused, her chest rising and falling quickly, her nipples puckered tightly.

Complete, utter beauty.

He kissed her mound again lightly and trailed kisses up

her center until he reached her mouth, then he kissed her deeply, sharing her own taste, her own orgasm with her.

"So perfect," he whispered against her lips. "So fucking perfect, sweetheart. Thank you for that gift."

If possible, her eyes became even softer around the edges. "I think you have that wrong, honey. I should be thanking you."

"Back then, I thought we were perfect, that how we were couldn't get any better. I was so fucking wrong. The kitchen, the bathroom, this bed. You didn't hold back. You weren't embarrassed or self-conscious. You showed me true beauty."

"I'm only showing you a reflection of what I see. You are the beautiful one, Trace. It's you. You bring it out in me."

She had that wrong. If she saw any kind of beauty in him, it was her doing. She brought it out in him.

Chapter Eleven

THE CHICKEN HAD TURNED to rubber. The mashed potatoes to glue. But he didn't give a shit that they'd delayed dinner so long it was ruined. It was worth it.

They ended up tossing it all and he grilled NY strips while Ellie sautéed a bunch of veggies instead, promising dinner the next night would be better.

He looked forward to it because the chicken had smelled fucking great when he had first arrived home and the cheesy garlic mashed potatoes even better.

And if it tasted as good as it looked...

Like Ellie.

They sat out on the deck at the wrought iron table set his sister had bought him as a house-warming gift. He wasn't sure he'd ever use it, but here they were.

"You grill steaks perfectly."

"I'm a man. If I can't grill, they'll take my man card."

Ellie snorted softly, pulling a smile from him. "I doubt it."

"When we're born with testicles, we have to agree to certain things. Becoming a grill master is one of them."

She grinned down at her plate as she forked a slice of zucchini.

He wanted to fork her.

He lifted his beer and took a long draw from the bottle. His gaze landed on her glass of red wine. He didn't remember that on the shopping list, but he hadn't looked too closely at it before forwarding it to Jesse.

If she had asked for everything in the entire grocery store, he would have paid for it.

He set his bottle on the table. "Wine instead of beer?" Even though both of them had been underage at the time, he had been able to sneak a few beers every once in a while from his father's supply in the garage fridge.

"I never really liked beer," she admitted. "I only drank it because it was all we had."

"If I knew you liked wine, I would have found a way to snag some."

"I didn't know I liked wine until..."

Until...

Bet she developed a taste for champagne, too.

He wanted to change the subject but since his mind was on McMotherfucker, there was no better time than the present to discuss what they'd found earlier.

"Hunter and I are meeting at the warehouse tomorrow morning to do more digital digging, but we've made plans to leave for Denver the day after. You'll be here alone for at least two days, maybe longer. Depends on what we uncover when we get out there."

She placed her fork on her plate and took a long sip of wine, his eyes glued to her throat as she swallowed. He lifted his gaze again when she asked, "What did you find so far?"

"Nothing concrete except the obvious. He was drowning in debt, which you were aware of. But it was deeper than you knew. I'm surprised you had any equity left in your house. As you know, your credit cards were all maxed out."

She made a small noise.

"Your joint bank accounts were empty, but so were his business accounts. Do you know if he had any offshore accounts he was funneling money into? Somewhere he was hiding his money from creditors?"

"No. He didn't talk business with me. I don't think he thought I was smart enough to understand."

It was Walker's turn to make a noise, which came out more like a low growl. Ellie was far from stupid. "Arm candy," he muttered.

She lifted her gaze to his. "What?"

"He treated you like arm candy."

"Maybe."

"He buy you fancy clothes, shoes, jewelry, brand name purses?"

She shrugged one bare shoulder. "Yes, he liked me to dress a certain way when we went out to dinner or parties, or to meet friends."

Walker studied Ellie. She had never been high maintenance. He could never picture her being that way, either. She had always been down to earth. Barefoot, pretty summer dresses, loose hair, the only color on her face from the sun. Her genuine smile and her emerald green eyes a thousand times better than diamonds or gold.

"Did you mind?"

She shook her head. "Not at first. It was fun dressing up. It was something I never had, never expected to have. Though, I was glad I didn't have to do it all the time. It wasn't important to me. I was always happier in a pair of jeans and sandals."

Not sandals. "Barefoot."

She tilted her head as she considered him. "Yes, you always teased me about keeping me—"

"Barefoot and pregnant in the kitchen," he finished for her. He remembered.

A small smile played on her lips. "Yes."

While he did tease her with that, he also dreamed about the day it would be true. He looked forward to eventually coming home after a long day of work to see her barefoot, preparing dinner and carrying his baby.

She'd be making their home and family. He'd be providing for them.

And to make sure he could do so, he had joined the Army.

Doing what he thought best had fucking destroyed that dream.

"You never had kids with him." For fuck's sake, he didn't want to go there, but he couldn't resist going there.

She didn't answer.

"Why?" he prodded. "Why, El? You always wanted kids. You insisted on at least two."

She pushed her plate away and grabbed her wine glass, avoiding his gaze. "*We* wanted kids. If I had children, they were supposed to be yours."

A sharp pain sliced through him. "But you fucking married someone else."

Her brow furrowed and she sighed impatiently. "Again, Trace? We talked about this."

"We talked about pieces of our fucking past. That was it."

"And as I said, I can't keep doing this, *we* can't keep doing this. The past has already been written. Neither of us can go back and erase it."

"No, but we can learn from it by understanding it, Ellie."

"For what reason?"

"Maybe because I fucking need it!" he yelled, then closed his eyes, unclenched his fists and took a long breath.

Her whisper was enough for him to open his eyes again.

"George was something to me, but you were my everything."

"But not enough to wait."

The next part didn't come as a soft whisper, the words were harsh, full of frustration. "And I already explained why. Put yourself in my shoes. Especially with how I lost my father."

He sat back and tried to do just that. Ellie coming to him to tell him she was leaving for the next four years. Not asking but *telling* him he needed to put his life and their plans on hold. Simply wait. And then hope that everything worked out in the end and she came home safe.

Would he have waited while she went and put herself in harm's way? Could he have sat home and worried, wondering if that call or knock on the door would ever come?

He wasn't sure if he could.

There was a saying he'd heard different versions of, but the one that stuck with him the most was, "If you love someone, set them free. If they come back, they're yours; if they don't, they never were."

He thought he was doing what was best for them.

Maybe she did, too, when she had set him free.

But now she was back.

"You should've had kids, Ellie." She would've made a great mom. "You missed out."

"So did you. And," her shoulders lifted slightly, "I still have time."

"You're turning thirty-seven soon. Your clock is ticking."

She rolled her eyes. "Thanks for the reminder."

"Why didn't you? Why was he good enough to marry, but not good enough to have children with?"

She didn't answer right away. "I don't know. Maybe deep down I knew something wasn't right. I couldn't put a finger on it. Honestly, I was worried I'd regret having children with him. And I didn't want to burden any innocent child with that. That wouldn't be fair to them because of my decisions or even indecisions."

"But he wanted them with you." Of course, he did. What man wouldn't?

"Yes."

Then it struck him. "And that's why you have an IUD. It's undetectable."

Her eyes slid away. "For the most part, yes."

"Did you lie to him?"

She lifted her chin and her green eyes slid back and hit his. Not sweet, soft Ellie. Oh, fuck no. A woman full of quiet strength and determination. "Yes. I'd been on the pill when we got married. After a year, he insisted I go off. I wasn't ready and told him that, but he pushed it. I wasn't sure when I'd be ready, but I didn't want to fight about it, so I had the IUD implanted instead. I wanted to be sure. I didn't take having children lightly."

This was a fierce Ellie, standing behind her decision. Not letting anyone make that choice for her.

And while in one way he was relieved with her deception, in another he wasn't.

What if he hadn't gone away? What if they had gotten married?

What if she'd done that to him?

To find out your wife was secretly on birth control because she wasn't sure of a lifetime commitment...

"You loved him, though."

"I thought I did."

"You had to love him enough to marry him." If she didn't marry him for his money, it had to be for love, right?

"I thought I did. But in the end, I guess I didn't know him as well as I thought. Marrying him was a knee-jerk reaction to you abandoning me."

He ground his teeth at her word choice. "I didn't fucking abandon you."

"That's what it felt like at eighteen, Trace. Today I might look at it differently. We were so damn young."

"And now we're not."

"Now we're not," she repeated softly.

"Now we both have to live with our decisions."

Again, a slight shrug, and an expression of sadness. "That's life, Trace."

Yes, it fucking was.

———

SHE FOUND it interesting that Trace had three prostheses that she knew of. The one with a boot, one with a foot and one with a blade.

Of course, the one with the boot went with him to Denver. Since his crutches remained behind, she wondered how he managed without them.

He was probably pretty good at managing a lot of things. Or figuring out alternatives. Like MacGyver.

The one with the blade, the one he used for running, reminded her of something the Bionic Man would be equipped with. When she told him that yesterday morning as he left for a run before meeting Hunter again, he said nothing.

So, she let it drop. She was still dying to know how he'd lost his lower leg. But since he wasn't willing to talk about it, at least not yet, conversation last night ended up being about whether he had found any worthwhile information on their second day of searching instead.

They hadn't and hoped to find some better leads in Colorado.

She wasn't sure she could deal with being stuck in Trace's house for the next week. Especially when he flew out that morning, leaving her alone for the next couple of nights.

Alone in his bed. Alone in his house.

But then, she was used to being alone. She'd been that way since she left George. When she thought about it, she had felt alone even before then.

Even so, she was back in Trace's life all because of her late husband.

He'd probably hate knowing that. He hated Trace. For some reason, George had a deep-rooted jealousy of him that she didn't discover until much later because he hid it well. But a couple years after they'd married, once she uncovered it, she realized why he pursued her so diligently after Trace left to join the Army.

He approached her first as a friend, used his McMaster charm and spent time with her when she was lonely and heartbroken. He slowly convinced her he'd give her a good life and would never leave her behind. He swore to give her the family and stability she sought.

The life she wanted with Trace.

In the end, George was determined to get the girl Trace had. Why? She had no idea.

Trace had his choice of girls in high school. So did George.

But it turned out George was the kind of man who wanted things he couldn't have. If someone else in town had a nicer car, he did everything he could to one up them. He made sure to have the best clothes, watches, everything. That's why she didn't understand his fascination with her.

She had nothing to offer him. Just herself.

She didn't come from money. And she wasn't looking to marry into it, either. Which made her believe his interest in her was genuine and true.

And later, after George had made several snide remarks about Trace, she had no idea why he'd be jealous of him.

Like her, Trace didn't come from money, either. He had a handed-down beat-up Ford pickup, clothes that were clean but not fancy, no expensive watch, no money even for college.

But Trace lived an honest life. His father, a carpenter, was loved and respected in their town. His dad passed on his traits of being a hard-worker and being appreciative of everything that he did have. Even though it wasn't much, it was his and he earned it.

Maybe that was it, George was never satisfied with what he had. He always wanted better, wanted more. And if there was something he couldn't have, he did whatever he needed to do to get it.

Like his pursuit of Ellie.

Once, he had mentioned she was a "clean slate." When she asked what he meant, he made a comment about how she wasn't jaded like some others.

But that stuck with her since his excuse didn't sound genuine.

Eventually, she figured out why.

She *was* a clean slate to him. He could mold her to anything he wanted. Or at least, that's what George thought.

While he had generously put her through college, afterward he wouldn't let her go out and use her degree by working or starting a career. Her education was reduced to a useless piece of paper in a frame.

Her "job," she was reminded every time she mentioned it, was to be the lady of the house.

Though it was difficult to even be that when he hired everyone to do everything she could do when it came to running the household.

She wanted to contribute to their marriage, to their life. She even offered to help at the office.

With everything George wanted to give her, with how he

wanted her to be, he ended up smothering her instead of "molding" her into becoming the perfect wife.

She was no longer Ellie. She was Mrs. McMaster. George's wife.

The lady of the fucking house.

What kind of title was that, anyway?

Mother, wife, yes. Lady of the house? No.

She didn't want to turn into a woman like George's mother. A socialite who loved to shop in New York City. Who enjoyed spending lots and lots of money. Surrounded herself with snobby friends of the same financial caliber.

While Trace might have joked about it, deep down she believed that was what he wanted: her barefoot and pregnant in the kitchen. George? Never. That thought would be appalling to him, even to simply mention it.

But, in truth, that was all she wanted and needed, too.

Love. Family. Happiness.

In the end, the life she hoped to build came tumbling down around her.

Love? Gone.

Family? Non-existent.

Happiness? After being forced to live in a box not of her own making, it was hard to find.

She existed in her marriage.

She existed in her big house.

She did what was required of her to be "George's wife."

She simply existed.

Until Ellie Cooke no longer did.

Living like that for so many years, she didn't even realize it happened until she left.

Then she looked back on her life and saw it clearly.

Ellie Cooke had completely disappeared. Nothing had remained of her for a very long time.

However, she was determined to find herself again and

was working on doing so when George was killed, and she was dragged unwillingly back to being Mrs. McMaster.

What scared her the most, when she received the pictures of a dead, tortured George, was that she didn't even shed one tear. Not one. She felt nothing.

She felt about as dead as George appeared.

She had been married to the man for sixteen years and while she thought what they did to him was horrible, she felt almost detached.

Did those sixteen years make her numb?

Possibly. Because her heart began to beat again when Trace stepped into that room at the warehouse. She began to breathe. The numbness seemed to wash away.

But now as she sat in his house alone, she remembered what he said about her leaving as soon as this was over. Once he and his team "fixed" her problem.

But wouldn't it be easier for her to just disappear like she planned?

Simple. Neat.

It was why she came to him, because she had no idea how to do it right.

To no longer be Mrs. George McMaster.

To no longer be Ellie Cooke.

To become someone new.

Start fresh.

Start a new life without any threats hanging over her head.

She'd be alone, but she was okay with that. She was used to it. She could survive.

Yes, when she talked to him next, she would convince him to give up what he was trying to do and tell him what she needed to do.

She just needed him to see how it should be.

I⊤ was late and Shadow Valley was two hours ahead of him. He sat in a rental in front of an office building on the outskirts of Denver. The building was dark and so was the interior of the car.

Hunter sat next to him in the driver's seat, itching to get out of the vehicle.

"If you want to get out, get out. I need to make a call first."

Hunter twisted his head toward Walker, and even in the dark, Walker could see the gleam of his grin. "To home?"

Home.

"Yeah." When Hunter opened his mouth, Walker raised his palm. "Not one fucking word."

Hunter chuckled and shoved the driver's door open, unfolding himself from the seat. He leaned back into the car to say, "Keep it quick. We need to get in there and get out. You could've done this back in your room."

"It's getting too late."

"She got somewhere to go in the morning?" Then the door slammed.

He found her in his contacts, pressed Send and closed his eyes, waiting for her voice to fill his ear.

"Trace."

"Were you sleeping?"

"No." She paused. "Is everything all right?"

"Yeah. We might have a lead. We're going to follow it tomorrow to see if it pans out."

He glanced out of the windshield at the dark building. But tonight, they were breaking into McMotherfucker's offices and were going to spend the night searching through it, trying to uncover anything they could.

"Are you at a motel?"

"Yeah," he lied. "Are you in my bed?"

Another long hesitation. "Does it matter since you're not here?"

Fuck yes, it did. "Whatever makes you most comfortable," he lied again.

More silence.

Then he heard it. A long shaky breath. That didn't give him the warm fuzzies.

"Trace?"

Ah, fuck. Something was brewing and he wasn't going to like what it was. It was starting to remind him of another conversation he'd never forget. He closed his eyes and dropped his head. "Yeah, sweetheart?" He did the only thing he could do. He braced.

"I'm sorry for everything. Then. Now."

She wasn't the only one.

"I... I... just need to go."

He let those words slide through him. Finally, he simply repeated, "Go."

"I think that's for the best. I don't want you, your team... I don't want anyone to get hurt."

"No one's going to get hurt, El."

"You can't guarantee that."

"Ellie..."

"I shouldn't have brought this to you. I never should have called Crissy."

But she did and now it was too late. "El..."

"Trace, it's for the best."

Fuck. He lifted his head, his jaw set. "Why don't you let me worry about what's best?"

"I don't want to give those men what they want."

"Wasn't planning on it, Ellie. That's why we're here. To find out who the fuck they are and figure another way."

"But that's not why I came to you."

"Are you regretting coming to me? Because, for fuck's sake, Ellie, both of us have enough motherfucking regrets already."

Silence answered him.

"If we make you disappear, El, you'll have no one and nothing."

"I have that now."

Walker glanced in the side mirror and saw Hunter pacing back and forth behind the car. He needed to get off the phone and get the job they were there for done. He never should have called her. "You have me."

"You said just until—"

"I know what I fucking said."

Again a long silence that made him want to scream. Finally, "Has that changed?"

Walker's nostrils flared as he sucked in a breath. "I don't know, El, we don't know each other anymore. We've been apart longer than we were together. We're different people now. I don't fucking know what any of this will bring."

You were with McMaster so much longer than you were with me.

He bit back a growl. "I gotta get back to work."

"I thought you were in your motel?"

Fuck. He was slipping. "Yeah, meeting Hunter in his room to go over some shit."

"Okay."

"I'll call you tomorrow night, El. Keep your phone on. It might be late."

"Okay."

Fuck. There she went with those fucking "okay" submissive answers again. He hated every time she agreed with him like that.

Every fucking time.

She lost herself along the way and that just made him want to kill McMaster if the asshole wasn't already dead.

"I'll text tomorrow if I need any info from you."

He ground his teeth when she answered with another, "Okay."

He wasn't going to ask her any more questions or give

her any more orders because he didn't want to hear her say it again. "Night, Ellie."

"Trace..." filled his ear.

"Yeah?"

"Be safe."

"Yeah," he breathed, then hit the End button on his phone.

He stared at it for a few seconds, then went back to scrolling through his contacts. He checked the side mirror again to make sure Hunter was still back there before Walker hit Send once more and put the ear to his phone.

It was late, but the woman he was calling would take his call. And because her man wasn't in her bed tonight, he had no doubt her phone would still be on.

Of course, he was fucking right.

Chapter Twelve

"HEY!"

"Hi!"

"Hello!"

Ellie blinked at the three women standing on the front stoop of Trace's house. Three very pretty—no, *gorgeous*—women who had a lot of curves between them. Way more than Ellie had, or would ever have.

A tall, voluptuous woman with long dark blonde hair, a younger blonde not quite as tall, and then a—what Ellie guessed—Latina by the coloring of her skin, eyes and hair. Darker than the other two and no less stunning.

Ellie's hand automatically went up to her hair which she had put in a messy knot at the top of her head. She wore no makeup, was barefoot and hadn't even bothered to don a bra that morning.

But clearly, she didn't need to ever wear one in comparison to the women before her.

Worse, she was still wearing her old, loose cotton shorts and one of Trace's extra-large T-shirts she had dug out from his drawer. Which meant she was swimming in it.

She hadn't been expecting visitors this morning. Or...

even today, for that matter. She had planned on spending the rest of the afternoon cooking casseroles and other things she could freeze for Trace, so he'd have some homemade meals once she was gone.

She had spotted a small chest freezer in the corner of his garage. When she opened it, she only saw a couple frozen pre-packaged meals at the bottom, so it was basically empty, wasting electricity.

Not that Trace couldn't afford his electric bill, with the house and vehicles he had, the man was clearly not hurting for money.

"I'm pretty sure you've met our men," The tallest one with the biggest boobs announced, drawing Ellie's attention back to the stoop.

She frowned. "Umm. Maybe?" She had no idea who their men were.

"I'm Parris," the woman continued, holding out her hand, which had a huge rock on her left ring finger. Huge. Like blindingly big. Probably three times as large as the diamond George had bought her.

In fact, if he'd seen something like that on one of his friend's fiancée's or wife's finger, he probably would have traded her engagement ring in for one that was even bigger.

But this woman's rock wasn't just a diamond, it was a stunning rectangular-cut blue diamond. Ellie realized the rare stone matched Parris's eyes.

"Mercy belongs to me," she said with a smile as Ellie took her hand and shook it.

That was a weird way to put it.

"Ellie Mc—" She swallowed that last name down. "Cooke."

"McCooke?" the shorter blonde asked with amusement dancing in her blue eyes.

"Just Cooke."

"Thought so. And just call her Rissa. *No one* calls her Parris."

Ellie's gaze went back to Parris aka Rissa, who shrugged. "I've given up trying."

The younger blonde then gave her a little wave. "I'm Kelsea, by the way. Ryder belongs to me."

The dark-haired woman also held out her hand, which Ellie accepted and gave a quick, firm shake. "Frankie. Hunter's mine."

Ellie's eyebrows drew together since she never heard women claim their men like that.

Maybe it was a local thing.

"Then, yes, I've met your husbands."

Three loud snorts went up, drawing Ellie's lips into a deeper frown. "Your men," she corrected.

"That's what they said," Rissa stated, then lifted the wine bottle she was holding in her left hand. "I brought wine."

Kelsea lifted a pink box that was labeled "Sophie's Sweet Treats" on the top. "I brought cupcakes."

Frankie lifted another bottle of wine. "More wine because one bottle is never enough."

Ellie would have to agree with that statement.

"Not living with our men, it's not," Rissa muttered.

"So..." Kelsea said quickly and raised her brows, looking over Ellie's shoulder into the house.

So...

Oh.

Shit.

Ellie stepped back and opened the door wider. "Please, come in."

She hoped Trace wouldn't mind a gaggle of women being in his house when he wasn't home.

All three women smiled, walked in and kept going.

Uh...

149

Ellie closed the door, locked it and quickly followed them into the kitchen.

"I hope we didn't ruin your plans by just showing up," Rissa said, not sounding sorry in the least and heading right to the cabinets to dig around until she found four stemless wine glasses.

"I *know* Walker did not buy those," Frankie stated, grabbing a couple glasses from Rissa.

"Mmm, no. I gave them to him as a house-warming gift. He'd probably serve wine in a leftover jar," Kelsea said. "How are you going to get laid serving a woman wine in a glass jar with tomato sauce residue in it?"

All three ladies scrunched up their faces.

"Umm," Ellie started, not comfortable hearing about Trace getting laid.

All eyes landed on her.

"It's beautiful out," Frankie stated, ignoring Ellie's discomfort, then went to the French doors, opening one side. "Let's sit outside."

The three women wandered out the door, leaving Ellie standing in the kitchen, holding the empty wine glass Rissa had handed her. She looked at it, looked at the door, found the bottle opener she had used on the wine Jesse had bought and headed outside.

It didn't take long for her to figure out how much she liked these women. They were fun, they didn't hide how much they loved "their" men and the cupcakes were to die for.

It also didn't take long for her to be buzzing on sugar and wine.

She quickly realized she could get used to other women like them coming over and hanging out. Especially these three since they were sharp-witted and had a great sense of humor.

They sat drinking wine, eating cupcakes and chit-chatting about nothing important. Occasionally they mentioned a "sisterhood," saying if she remained in town—which wasn't the plan, but she didn't correct them on that—she'd be inducted into it. Kelsea said something about this sisterhood being full of old ladies.

The three women who were sitting on Trace's deck were certainly not old, so when she asked about it, it was explained that she'd misunderstood. The women were "ol' ladies" and not elderly women.

Then Ellie was schooled on what being an ol' lady was to a biker and Kelsea spent the next hour going down a rabbit hole about the whole MC life.

She found it fascinating but didn't think being an ol' lady was for her, which made them break out in laughter.

Then she was told being with Trace, she'd never be an ol' lady since, though he worked for MC member Diesel, he wasn't a part of the MC itself. And while she was relieved she'd never hold the official title of "ol' lady"—which she disliked as much as "the lady of the house"—she also informed them she wasn't "with" Trace.

That was greeted with a chorus of soft snorts, "*mmm hmms*," "*rights*" and "*sures*." But she wasn't going to argue with her companions. She liked them too much, the afternoon had been a blast and she didn't want to ruin it.

Eventually, after her third glass of fermented grapes and her second cupcake sugar-high, she felt relaxed and comfortable enough around them, to blurt out, "Do you know he doesn't have his leg?" She covered her mouth in horror once she heard the question come out of her mouth.

She needed to leave it to Trace to tell her what happened, not ask some strangers.

Who she, in truth, no longer considered strangers after wiping out two bottles of wine and almost a dozen gourmet cupcakes.

"He doesn't?" asked Kelsea in surprise. Ellie had curiously noted that she had only sipped at one glass of wine for the past couple hours. Unlike the rest of them.

Frankie's head shot up and she glanced around the table in shock. "Did he lose it?"

"Could have sworn I saw him running with it the other morning. Did he misplace it?" Rissa asked, a gleam in her eye.

Ellie rolled her eyes and muttered, "Funny."

Kelsea slapped the table and laughed. "Let me give you a little head's up about living in this compound." She lifted her index finger into the air. "One, like we discussed earlier, it's full of bikers. They don't wear skimpy, *nutastic* shorts when they run. Why? Because they don't run. If they did—and didn't die instantly doing so—their legs would blind you because they never see the light of day, unless they're fucking. Their jeans only come off to fuck, shower and sleep. And sometimes to get thrown in the wash. That's it." She took a breath and continued by adding a second finger to the one she was still holding up and looked toward the sky. "Two, those shorts *our* boys wear are God's gift to women. Especially for us since we put up with them." She added a third finger. "Three, when one of them goes for a run and he's spotted? Everyone in this neighborhood who doesn't have a dick gets a text. *Everyone*. It's the law. Because it would be a damn shame if any one of us missed it."

Frankie leaned forward and half-whispered, "*Oooor* if you *know* your man is heading out for a run, you send out a group text immediately. No exceptions."

Ellie closed her gaping mouth. "Do your men know about this?"

The ladies all shouted, "No!" at the same time around the table, making her jump.

"No, we made a pact with the sisterhood to not get caught gawking or ever tell our men. It's a secret of the sisterhood," Kelsea informed her.

"Among others," Rissa quickly added under her breath.

Frankie nodded. "Anyone snitching gets the boot."

"Snitches get stitches," Kelsea added seriously. "Also, it's a law that whatever barbecue, kid's party, or *whatever* Axel gets invited to? Someone must bring cupcakes."

Ellie had no idea who this Axel was. "Why?"

Rissa leaned into her arm and said, just as seriously as Kelsea, "Trust me. You do not want to miss Axel licking the icing off the top, then scooping out the filling of one of Bella's stuffed cupcakes with his tongue. Our men may have Ranger Panties, but Bella's a lucky bitch since her man has a golden tongue."

Ellie wondered if this Axel's tongue beat Trace's. Impossible. "Is Bella a part of the sisterhood?"

"Yes," all three answered at once.

"Is Axel one of the bikers?"

"Yes and no," Kelsea answered carefully. "Heavy on the no."

"Is he a Shadow?" She didn't remember him being at the warehouse. But that didn't mean he wasn't and simply hadn't been somewhere else.

"No, he's..." Rissa rolled her eyes up at sky for a second, then answered, "an exception."

Kelsea nodded. "It's complicated."

As fascinated as she was to learn more about the golden-tongued exception named Axel, Ellie needed to steer this conversation back to Trace since it was going off the rails. "So, you all watch Walker when he runs."

Mmm hmm's and dreamy smiles went around the table.

"That means you know about his leg." Of course they did, but she was trying to snap them all out of the fantasies they fell into while they discussed Ranger Panties—which now she had an official name for all that clingy goodness—and the tonguing of icing.

"Hard to miss," Kelsea said on a giggle before taking a long sip of her remaining wine.

"Do any of you know how it happened?"

All three of the ladies' heads snapped up and eyes narrowed on her.

Rissa lifted a hand. "Wait. He didn't tell you?"

"We assumed you two were knocking boots," Kelsea added. "Or *boot*, in his case."

Frankie leaned forward with a look of concern. "Hunter said something about the two of you being lost loves. We figured you were rekindling the flames. In fact, he..."

"He?" Ellie prodded when she didn't continue. She most certainly wanted to hear the rest since it was Hunter who was in Denver with Trace.

"Uh. He was concerned that you were left here alone and thought you might want company."

That sounded like a fib. "You ladies—"

Kelsea snorted.

Ellie began again. "You ladies came over here because Trace asked you to?"

"Trace?" went up around the table in stereo. The women looked at each other first before turning back to Ellie.

"Damn, that name is hot," Kelsea murmured. "Better than Dwight."

"I like the name Dwight," Frankie told her. "It's solid. Who names their kid Danny instead of Daniel? Not only Danny, but Danny Diego Delgado, Jr.? I mean, seriously? Triple D's?"

Ellie smothered her laugh with her hand.

"I take it Danny Diego Delgado, the third, is out for a boy's name," Rissa said dryly, though her eyes had a sparkle to them.

"Oh, I informed him of that as soon as I heard his whole name. We're having a girl anyway."

Ellie stared at the empty wine glass in front of Frankie. "You're pregnant?"

"No. Not yet."

Kelsea curved a hand around the side of her mouth and stage whispered. "They're practicing. *A lot.*"

Rissa arched a brow at Kelsea. "And you two aren't? The only good thing about Walker building his house between both of ours, is now there's a sound barrier and I don't hear Ryder's southern accent getting thick because we have all figured out why that happens."

Kelsea's lips twitched. "If that's all you heard, then you're lucky."

Rissa rolled her eyes. "No, that's not all we heard. But we'll leave it at that."

Heat rushed into Ellie's face. "I figured since these houses were newer, they'd have thicker walls."

"They do, but some of us are louder than others." Rissa faked coughed into her hand. "Kels."

Kelsea's grin widened and shrugged. "You must not hear yourself. '*Ooooh*, Ryan! Give it to me, big boy!'"

"I don't call him big boy," Rissa's hiss ended with a tipsy giggle.

"Your blush is telling us you two are getting it on," Frankie murmured, ignoring the other two, her dark eyes glued to Ellie's face.

"Please tell us you are," Kelsea added.

"It's... It's..."

"Oh fuck. It's *temporary?*" Frankie asked with a raised brow.

Ellie wasn't sure she should admit it, but she nodded.

All three women slammed into the back of their chairs and howled with laughter.

"Um..." Ellie stared at her wine glass, wishing it wasn't empty. She pushed to her feet. "I'm going to grab another bottle of wine."

Kelsea reached out, snagged her wrist and tugged her back into her seat. "No, hold on. We didn't mean to laugh."

"Yes, we did," Frankie corrected her, then shook her head. "Of course it's temporary."

"This is going to be fun to watch," Rissa added.

"Only because we've all dealt with this same 'temporary' bullshit," Frankie said, her head tilted as she studied Ellie. "They ride in on their white horses and plan on riding back out once they're the hero. However, on that ride back into the sunset, their horse breaks a damn leg." She rolled her eyes and got serious. "You two were together once, right?"

"Yes, but we were young."

"Weren't we all," Rissa murmured. "When I had a smaller ass and could fit into a double D bra." She sighed.

"Mercy loves your tits and ass, so shut it," Kelsea told her. "All the boys love your quadruple Q tits, they're just too scared to look at them."

Rissa laughed. "Oh, they're not too scared. I've caught them all." She quickly looked at Kelsea and Frankie. "Except for Hunter and Ryder, I mean."

Frankie and Kelsea rolled their eyes.

Frankie swatted her hand in the air. "You don't have to cover for them. We know how they are. Anyway, how long were you two together?"

"Just a couple years."

"And then?"

"And then he went in the Army," Ellie answered Frankie.

"And?"

"And," Ellie shrugged. "And that was it."

"He broke up with you to go into the Army?" Rissa asked in a sharp whisper.

"No, I..." Ellie took a deep inhale. "I broke up with him."

"When he was overseas?"

"Yes."

The women around the table got quiet.

Finally, Frankie asked, "You let your man go because he enlisted in the Army?"

Ellie closed her eyes, her fingers wrapping tightly around the stem of her empty wine glass. "I was young and stupid and scared."

"Scared of what?"

"Losing him."

"But you lost him by letting him go," Frankie whispered.

She didn't let him go, in truth, she pushed him away. "I let him go before he could be taken from me. Again, it was stupid. I never should have done it."

"You loved him," Rissa stated, her eyes watching Ellie way too carefully.

"Yes."

"You still love him?"

Ellie rose her eyes to Rissa's. "Yes."

"You married someone else." It wasn't a question that came from Kelsea, it sounded more like an accusation.

She didn't need to feel any worse about it than she already did. Ellie shoved her chair back and got to her feet. "I appreciate you ladies stopping by and keeping me company while Trace is gone, but now I have some things I need to do."

"Ellie, wait," Kelsea said as they all stood up. "We've all fucked up. We've all made mistakes. And Frankie was right when she said they ride in on their white horses—though, in reality, they're dark horses—to be the hero and save our asses. Ryder saved my fucking ass. No joke. I was in a dark, dark place that he pulled me out of. If it wasn't for him, I'm not sure where I'd be."

Rissa spoke up next. "I made the mistake of trusting a good friend of mine, who, in the end, wasn't as good of a person as I thought he was. His illegal activities got me into a dangerous jam that Mercy got me out of, luckily. He saved my ass."

Ellie's eyes slid to Frankie as she began to speak. "I can't even begin to tell you how Hunter helped me and Leo because of a major mistake I made, too. If it wasn't for him..." Her lips flattened out.

"My point was," Kelsea continued, "we make mistakes, we learn from them, we move on as best as we can. We might bitch about our men, and I'm sure they bitch about us, but I can tell you..." Her voice caught. "I can tell you if you think whatever you had with Walker is worth fighting for, then you need to fight hard. Just like us, these men are far from perfect. They're stubborn and hard-headed, but so are we. But, *fuck*, they will never hesitate to tell you flat out that we make them a better man. And I can tell you, no bullshit, they make us better women. I was barely existing until Ryder took me, shook me and then threw me back out into the world. I'm thankful for that every damn day."

"Everybody is thankful for that," Rissa said softly. "We're not judging you, Ellie, and never will. But we're here for you because we live with and love men who are just like Walker. So, if anyone understands, we do. None of us met our men in perfect conditions. You know why? Because there are no perfect conditions. There are no fairy tales. There's life. And sometimes it's really hard. While other times it's simply hard to deal with. But we're just as strong as our men, so we deal with just as much shit as they can. Even so, it's sure nice to have someone, whether it's our men, or the sisterhood, at our back. So... if you ever want to talk..."

Kelsea tipped her head toward the taller woman as she snagged the two empty wine bottles off the table. "She's a therapist. A good one. Trust me."

Every muscle locked in her body. "I don't need a therapist."

"We *all* need a therapist," Frankie said with a sharp

laugh, gathering the empty wine glasses. "Including our men, though they'd never admit it."

Most men like that wouldn't. They'd rather suffer before asking for help.

Rissa said, "We'll leave the cupcakes here since they always tend to help."

She didn't need the help they were talking about. She only needed help to disappear. That was it.

Problem solved.

"I need to get Leo from Diamond," Frankie said. "If you need anything, Ellie, let me know. Walker and Hunter are close. That means if you stick around, I hope we become close, too."

"All the boys are close," Kelsea said with a wink. "But some of them a little more than the others. I had to deal with that when it came to Steel feeling the need to protect Ryder and doing it to my face. Like she said, anything you need, we're here for you." She followed Frankie into the house. "I'll walk you out, Frankie."

Then it was just her and Rissa on the back deck. "I'm sorry, I didn't mean to ruin our afternoon. I loved it and I appreciate you all coming over. According to Trace, I might be here for a few more days, so I'd love to get together with you ladies again."

Rissa stood by the French doors, studying Ellie. "You'd be a fool to let him go again. He's a good man. They all are."

"I might not have a choice this time."

"Mercy said you came here asking for their help to disappear."

Ellie was surprised Rissa knew that. "Do they normally talk about their cases?"

"No. But this one's special, I guess. Look, our men are typical in the sense they don't talk about feelings. They think they're invincible and nothing will break them. But they're not typical because they all know each other very well and, though it's not discussed, they know what each other's needs are. Sometimes it's a little scary how in tune they are with each other. Even Diesel. But then, I guess that's what makes a good team."

"Pieces of a puzzle," Ellie murmured.

Rissa gave her a soft smile. "Yes, they're puzzle pieces. But they not only have to fit perfectly with the other men, but with their other halves, which are their women. Sometimes it's a lot for them. In fact, I'm not sure any of them expected to find the woman who—how should I say it?—soothed their soul. Completed them. But in truth, they do the same for us. These guys are intense, and I have to say mine is the worst. Every day is a struggle with him, but I do it because I know it's worth it. Let me let you in on something Walker may never tell you. With what they do, they hold onto a lot of secrets, a lot of memories that would haunt others. They do things they never talk about. Not to anyone but amongst themselves. Sometimes not even then. Sometimes they're alone with the things they've done or might have to do. They might think they're strong enough to deal with it, but, honestly, it has to wear on their psyche at some point. To do some of those things, they have to turn off their conscience. And that's not healthy. It affects them more than they realize. Because while sometimes they can come off cold and uncaring, in truth, they love and care intensely. You just have to know it's there, even when you can't see it. Luckily, Walker isn't as bad as Mercy or even Steel. But even so, I'm sure he'd rather hide his vulnerability than expose it."

"And I'm his vulnerability?"

"I'd guess one of them. Just like I'm Mercy's. Frankie and Leo, their son, are Hunter's. And Kelsea is Ryder's. And we won't even discuss Diesel. That fucking man..." Rissa sighed and shook her head. "Mercy is the coldest man I've ever met, but he also burns the hottest. So even if Walker shuts you out, don't think you've lost him. If he's worth it, never give up."

"I gave up."

Rissa smiled. "And now you're going to fix that."

"I wish it was that simple."

"It *is* that simple."

"But these men who want their money... They won't stop until they get it."

"Trust the Shadows, Ellie. Trust Walker. If he loves you, and my guess is he does, then he won't stop until you're safe. All you have to do is believe."

Believe.

"What if this is bigger than what they can handle?"

Rissa tilted her head and smiled. "Then you don't know these men, Ellie. They can handle anything."

At what cost? Ellie wanted to ask.

"I can see myself out. I'll write our numbers down and put them on the counter. I'll make sure you get on the texting tree for when the boys are out running. Then you'll also have our numbers if you need them. Don't forget, I'm right next door. So is Kelsea."

With that, Rissa gave her a last smile and walked inside.

Chapter Thirteen

AFTER SHE PLUGGED ALL the numbers on the list Rissa left on the counter into her phone, she made a large pan of baked ziti, ate a plateful before freezing the rest in some containers she found in one of the kitchen cabinets. She marked the date and what it was on the lid and stacked them into his garage freezer.

She'd make a new list of groceries, text them to Walker to send to Jesse so she had enough ingredients to prepare him a variety of meals for the future. It was the least she could do for what he was doing, or trying to do, for her.

She had popped the cork on her last bottle of red. She needed to add that to the shopping list, too.

She filled her glass almost to the rim and while she cooked, ate, and then wandered into his living room to figure out his multitude of remotes for the TV and all the boxes attached, she managed to drink almost the whole bottle without even realizing it.

At least, until she went to get her next glass and when she turned the bottle over, it was empty.

Damn.

She had realized after the ladies left, not one of them

had mentioned how Trace lost his leg. But she couldn't imagine why it would be a secret. Though, since Trace hadn't shared about it with her, maybe they didn't know, either.

But one thing they said was to fight for Trace.

However, to do that, she would have to stay. And, even if she wanted to, she wasn't sure if that would be possible. She hadn't heard from him all day, so she didn't know what he found, if anything.

Despite his best efforts, he might end up agreeing that she would need to disappear.

In the meantime, did she really want to become attached all over again to a man she might not be able to have? Or who might not want her once this was over?

She sat there, staring blankly at the TV, so tied up in her own head, which was swimming from all the wine she drank, when her phone rang next to her, making her jump.

She quickly grabbed it and glanced at the screen.

He now unblocked his number whenever he called her, so she knew it was him and not those other men. She was surprised to see how late it was, just after midnight.

She swiped her finger over the screen and put the phone to her ear. "Trace," she breathed.

And when he answered, everything on her tingled and clenched. "Ellie."

Did his voice sound more erotic to her because it was late, and she was thoroughly pickled?

Or was it like that all the time?

"I had visitors today." She bit back the giggle wanting to bubble up.

She got nothing but a long pause. As if he waited for her to continue. So, she did. "I like them. They're really nice."

"Good women," came his answer.

"They brought cupcakes and wine."

"I think that's standard for them, sweetheart."

Ellie closed her eyes at his "sweetheart." "It's a good one to have."

His low chuckle filled her ear.

"Trace," she began.

"Yeah, baby?"

"Are you coming home soon?"

"Yeah. Flying out tomorrow. Found a lead. Need to follow it. But I'm not sure how long I'll be staying."

Ellie frowned. "You're coming home and then leaving right away?"

"Plan to be home a night or two, then I'll go."

That would be three more days closer to the looming deadline. "I told you how you could make this easier for both of us."

"Yeah, and I heard you. Doesn't mean it's the best option."

"But it would be easier for everyone involved." When he didn't say anything she added, "Your boss isn't going to be happy. Fifteen hundred won't go far when it comes to all of this travel."

"Sweetheart, that fifteen hundred was spent the first morning. He charges premium for our time. That's why it's a good gig for me."

He did have a nice house, car, motorcycle... And he'd restored the Ford. None of that was cheap. "I can't afford to pay—"

"I've got it covered."

"Trace..."

"Said I got it covered, El."

She pressed her fingertips to her bottom lip and dropped her head. "Why?"

"Because I put myself in your shoes, as you asked. We were both wrong back then. And now I want to make it right."

"For me?"

"With you. Can't do that if we erase your existence."

"I could change my name, my hair color..."

"What I'm finding, El, is that wouldn't be enough. Not with this... outfit. We would need to fake your death, get you all new documents and then set you up somewhere they would never look."

"That sounds more complicated than I thought."

"Yeah, it's not just you getting a fake passport and hopping on a plane to live on some tropical island, Ellie. Not with these guys. They don't fuck around when it comes to their money. Your husband picked the wrong men to screw over. I wouldn't doubt they don't put the screws to your father-in-law next, if they haven't already. McMaster put his whole family at risk. They won't stop until they get what they're after. They're rich and powerful, and you don't get that way by backing down or excusing debts. This is some serious shit."

His serious words were compounded by his serious tone. "So, it's worse than I thought."

"Worse than any of us thought."

"I told you I don't want to put anyone at risk. I meant that. Not you. Not your team. Not anyone who lives in this compound, Trace." Including the women she not only met today, but the women she still hadn't met or any of their children. "I don't want what George did to mess up anyone else's life."

"Too late on that one, sweetheart."

But it could minimize the damage. He had a plan she just needed to let him do whatever he did with it. "So, who are they?"

"Not now. We can talk about that when I get back. That's not why I called."

Ellie raised her head and sat up. "Did you call to tell me how you lost your leg?" She winced when that came out. Damn wine.

"No."

"Are you ever going to tell me?"

"I've relived it a million times, El, not sure I want to relive it one more."

"I'd like to know."

"Is it that important to you?"

"Yes."

"Why?" he echoed her earlier question.

"Because I love you and I wasn't there for you when it happened. I wasn't there during your recovery, however long that was."

"El..." he breathed.

"And I want to know everything that I missed. And you're wrong about something."

His voice had a catch in it when he asked, "What's that, sweetheart?"

"Maybe we both did the wrong thing, but I did it for selfish reasons."

"No."

"Yes. I did what was best for me, not you."

"Again, I put myself in your shoes, El. I probably would have been out of my mind if the roles had been reversed."

"Enough to leave me?"

He was quiet. His breathing the only sound on the other end of the phone.

"How come it took this long for us to figure it out?" She tried to keep the shake from her voice, but it was impossible. She always got more maudlin when she drank too much wine.

"Because it happened and we both moved on. That's how life is. Shit happens, and unless you wallow in it, you get swept up with everything else going on around you. Next thing you know, the woman—the girl you loved—loves someone else, gets married to him and plans to have his babies."

But she didn't have his babies. She should've known then she'd made a mistake. An even bigger one than breaking up with Trace.

"I'm sorry."

"Sweetheart, sorries aren't going to change the past."

"But that's all I have to give."

"Fuck, El," he said on a low groan.

She refocused on something else he said. "You said 'loved.'"

No answer.

When she told him she loved him, it was present tense. "Past tense."

"We spent more years apart than we did together, El. And the couple years we were together were a long time ago."

But true love never died, wasn't that right?

Maybe his love for her had never been true.

"You're right," she said softly, feeling a sting in her eyes. She was not going to break down while on the phone with him. She could not expect him to pick up his feelings after nineteen years, brush them off, and slap them back into his chest.

And she reminded herself again, maybe that was for the best. In case she did have to disappear. She ripped his heart out once, she didn't want to do it again.

"None of this was why I called."

"Why'd you call?"

"I'm an expert at dirty talk. Remember?"

"You called for phone sex?" she squeaked, his unexpected reason for calling sweeping away the sadness that had settled into her bones.

"You made me an expert at it, sweetheart."

"All those late nights on the phone."

"Yeah. When I was at a safe distance from you and I could do what I wanted to you without getting in trouble."

"If anyone had found out, you still would've gotten in trouble."

"I'll rephrase. Ended up behind bars."

Ellie smiled. "You did some very naughty things to me over the phone, Mr. Walker."

"And you drove me out of my mind, Miss Cooke. All those showers were never enough. I had to improvise."

"Like MacGyver," she whispered.

"You didn't enjoy those conversations?" he teased.

"You know I did."

His low chuckle came through the phone again.

"You know that's why at 12:01 on my birthday we were in the back of your pickup by the lake."

"My plan worked."

Ellie's smile widened. "No, honey. *My* plan worked." She wanted him just as much as he had wanted her.

"Where are you?"

"On your couch."

"You sleep in my bed last night?" The softness in his voice was now gone. In its place was a firm tone.

"Yes."

"Did you touch yourself, too?"

"Yes." Heat crawled into her cheeks, and it wasn't from the wine. "A little," she fibbed. She didn't have a lot in her two suitcases, but she had packed her favorite vibrator, hoping TSA didn't find it if they searched her luggage.

"Were you thinking about me when you did it?"

"No."

He laughed. "Such a liar. What if I told you I thought about you very early this morning?"

"I wouldn't be surprised."

He barked out a laugh. "Damn, El."

"Is it a compliment that you think about me when you masturbate?"

"Yes."

"Really?"

"Only if it's me, though."

"Oh, *then* it's okay. I see how it is."

"I'm glad you see it."

She faked yawned. "Okay, time for me to get some sleep. I didn't realize it's this late."

"Yeah, sweetheart, you need to go to bed."

"That's my plan."

"Go to my room, do what you have to do to prepare for bed, then call me back."

"For?"

"You know what for."

Warmth swirled through her, curling her toes. "With you there and me here, you won't be able to control when I come."

"You don't think so?"

A shiver ran through her at his question which wasn't one, but more like a challenge. "I'll be in control."

"We'll see. Go to bed, El. You've got five minutes to call me back. Which means you need to hustle."

The call ended and she pulled it away from her ear to stare at it for a second.

But only a second, because she only had five minutes.

Which meant she needed to hustle.

———

WALKER HAD one arm crooked behind his head, which was on two stacked pillows.

Five minutes seemed like a fucking half hour. But he watched the time on his phone and about ten seconds before her deadline, his phone lit up. He hit the Answer button and put her on speaker phone. "That was close."

"I took my time," she answered, sounding slightly out of breath.

Right she did.

Jesus, laying naked in a bed talking to Ellie, while she lay in his, brought memories crashing forward.

His mother probably wondered why he went through so many boxes of tissues when he didn't have a cold or allergies.

There was many a night where he and Ellie got off in the back of his truck with them managing not to go all the way, but sometimes he could only take so much and took her home early because he had his limits. Then he'd call her from his room, hoping neither of his parents would pick up the line.

Or hoping like hell her mother or stepfather didn't pick up hers.

He had promised them they would wait, and they did, but there were plenty of times when he thought he might have to break that promise.

Thank fuck for a good imagination and phones.

Like tonight.

Because what he found out last night in McMaster's offices, what information he dug up today, was not good.

He wasn't sure how to get Ellie out of this jam. He didn't have enough money himself to pay the debt. If he could, he would, just to keep her safe.

Even if he sold everything he owned and liquidated his investments, he still wouldn't be close. He could borrow it, if he needed to, but—

"Trace, are you there?"

He shook himself mentally. "Yeah, I'm here. You in my bed now?"

"Yes."

He closed his eyes and pictured her there, ready and waiting. And something he wasn't ready to admit rushed through him like a freight train.

Feelings he hadn't felt in a long damn time.

Fucking goddamn.

"El, you naked?"

"No. I'm in panties and your T-shirt."

His lips curled up at the thought of her wearing his shirt. "Panties off. Leave my shirt on."

Fuck yes. She'd be wrapped up in something of his when she came. Just like the old Rolling Stones shirt he used to own that she had confiscated when they were young. She had told him she slept in it every night.

Bet she didn't sleep in anything but expensive nighties once McMaster got a hold of her.

Fuck the nighties. He wanted her in his shirt.

He wrapped his fingers around the root of his cock and squeezed them tight, trapping the flow of blood, watching his cock darken, the veins protrude.

He wanted her mouth on him right now. He wanted the tip of her tongue touching him, whisking off that bead of precum at the tip.

He hated that he was so far away from her.

He released the root of his cock and studied it as it turned back to its normal color.

"Panties are off, shirt's still on. Now what?"

He shook his head and smiled. She knew exactly what. They'd done this dozens of times. Maybe even more.

It *was* a miracle they never got caught.

"Now you become an expert at dirty talk."

Her rush of breath hit his ear. "I—"

"Don't say you can't. If anyone knows how innocent you *aren't*, it's me."

"Which is all your fault," she reminded him.

His grin got bigger. He would be glad to take the credit. She might have looked sweet and innocent on the outside when she was in high school, but he knew the truth. She burned hot deep down inside.

172

She hadn't been easy, but she'd been worth every fucking second he had to wait.

"I was only like that with you."

Thank fuck for that. "That's because you were mine, El."

"But I never... Even then... It was always you doing it."

"And tonight, it will be you."

"What if I'm not good at it?"

He glanced down at his cock, which was leaking onto his hip. "Sweetheart, I'm hard as fuck for you right now. So fucking hard just thinking about what you're going to be whispering in my ear, what you're going to be doing in my bed, wearing my shirt... Even if you suck, it'll be okay."

She huffed. "I'm not going to suck."

"There's my girl."

"I'm not a girl anymore, Trace."

"No shit. I've noticed. And knowing that makes me even harder. You were great back then; you are even better now."

"I..."

"Baby, I don't want to rush you, but I don't have all night. I got an early flight and another phone call to make after this."

"This late?"

"Yeah."

"To who?"

The last thing he wanted to talk about with her in his bed and his fist wrapped around his cock was her case. "Doesn't matter. What matters is, we're on the phone and my dick is hard. And if you touch yourself, you're probably already wet."

No answer.

He grinned and stroked his cock. "Right?"

"Mmm hmm."

He laughed. "Thought so."

"But the wine helped."

"How much did you drink?"

"A bit."

"Enough for you to do things you normally wouldn't do?"

"No."

"Damn," he whispered. "I'll save that for when I'm in the same room."

"Okay, so now what?"

"Now you make us come."

"Quickly or slowly?"

"Your call."

"Hmm. Okay. So, if I was drunk enough, what would you want to do to me?"

"This is supposed to be you, El, not me."

"Just give me this and I'll take it from there."

He bit back a laugh. "Okay. I've touched every part of you. Claimed every part, too. Except for one. You never let me go there."

"No, I—"

"I want to go there, El. Take me there tonight."

He heard her breath hiss raggedly.

He barely stopped his from doing the same when he fisted his cock again from the root to the tip. It was already slick and shiny from the coconut oil he'd put on his stump after taking off his leg. What he used to keep the skin on his residual limb pliable also made a great natural lube.

And he'd be using it on her when he finally got to take her ass for real.

But, for now, he would have this fantasy.

If Ellie got on board.

"El?"

"I'm here."

"What are you doing?"

"Trying to figure out if I should be on my back or my stomach."

Damn. "Let me know what you decide."

A giggle filled his ear. "If you were here, how would you want me?"

"That's cheating."

"But I have no experience with this."

Thank fuck for that, too. That was what he wanted to hear. "You'll figure it out, sweetheart. Do whatever you're comfortable with."

"Okay."

"Okay?"

"Yes, I'm on my knees."

Fuck me. "Where are your hands?"

"I'm going to have to put you on speaker." He heard a rustle. "Okay, I have my head on the pillow and the phone next to my face. Can you hear me all right?"

"I hear you." He dropped his phone onto his chest and with his other hand he cupped his balls, squeezing lightly. "Can you hear me?"

"Yesss," came out of her on a hiss.

"You touching yourself already?"

Silence.

What the fuck? "El? You need to talk, not just get into your own head."

She giggled again. "Sorry. I'll do better."

He waited. More silence.

"Ellie," he barked.

"I... I'm going to come."

"Already?" He kicked his head back on the pillow and stared at the ceiling in frustration. "Don't!"

"Too late," she whispered. "Told you that you wouldn't be able to control my orgasm."

"Singular."

"What?"

"That was only the first one, sweetheart. And I'm still laying here with a throbbing cock in my hand." He sighed. "There's a container of coconut oil next to the bed."

"I know."

"Put some on your fingers."

"I'm supposed to be doing this, Trace."

"Then do it. You're killing me here."

He heard more rustling, then she was back. "Now what?"

"What do you think?"

"Oh."

"Talk me through it, El. Tell me everything you're doing, how you're doing it and how it feels."

"When you give me orders, it makes me clench tightly around you."

Fuck yes. He could imagine that, too.

"Trace."

"Yes?"

"I like it when you give me orders."

Jesus. This woman really was going to kill him.

"Okay, baby. Then I'll take over." He settled deeper into the mattress and began to stroke himself, his palm easily sliding up and down his erection. He smoothed the coconut oil over the head, gathering the precum along with it. "Thumb on your clit, El. That's my tongue touching you there, stroking it. Tell me how that feels."

"Good."

"Just good?"

"Good enough to make me want to come again."

He almost yelled out "Already?" again, but he bit it back. If she was that worked up, then he shouldn't complain. "You want to come again?"

"Yes."

"Then I'll make you come."

Chapter Fourteen

"You taste so fucking good, El."

Ellie groaned when she heard that.

Her eyes were closed and his voice—deep and a bit growly because of his impatience with her—made goosebumps break out.

But she was relieved he took over. She didn't want to have to worry about expressing her thoughts out loud when she was on the verge of coming. In fact, she might end up babbling nonsense and that wouldn't do him any good.

He had instructed her what to do with her thumb and she imagined it being his tongue.

And once again, she came seconds later with a gasp. "Trace."

"Yeah, baby. You're so fucking wet. So ready for me to fuck you."

"Yes."

"But you're not going to get what you want. I'm going to get what I want."

"Okay."

"And you know what I want."

She did.

And while she was okay with it on the phone, she wasn't sure if she'd ever be ready to give him what he wanted in person.

She might need more wine than what she drank.

"You don't know how good you taste, El. So fucking good. It was something I never forgot, and I can never get enough of. Are your fingers oiled up?"

A shudder ran through her. "Yes."

"Get ready for me."

"I—"

"El, do this for me."

She slid her hand between her thighs, reaching up and around behind herself, to slide her oiled fingers over her anus.

"Make sure you get it in there good, baby. Outside and inside, too."

"For me to get in on the inside—"

"El." Her name held a warning, as if he only had so much patience.

She continued, rubbing the tips of her two lubed fingers over her hole, surprised how good—but different—it felt.

"Inside, El."

She tentatively slid the tip of her middle finger to the center and pressed in. At first it felt weird and she tightened up.

"Relax, baby, just let it happen. It'll be good, I promise."

She pushed the tip barely inside her, let her mind wrap around what he wanted her to do and forced herself to relax.

"Is it tight?"

"Yes."

"Keep going. If my cock is going to fit, you need to get used to your fingers. Once you do, I'll take over."

Okay, okay, okay.

She pushed one finger deeper inside her until it couldn't

go any farther because of her awkward position. She was hardly flexible enough to make it easy. "You're inside me now."

"No, baby, that's you. I'll let you know when I'm inside you."

Her eyes rolled back as she worked her finger in and out of her as best as she could, imagining what it would feel like for Trace to be doing this with his much thicker fingers and then his cock.

She tensed for a moment, thinking about it. Then she blew out a breath and made herself continue.

"Add another finger."

"Trace."

"Yeah, baby?" He had a hitch in his answer. And she realized his breathing was coming louder through the phone.

"What are you doing?"

"Sliding my slick cock up and down your crease. Slowly pressing in, but not taking your ass just yet. Getting you used to what it's going to feel like when I take you there. When I take that place that will solely be mine and mine alone."

"I want you here."

He ignored that, saying instead, "My cock is so hard for you, Ellie. I want to be inside you. But I'm going to take my time. Make sure you enjoy it. You okay with that?"

Of course she was.

"Are you ready for me?"

"Yes," she whispered, hoping he heard her. "I'm ready for you, Trace."

"Are you sure?"

"Yes."

"Pull your fingers out, I'm coming in."

She let her fingers slip loose.

"The head of my cock is right there, Ellie. Asking for entrance."

Ellie pressed the tip of both fingers against herself again and with her eyes closed and her mind wrapping around his words, her fingers turned into his cock. He was there in the room with her. Ready to take her.

"Are you going to let me in, El?"

"Yes."

"Then let me in."

That demand ended with a groan and Ellie pushed her two fingers past her tight rim, allowing Trace access to somewhere he'd never been before. Where no one had ever been before.

"Fuck, Ellie, you're so fucking tight. Hot. Squeezing my cock."

As she sank her fingers as far as she could go, everything clenched on her. Her anus, her core. Her clit even throbbed. Her nipples had pebbled as they pressed to the sheet.

She pushed her face deeper into the pillow and her shoulders harder into the mattress.

His voice came from a distance. Telling her everything he was doing to her. And she was there. In the room with him as he took her this way. She pressed two fingers from her other hand against her clit, circling and pressing against it. And her whole body shuddered.

What he was doing to her was amazing. Unexpected. She wasn't sure she'd like it, but, *hell*, she loved it.

He was now plunging in and out of her, taking her harder, faster. His breath coming like a freight train and she could hardly catch hers.

"Trace," she called out.

"Fuck, Ellie, you feel so fucking good."

"So do you."

"Like it?"

"Yes."

"Going to fuck you harder now."

She didn't answer him, instead, began to rock back and

forth harder on her knees, faster, as she took his cock and rode his fingers at the same time.

"Fuck, Ellie." She heard his rush of breath. "Going to come?"

"Soon," she barely got out herself.

"No, not soon. When I tell you to come, I'm going to come deep inside you. I'm going to fill your ass up with my cum. You're going to come at the same time."

Her eyes rolled back at his words. She wanted to tell him, "Okay," but she couldn't get it passed her lips.

"Feel how hard I am inside you?"

Yes.

"Feel how much I want you?"

Yes.

"You're going to come when I tell you."

Yes.

"Now." A deep groan filled her ear. "Come now."

She clamped down hard on her fingers and her pussy clenched at the same time as the intense climax spiraled out from her center, around her fingers, sweeping through her, making her cry out his name until she had no voice left.

Then all she heard was her pounding heart and her own ragged breathing in her ears.

It took her a little bit to gather her senses, but when she did, she opened her eyes, saw the phone had slid off the pillow. It had gone dark and she wondered if he had hung up.

She collapsed to the mattress, snagged a tissue from the box next to the bed to wipe off the oil from her fingers and called out, "Trace?"

"I'm here." He was still out of breath, too.

"I need to clean up."

"Me, too."

She smiled as she rolled over and sat up. "I don't want to touch my phone yet."

"Mine's collateral damage. I had it sitting on my chest."

"And you..."

"Yeah, I even got some in my mouth."

Damn. Ellie bit back her giggle. "That sounds kind of hot."

"Trust me, it wasn't."

This time she didn't hold back, she laughed as she climbed from the bed. "I'm leaving you there. I'm going to go wash up quick. Are you going to wait?"

"Do your thing. I'll call you back in a couple minutes."

She rushed from the bed, cleaned up, brushed her teeth quickly, relieved her bladder and then hurried back, just in time to see her phone lighting up again. She grabbed it from the bed and put it to her ear.

"Did you get the spill cleaned up?" she asked.

"Yeah, but the whole time I was imagining it was you doing it with your tongue. Now, *that* was fucking hot."

She settled on the bed. "I thought you needed to make another phone call."

"After that, I'm not in the mood to call who I need to call. It can wait until I get back tomorrow."

She smothered a yawn. Between the pasta, the wine and now the phone sex, she was ready to crash.

"You settled in my bed?"

She turned off the bedside lamp and the room went dark. "Yes."

"I'll be in it with you tomorrow night. Tonight was practice for the real thing."

"I'm not sure I'm ready for that. I really liked it, but I'm also realistic about size."

She heard him chuckle softly. "Thanks for the ego boost."

"I'm not saying you're overly large—"

"How about we leave it the way you said it."

She smiled up at the dark ceiling. "I might fall asleep on you."

"You've done that plenty of times in the past, El."

"Sorry."

"Didn't mean it like that. I loved listening to you fall asleep, wishing I was next to you in your bed, holding you as you did it. Knowing one day that would come true, we'd fall asleep together every night and wake up together every morning."

"But it never happened." *Damn*, did she regret that.

"It did, El. In the bed you're lying in right now."

That was true.

"And I'll be home for a couple nights and I plan on fucking you until you can't help but fall asleep on me, and then in the morning when we wake, I'm going to fuck you again."

The blood rushed through her in anticipation.

"And more phone sex when you're gone?"

"We'll see. I'm not sure how things will go."

That didn't sound good. When she opened her mouth to ask, he cut her off. "Not now, El. Let's savor what we just had for a little while longer. Plenty of time to talk about the ugly stuff."

The ugly stuff.

That really didn't sound good.

But he was right. She wanted to enjoy the remaining euphoria from their phone sex.

When he didn't say anything for a while, she thought maybe it was he who fell asleep on her.

"We should've done it sooner," she whispered, not wanting to wake him if he did.

"Hmm?" came his murmur.

"We should've done it sooner," she repeated louder.

Amazingly enough, he knew exactly what she meant.

"You weren't old enough. I didn't want you to ever regret it."

"Everybody else our age was doing it."

It took him a long while before he murmured, "We weren't everybody else."

No, they weren't.

She'd been the last one of her friends to lose her virginity and sometimes that got frustrating.

Especially when there were days—and nights—where they almost didn't make it. Nights when they almost gave in to the temptation.

But Trace had been strong. Strong enough for both of them. He had the willpower of steel.

When she looked back now, she wasn't sure how a boy on the cusp of being a man had that. Especially at eighteen, nineteen, even twenty, when his hormones were raging.

But at the time, he loved her enough to wait until the moment was right.

She wished he still loved her. She wished things had turned out differently. *Hell*, she wished a lot of things.

"Trace?"

No answer.

Listening carefully, she heard it. The soft, steady breathing of a man who had fallen asleep over fourteen hundred miles away.

"Goodnight," she whispered into the phone, then added, "I love you, Trace."

Before hanging up, she waited a moment to see if he would answer.

He didn't.

————

WALKER GRIPPED the phone in his hand so tightly he thought it might shatter. "Do you know what your fucking son was involved in? Do you know how he risked your daughter-in-law's life? Hell, she's still at risk. She said she went to you for help and you fucking turned her away."

"I don't owe her anything."

His chest rose as he inhaled in a deep breath and held it long enough to keep the last string attached to his temper from breaking. "But your son does."

"My son is dead," Gerald McMaster answered.

And Walker wouldn't shed one fucking tear about that. Not a fucking one.

"I remember you, Trace Walker. My son said you took his wife's virginity and then left her once you got it. Georgie had to step in and take care of what you left behind."

Georgie.

He wanted to puke, but instead he growled, "I didn't leave shit behind."

"Yes, you did, boy."

Walker gritted his teeth at the man's use of "boy." *Condescending asshole.* "I was doing it for her." Why the fuck was he explaining himself to this motherfucker?

"No, Walker, you got what you wanted from her, then abandoned her. My son had to step in—against my wishes, mind you—to take care of her. She had nothing. Her family couldn't afford her education, so I paid for it at Georgie's request. He bought her everything she needed. Lifted her up from the poverty she lived in."

Jesus. Ellie's family might have not been rich, but they certainly hadn't been living in squalor or in a tent under a fucking bridge. She had a good home with a loving mother and stepfather who provided the necessities.

"Contrary to what you believe, Walker, you didn't turn her into a woman when you stole her innocence. After you left her, she turned into nothing but skin and bones, an unattractive skeleton. Her eyes were haunted. She became a hollow shell. My son took pity on her and fixed your mistake."

Your mistake. Had she lost weight after he left? Had she been that worried that it physically made her sick? If so, he never knew. She'd said nothing when she had called him to end it.

"So, who turned her into a woman, Walker? Not you. You destroyed her. My son saved her, made her who she is by educating her and giving her a life worth living. A better life than what she had or what you would've ever given her."

"A life he died for because he was a greedy fuck. While he knew how to groom a woman to be his *perfect* wife, he didn't know how to run a fucking business. He ran that business—the one *you* set him up in—into the ground. He got involved in shady and dangerous business dealings with even shadier people. So, don't paint him to be some kind of fucking saint. He wasn't. He was far from it. But that's not why I'm calling you, Jerry."

"Cursing is unnecessary, and I didn't give you permission to call me by my first name."

Walker could just imagine the pompous old ass's jowls flapping and his hand clutching at his collar in indignation. "I'll take that into consideration, *Jerry*. I need to know whether anyone has contacted you regarding that 1.3-million-dollar debt."

His long pause was telling. "If they did, why the hell would I discuss it with you?"

Walker glanced toward the door. He had just arrived home and hadn't gone into the house yet because he wanted to get this business out of the way first. He had stayed in the garage so Ellie wouldn't hear the conversation with her *loving* former father-in-law. "Because it would be in your best interest to do so. Have you seen what they did to your son? Is that what you want to happen to Ellie?"

"I don't care about Ellie."

He felt his upper lip curling into a sneer. "How about your wife, *Jerry*? Or how about you, you selfish prick? Do you think they simply killed him? That it was quick? Fuck no, they made your *Georgie* suffer. I'm sure he cried, begged and shit his fucking pants, *Jerry*. They tortured him slowly. They made him feel every single cut they made. They knew what the fuck they were doing. How to keep him alive as long as possible when he wished he was dead. And, believe me, *Jerry*, you don't want them doing that to you."

"I don't owe them that money," McMaster said faintly.

"Neither does Ellie."

"It was because of her that Georgie went into debt. He was desperate to keep her happy. Her tastes became expensive once she got to experience everything she could have. My son said she was always demanding bigger and better."

Yeah, a man with bigger balls and better morals.

"Bullshit. It was your son who wanted the best of everything." His trip to Denver made that very clear after speaking with people who knew him well. "Not her. She was never like that and still isn't."

After a long hesitation, McMaster asked, "She's with you? She came to you for the money?"

Yeah, you cunt, she's back in my bed where she belongs. "She came to me for help because you don't have a conscience big enough to do the right thing."

McMaster clicked his tongue, making Walker want to reach through the phone and rip it out.

"She was never good enough for my son. She wasn't even good enough to be a brood bitch. For all the money we spent on her and all the time Georgie invested in her, she could have at least given me grandchildren."

Walker ground his molars together so hard, his jaws popped.

"The *right thing* to do was to wash my hands of that girl. I did. It's done. Now I'm done with you. I don't care what they do to her."

"And when they do it and still don't have their money and they text you the pictures of her not only tortured but filleted open, then what? Who do you think they're going after next? These men are not going to walk away empty-handed, *Jerry*. I promise you that."

"Then give them what they want."

Walker closed his eyes and inhaled slowly through his nose, filling his lungs until they couldn't take any more, until he felt as though he'd explode. Just as slowly, he released it. When he was done, when he no longer felt like throwing his phone across the garage and stomping it with his boot until it was in pieces, he said, "And that's what I'll do, *Jerry*."

His cell phone went dead.

He needed to convince the cartel that McMaster was the better target. That if anyone could get them their money, it was him.

All Ellie had to give was her life and them taking it wasn't going to get them paid. In fact, it would get them dead, because if that happened...

If that happened...

He rubbed his hand over his eyes, trying to wipe away the image of Ellie sitting in a chair in the same condition as her husband was. Where death would be a blessing compared to the suffering that came before.

He strode over to the garage door opener on the wall and whacked it. The middle door rose as he snagged his key out of his key cabinet and then strode quickly to his bike.

The door into the house opened and Ellie stood in the doorway, eyes wide. "Where are you going? You just got back!"

"Going for a fucking ride."

Her gaze slid over him, clearly assessing his mood. And

he knew when she figured out how pissed off he was when she said, "I'm going with you."

She was wearing shorts and a T-shirt, as well as completely barefoot. There was no way she was riding like that. Especially when he was in a mood to ride his bike like it was stolen and he had a parade of cops on his tail.

"No. Stay here."

She stepped into the garage. "Trace, I—"

"Stay here!" he yelled at her.

She stumbled back a half step and her green eyes went wide.

Then he watched his soft, sweet Ellie disappear. Her face got hard and she got a determined look in her narrowed eyes. "No. I'm coming with you."

He raked his eyes down her body. "Not like that you're not."

"Then tell me what to wear."

Fuck him. He scrubbed a hand over his hair and blew out a breath before he said something to her he'd regret. "Jeans, socks, solid shoes. Jacket, if you got one. I'll dig out a fucking helmet. But hurry the fuck up. You've got five minutes."

She turned and ran inside, screaming, "You and your five fucking minutes!"

If he wasn't so fucking pissed and ready to kill someone, he would've been amused with her yelling at him. But he wasn't.

And he really didn't want her to go along. But, for some reason, he also couldn't deny her.

With a shake of his head, he grabbed a helmet off one of the shelves. It would be too big for her, but it was better than nothing.

He put it on the hood of his truck, mounted his bike and crab-walked it backward out into the driveway. By the time he had it turned around and warming up, she was there, dressed exactly like he told her, holding the helmet to her stomach.

"Put your helmet on, get on, then hold the fuck on."

She opened her mouth, snapped it shut, gave him a nod, and pulled on the helmet. Before she could secure it, he brushed her hands away and did it for her to make sure it was as snug as possible.

Something twisted in his gut when she climbed on behind him, wiggling forward until she was snug against him with her arms wrapped tightly around his waist.

Once she was done with her adjustments, he hit the throttle so hard he thought he was going to lose her off the back. But she caught herself and clung to him even tighter.

The second he was past the compound gates, he twisted the throttle harder and leaned forward into the wind with Ellie pressed to him like a second skin.

He took them through the winding back roads out of Shadow Valley, taking each curve as fast as his old restored Harley could handle without wiping out.

And it felt fucking great.

Not only to clear his head and to have his girl between his legs, but his girl holding on to him.

Trusting him with her life. Not only with her situation, but on his bike as he tried to drive away his frustration.

But then, she was on the back of his dirt bike more times than he could remember. She had loved the wind in her air and used to hoot and holler in his ear the faster he took them.

Now, looking back, he'd done some stupid shit on that bike with his girl on the back. He could have killed them both.

However, he didn't and those were some of the memories that were worth holding onto.

Now, instead of his girl against his back, he had his woman.

She just happened to be one and the same.

After the first twenty minutes, he eased off the throttle, relaxed and Ellie loosened up against him.

After two hours of having her thighs pressed against his hips, her pussy against his ass, he headed back. Once he pulled his girls back into the garage, she dismounted, took off her helmet and shook out her hair.

Her cheeks held color, her eyes a spark, and his woman was fucking beautiful.

She combed her fingers through her long, auburn hair, working out some of the tangles. "It's going to take me a long time to get the knots out."

"Next time remember to put your hair up first."

He closed his eyes. *His woman. Next time.*

He was sinking fast.

But then, he wasn't really fighting that pull, either.

Her "I'm surprised you still ride," had him reopening his eyes to see her stashing the helmet on the shelf.

As she reached up on her tiptoes, his eyes explored her ass in her jeans. When she turned around, he lifted his gaze as she shed the light windbreaker she wore. Her nipples pressing against her thin baby blue T-shirt caught his attention next.

His mouth finally reconnected to his brain. "When he restored it, Jag customized it for me. I have a hand shifter instead of a foot shifter."

"I thought something was different. I wasn't sure if dirt bikes were designed the same."

"No, same concept. One was a boy's toy," he ran his hand over the perfectly restored gas tank with care, "this toy is a man's."

Jesus fuck, did he really puff out his chest at that? He certainly fucking did.

"It's beautiful."

Like you. He dismounted.

"Thank you for putting up with me."

He tilted his head. "On the ride?"

"Yes. On the ride." She waved a hand around. "With this whole thing. I appreciate everything you're doing. Or trying to do."

"You got fucked, Ellie, and not in a good way. I can't sit back and watch you suffer—even die—because of some greedy motherfucker. Even if that motherfucker was your husband."

That word, just thinking about Ellie being married to McMaster, left a bad taste in his mouth.

But it was over. Done. McMaster was no more.

He just needed to figure out how to keep Ellie alive by getting her clear from her so-called obligation to this dangerous cartel.

He also needed to sit her down and go over what he found. He'd like to shield her from it, but it wouldn't be fair to hide things from her. Especially when it involved her life.

After snagging his duffel out of his Hellcat, he followed her into the house, dropped his bag in the laundry room and went into the kitchen. The smell of something cooking made his stomach growl.

"Where'd you get that?" he asked, lifting his chin toward a crockpot on the counter. He knew he didn't own one.

"Frankie. She let me borrow it."

She lifted the lid to check whatever was cooking, then closed it before turning around to lean back against the counter.

"You look fucking good in jeans." That sight made his mouth water more than the smell of the food.

She smiled softly. "I hardly ever wear—*wore*— them. I miss it and that's going to change. We lived in jeans in high school, remember?"

"Yeah. I still live in them, or cargo pants, unless I'm home. Then it's easier to wear shorts."

"You look fucking good in jeans, too," she repeated.

"He didn't let you wear jeans?"

She did a half-shrug. "They weren't appropriate."

Jeans were always appropriate. Except for weddings and funerals, that was. "Did his controlling you bother you?"

"Not at first, because it was subtle. Eventually, it wasn't. Then, yes, it bothered me. It's one reason why I put off having kids. I didn't want them to be little controlled puppets. They could only wear this, only eat that. Teaching a child manners is one thing, dictating their every move is another."

The anger he'd lost on the ride was surging back up. "He dictated yours."

When she averted her eyes and didn't answer, he realized he didn't need an answer. His thoughts went back to something the senior McMaster said. "He put you through college."

She blinked, probably wondering how he knew that.

It shouldn't annoy the fuck out of him, but it did. And he knew it was because that was something he might not have ever been able to give to her. Not without financing it and going into debt.

Now? No problem. Then? Yeah. It wouldn't have been an option. He couldn't even do it for himself which was, again, why he joined the Army.

"Yes. He said a degree would open the world to me."

"Did it?" Of course, it didn't. He already knew that answer.

"No. It put me in a bubble. His bubble."

"I'm surprised he let you go away to school."

"He didn't. I took classes at Ithaca College."

"For what?"

She sighed and her expression turned sour. "My major was Art History. I assumed it was to expose me to more

193

culture, which apparently, I was lacking, according to his father. I guess knowing art, I could impress his friends."

"Did it?"

She huffed, "I never discussed art once with any of his friends. Total waste of time and money. Not that I don't appreciate art, it's just not something I wanted a degree in."

"What did you want to major in?"

"I don't know... Back then I thought the culinary arts. I wanted to expand my portfolio to more than grilled cheese sandwiches with tomatoes and ham."

His lips twitched. "Nothing wrong with those sandwiches."

"No, but still... I would have loved to open a cute little diner. Maybe one that was only open for breakfast and brunch. Or even a trendy food truck."

"Two of the DAMC women run a bakery in town." And from what Hunter had told him, Frankie had wanted to learn the culinary arts, too. She was planning on attending a local tech school just for that reason.

Maybe it was something the two women could team up to do together. As close as he and Hunter were, it would be good if their women were close, too.

Fuck, but only if Ellie stayed in Shadow Valley. And that could never happen if he didn't get his ass in gear to put a stop to the cartel's threat.

"Sophie's Sweet Treats?"

Her question pulled him out of his thoughts. "Yeah. I'm sure those are the cupcakes they brought."

"They were. They were to die for. I would love to be able to learn to bake like that."

"Maybe they can teach you. It'd be a start on your culinary dream."

She paused. "That means I would have to stay in Shadow Valley."

"Right." That meant she'd have a reason to stay. Especially since she no longer had a home in Denver. Maybe she didn't want to stay, though. Especially since she kept pushing him to help her go ghost. "You're right. Never mind."

"But it could be something to do while I'm here to keep my mind off everything. And until this mess is sorted."

Sorted.

It was going to take a lot of shoveling, not sorting. And they were running out of time.

"Right. If you're interested, I'll say something to Z."

"Z?"

"Zak, remember? The president of the DAMC. The club now owns the bakery through him and his wife. Bella also is a big part of it."

"Bella with the cupcake licking Axel?"

Say what? "Is that what you women talked about while sucking down wine?"

She grinned and shrugged. "Maybe."

"Fuck licking cupcakes. Did you tell them how much I like licking your pussy?"

He bit back his grin when color rushed into her cheeks. "Yes, because that's what we talked about. Which Shadow has the best tongue for cunnilingus." The sarcasm was strong.

"I suppose I won." And didn't his damn chest puff out again before he could stop it.

"You didn't."

His brows shot up. "Who won?"

"We all agreed we'd need more analysis before we could bring it to a fair vote."

His eyes slid from her to the slow cooker and back to her, wearing those hip hugging jeans. "How soon for dinner?"

"It's a crockpot meal. It won't get ruined like the chicken."

"Then as a candidate, I suddenly feel the need to impress my voters."

"Voter," she corrected.

"Right. Voter. Just you. If we have time before dinner, I can start my campaign."

She rolled her eyes at him. "You need to be *pretty* convincing to get my vote."

"I'll try my damnedest."

"Dinner will keep. Your voter is waiting."

Chapter Fifteen

HE HAD his woman plastered to his side. His stomach was full. His nuts were empty.

Fucking life couldn't get better than that, could it?

Yeah, it could.

His woman wouldn't be indebted to a fucking Mexican cartel for 1.3 million dollars, which was due in a few days. He needed to tell her what they'd found in Denver, but it was going to ruin their relaxed mood.

Her eyes were closed and occasionally she would let out a soft sigh as he combed his fingers through her hair. Her messy, knotted hair. That *he* caused.

He smiled up at the ceiling.

He was pretty sure before dinner he cemented her vote with his mouth on her pussy. But just to be *very* sure, he did it again after dinner.

She also got his vote when she wrapped her hot, wet mouth around his cock and took him right to the point of coming before he made her back off, so he could fuck her.

But, again, he needed to get her up to speed before he took off for California with whoever in his crew decided to join him.

They needed to get a better lock on the Castellano Cartel, which was based in San Diego but had their claws in quite a few other states.

He feared what they would find out there was something much bigger than he and his team could handle. And that fucking turned his stomach.

He dipped his chin and couldn't see her face since it was tucked into his neck. Her warm breath blew softly across his throat, her fingers were as active as his, but hers were pressed to his right pec, with her thumb softly brushing back and forth over one of his nipples.

"I gotta leave again Friday morning," he reluctantly reminded her.

"To where this time?" She didn't lift her head but moved her hand over to his dog tags and traced them with the tip of her finger.

"California. San Diego, to be exact. Hunter and I found out who they are."

She gripped his tags in her fist and lifted her head, meeting his eyes. "Who?"

"Sorry if this hurts you, but McMaster was a fucking stupid ass who deserved to die. Anyone in their right mind would never have gotten involved with this organization. You don't do business with a cartel like this and expect to walk away unscathed. It just doesn't happen."

She released his tags and sat up, folding her legs underneath her and to the side. "Cartel? Like a drug cartel?"

"Out of Mexico. The Castellanos. Does that name sound familiar?"

She shook her head. "No. Was George dealing drugs?"

"No. He didn't get involved with that aspect. Because he had an investment company he had the tools to launder money, which is something the cartel needs. He did it for their ring in Colorado. I'm assuming the organization has someone set up to do the same in every state they deal in."

"Every state?"

"Yeah, I suspect it's a few. They run drug rings dealing in black market marijuana in every state where pot was legalized. At least on the west coast from what we could find."

"If he was working for them, how did he become indebted to them? Wouldn't they pay for him to launder money? It might be an illegal one, but it was still a service he was providing."

The woman was smart as fuck and didn't need a damn degree in Art History to prove it.

"Right. So, the first night I called you from Denver, I was not in my room. We were about to break into his offices and I didn't want to tell you that over the phone. We got in and found shit that proved he was skimming. And for the amount of money he was laundering, even skimming a small percentage was a lot of money. It looked like he skimmed at least two or three million."

Her mouth opened, then snapped shut. "Damn," she whispered. "How? How did he do it?"

"He used a method called round-tripping. From what we found, it looked like the cartel would deposit money into an account in the Caymans for a shell corporation. Then McMaster would take that money, which was exempt from being taxed, and invest it. Eventually, the cartel would cash out the investments. Dirty money was now clean." Walker raised his hand before she could interrupt him. "That's not all he was doing. He also set up his own shell corporation in Colorado to purchase real estate. He was helping the cartel buy houses with the laundered money around Denver for them to turn into illegal grow houses. So, he was setting them up with the real estate, then laundering the drug money they made by buying investments in small increments before turning around and selling those investments in bulk."

"That all sounds complex."

"Complex but effective. But by getting involved with the cartel, he became mired in their shit. Similar to the mafia, once you get in business with them, you don't ever get out. At least alive. He might have realized his mistake and that's why he started skimming. I'm assuming that stolen money went into another offshore account where he would use it to eventually disappear once he had a shitload of it. Whether he planned on taking you with him or not, I have no fucking clue."

"I wouldn't have gone."

"But if you didn't, you might have ended up in the same situation you're in now. With your life on the line. Cartels are nothing to fuck around with, El. He not only fucked around with them, he fucked them over. That's an immediate death sentence. Even if he could've paid off the debt, the result would've remained the same. He would've been tortured and killed. I'm honestly surprised they didn't snag you at the same time. But maybe they hoped to gain access to that stolen money first. And by you being his wife, and heir, you'd have that access."

"They'd rather have their money than have me dead."

"Yeah, but they also don't like being fucked over. And, from what we found, McMaster fucked them over royally. I guess he didn't think they would be checking their books with a fucking fine-tooth comb. They were. Even if he hadn't skimmed the amount he had, he would've gotten caught eventually. At first, he was using the money to cover bad investments and deals gone wrong that he'd done. He took risks to make as much money as he could in as little time as possible, but all that shit collapsed around him. Then snowballed. Unfortunately, the asshole didn't know how to make a good deal. He didn't use his head, he used his thirst for the all-mighty dollar to make his decisions. And none of those decisions were good ones. I see why his father washed his hands of him."

"I knew something was off. He wouldn't discuss it and actually shut me out."

"Here's the thing, that's only what we uncovered in Denver. We're heading to San Diego to get a bead on the cartel. More recon is necessary to make solid decisions."

"About me."

"About your situation. How we're going to resolve it."

"I can't see how to resolve it other than me just going ghost, as you put it."

If anything, he wanted to leave that option as the final one. He wanted to avoid it if at all possible.

And mostly his reasoning was a selfish one. He knew it. So did his team.

Or if they didn't realize it yet, they would when he met with them in the morning. They had to find a way other than ghosting Ellie.

He had an idea but would run it by the others. Six minds— or seven, including Diesel—were better than one. They all had different strengths, which was why they worked well as a team.

Her cell phone lit up on his nightstand. Before she could grab it, he did.

It was the cartel with their daily countdown.

Once again, he was reminded that the clock was ticking.

No, it wasn't a fucking clock. More like a goddamn time bomb.

———

WALKER GLANCED OVER HIS SHOULDER. He'd kept the light off, but there was enough early morning light leaking around the curtains to see Ellie sleeping. Her bare back was to him, the bedding pushed down all the way to her waist.

He let his gaze sweep over the line of her spine, the way her long hair spilled over his pillow, the way her ribs rose and fell with each steady breath.

Fuck. They needed to come up with a solution this morning and fast. He wasn't going to lose her again. Not this time.

Whether she knew it or not, she was going to be permanently in his bed.

With one last look at her, he turned back to the large jar of coconut oil he kept next to the bed. When he reached for it, a hand shoved his arm away.

"Let me do it."

Jesus. The thought of her rubbing oil onto his stump shouldn't make his dick twitch, but it did.

"I thought you were sleeping."

She didn't answer as the mattress shifted and she came around the bed to stand in front of him.

Totally fucking naked.

As much as he liked it, that wasn't going to work.

"Sweetheart, put my shirt on if you're going to do it. Otherwise, I'm not going to get out of here on time."

His cock was already at half-chub in the boxer briefs he had pulled on. Her going to her knees at his feet naked would only make it worse.

As he reached for his crutches, she shook her head and blocked his access. "What do you need?"

He wasn't sure this was a good idea. He didn't ever want to be dependent on anyone else. He sighed in resignation. "Cargo pants and my boots."

"That it?"

"You'll find a liner, a regular sock and I'll need one of the shorter socks in my second drawer down."

"Shirt?"

"Black T-shirt in the top drawer."

She snagged the discarded T-shirt he'd tossed on the

floor last night, and pulled it over her head as she moved to his dresser, got what he'd need and then went back to his closet to bring out his leg with the boot attached.

He wasn't sure what he was feeling watching her carry it to him. He was resigned with what happened to him all those years ago, but seeing her accept him as-is kind of caught him off-guard. It shouldn't. He should be relieved.

It was a weird feeling.

He'd been with many women over the years, most of them just one night stands, some of them were just women like Sami. Just sex, nothing serious. He'd even had women freak out and back out last minute when he removed his leg before fucking them.

Sometimes to make it easy, he wouldn't. If it was just a quick bust-a-nut hookup, he'd take them against a wall or bent over where he only had to drop his pants enough to get the job done.

Then they never knew of his disability.

He was staring at his residual limb when her bare legs came into view.

"I've watched you do it a couple of times, but I want to help." She raised a palm. "And before you say you can do it yourself, I know that. But I *want* to do it. Just let me, please."

She dropped to her knees, a sight which would never get old, and he grabbed the jar and held it for her.

She dipped her fingers into the semi-solid oil and then tentatively began to rub it into his skin around the stump. "I've used coconut oil as a natural moisturizer."

"Makes great lube, too."

"You're not doing your job if I need lube."

"You'll be thankful for lube when I take your ass for real." Well, thinking that wasn't helping his cock from getting hard, either.

She glanced up from what she was doing. "*If* I let you take it."

"You'll let me take it."

She stuck her tongue out at him playfully and continued to rub the oil into his skin.

"Using some kind of lotion at the top of the liner helps prevent dragging on the skin," he murmured.

She nodded. "Makes sense. Is that enough?"

"I'll never get enough of you touching me," he admitted.

"I meant enough of the coconut oil."

"Yeah."

"Tell me what to do next."

His brow furrowed. He wasn't sure he wanted her taking care of him like this. He loved to be intimate with her, but this was a different type of intimacy.

He swallowed hard and cleared his throat to get the rough out before continuing. "Flip the liner inside out. Make sure the cup of the liner is secure against the end of my stump, and once it is... that's it, El. Good. Now, roll it up, making sure there aren't any air pockets."

Her hand slowly and gently smoothed the silicone liner up his residual limb. She took her time, making sure there were no air bubbles like he'd said.

He had to look away while she did it. He focused over her head on a picture he had hanging on the wall. Even though he couldn't see it from where he sat, he knew he wore a smile on his face while standing in front of a Black Hawk with the rest of his unit. The rest of them were smiling and laughing, too, since one of the guys had cracked an awful joke right before the picture was taken.

Some of his brothers in that photo never made it home. He did. He should consider himself lucky.

"Now what?"

He dropped his gaze to her upturned face as she squatted in front of him.

Fuck.

His voice was still a little raw when he said, "Roll the sock up next. All the way... That's it. Smooth it out, then hand me my cargos that are on that chair."

She popped up from her position on the floor and went to grab his pants, quickly returning. "Now what?"

"Now I put my pants on. And a sock on my other foot."

She watched as he pulled his cargos over his foot and up his legs. He worked them over his hips and then rolled his left pant leg up past his knee.

"I guess loose pants help?"

"Yeah. There are different ways to get your pants on, but loose pant legs help."

He straightened his left knee, pointing his stump and the pin at the bottom of the sleeve straight out. "Grab the leg, El, slide it over my stump, making sure the pin is set securely into the locking device of the socket."

As soon as she did so, he pushed up from the bed and the pin clicked into place, locking his leg on.

"The locking pin is how it stays on?"

"That and vacuum."

He sat back down, put a sock and boot on his right foot, lacing it tight.

She hadn't stepped back and was almost touching him. He could feel her body heat, she was that close.

Before he could grab his shirt and pull it over his head, she stopped him with a hand once again wrapped around his dog tags.

Her green eyes hit his and an ache swelled in his chest at the total love and devotion he saw in them.

A love that could easily be used as a weapon to destroy him if she wanted to.

He hoped to fuck she never wanted to.

He hoped to fuck he could find a solution to her problem.

He hoped to fuck that once he did, she'd stay.

What he was seeing made him think she'd say yes if he asked.

She dropped her gaze to his tags. "Tell me."

"I don't have time; I need to get to the warehouse."

"They can wait."

"El, your deadline is looming. We don't have time to waste."

"So, give me the abridged version. Give me something, honey. I want to know. You now know what happened to me during all those years. I need to know what happened to you."

"I joined the Army and got a disability discharge."

She shook her head. "No, Trace."

"Yes, El."

Her eyes turned sad, her lips turned downward as she captured the bottom one between her teeth.

For fuck's sake. He didn't want to make her sad. He didn't want to be the reason.

He had always been the one who was supposed to make her happy.

He failed.

Now was a chance to make up for that failure.

At least a small part of it.

Though, the story might rip her apart. And make her even sadder than him keeping it from her.

If she stayed, he'd have to tell her eventually. She was right. She needed to know.

Maybe he was a coward for putting it off.

He grabbed both of her cheeks and leaned down to kiss her, pulling that bottom lip free by separating her lips, sweeping his tongue through her mouth. But only briefly because it wouldn't take much to jerk his pants down enough to bend her over and fuck her again.

And then he'd really be late.

She sighed softly when he ended the kiss.

"I love you, El."

His words didn't push away her sadness, which he was hoping it would do. His story was only going to compound it.

"I won't have time to debrief you after I tell you, so be prepared for it to haunt you the rest of the day until I get back. Then we can discuss it in more detail, yeah?"

"Okay," she whispered.

"You need to talk in the meantime, shoot me a text. If I can, I'll call you back. But I really need to concentrate on the bigger, more important picture, which is keeping you alive and in my life." Fuck, if he was going to reveal all, he might as well bear his soul, too.

"Okay."

"This time I'm not letting you go so easily, El. I'm going to fight for you. Fight for what we can have. What we should've had all these years. I didn't fight back then. I should've."

"I should've fought, too."

"You did what you thought was best."

"So did you."

"So did I," he repeated, then sat back on the edge of the bed, pulling her with him. He settled her on his right thigh, with his arm around her waist. "Are you sure you want to hear this?"

"Yes. I feel like you're keeping a piece of you from me by not telling me."

He closed his eyes and reluctantly took himself back to that day. The one that changed his life forever.

He had three major life-altering moments he would never forget. The first time he spotted Ellie across that gymnasium. The day he called home and she broke up with him.

And that day in Iraq.

"We were tasked with extracting some soldiers who had

been caught behind enemy lines and needed a medical evacuation. We were to fly in at night, get them and get out." Instead, he ended up being the one behind enemy lines needing the medical evacuation.

"When I talked to you, you said you were headed to Afghanistan for Operation Enduring Freedom."

"Yeah, I was there for a while and then I ended up in Iraq under the same pretext. An operation of freedom." He did his best to keep the bitterness out of his voice, though it was difficult. "I was there until eight years ago when the Little Bird I was in crashed."

Her eyebrows knitted together. "Little Bird?"

"It's a smaller chopper, easier to maneuver for evacuations and rescues than something larger like a Black Hawk."

"Your chopper was shot down?"

He shook his head. "No. It was a mechanical problem. But we crashed in a hostile territory where it was hard to miss a downed chopper. I was the co-pilot and was lucky in the sense that I survived the crash. The pilot wasn't so lucky. When I came to, my leg was pinned. Crushed, actually."

"So, it was amputated."

Fuck. Yes, it was amputated, but not in the way she meant.

He closed his eyes and it all came back to him. The MH-6M was smoking, and though he hurt everywhere, he couldn't feel shit from right above his ankle down. For a while he tried to dig the hard, arid earth out from under his leg with his knife to see if he could slip free. Unfortunately, it was like chipping away at fucking concrete.

He was sure the crash site would be spotted by insurgents once day dawned and the smoke rose high into the sky. That was if the Little Bird didn't catch fire beforehand and burn him to fucking death.

His options of saving himself were limited. Try to wait it out until help arrived and risk being found and killed by unfriendly forces. Or get himself out of that situation and to somewhere where he could hide until he could be extracted.

He only had two hours before the sun would come up and he knew that time was ticking for him, just like it was for Ellie.

He couldn't just lie there and wait for his destiny. So, he did what he needed to do. He removed his belt and used it as a tourniquet. He wiped his knife off the best he could on his uniform and he...

Ellie let out a low, eerie howl from deep within her chest.

He opened his eyes to see her crying, his face clasped in her trembling hands.

He spent over an hour sawing through skin, flesh and bone to free himself. He had blacked out a few times but as soon as he came to, he forced himself to continue. And once he was done, when he was free, he crawled and dragged himself over the ground using his hands, elbows and his good leg, finding a radio, calling in a mayday and his location. He continued until he got to a place where he could hide in thick brush and wait for help to arrive.

The evacuator became the evacuee.

The help became the helpless.

One of the Night Stalkers' motto was "death waits in the dark." Unfortunately, it was waiting for him that time.

But he escaped the dark that night along with death.

He just didn't escape it whole.

Chapter Sixteen

"No point in heading west, Walker, now we know who we're dealing with. There's no point in wasting time or resources to see with our own eyes what we can see right here," Hunter said, looking up from one of the screens he was sitting behind.

Steel sat at the other computer next to Hunter, a toothpick moving at the corner of his mouth. "I don't know, brother. We're motherfucking badasses, if I say so myself, but they out-badass us. Sometimes you just have to admit defeat."

"And fucking with them may just stir the hornet's nest. Last thing we need is to bring the wrath of a cartel's army upon Shadow Valley," Mercy said. "D would shut that operation down in a fucking second. He and everybody else have too much at risk for one woman."

"We don't need to start a war we can't fucking win. And, brother, this is one we cannot win without total devastation," Brick said, leaning against the wall, one boot planted on it, and his arms crossed over his chest.

"Agreed. It's suicide to fuck with these people. They have

endless cash, weapons and connections. I'm not one to give up easily but I'm also not fuckin' stupid," Ryder said.

"Can't give up," Walker muttered, looking around the room at his teammates. Never, ever had he seen them ready to throw in the towel. They loved challenges, so if they were saying it was a no-go, they meant it.

"You might not have a choice," Mercy told him.

Then he had two choices left. Turn Ellie into a ghost before the cartel did or pay the fuckers off.

"Think they'll let her off the hook if they get their dough?" Steel put into words what Walker was thinking himself.

"Not sure. But unless any of you got 1.3 million in your wallet you're willing to loan me, it doesn't matter."

"If we did, it wouldn't be your debt, Walker. It would be hers," Mercy grumbled from the other side of the room. When Walker had entered into the room, he was surprised to see Mercy sitting behind a computer, too.

All hands were on deck for this mission. Paid or not.

"Or would it?" Steel asked, watching Walker too carefully for his taste.

"This cartel isn't small, Walker. It runs grow houses and drug rings in at least three states that we know of," Hunter reminded him. "We can't just go in and wipe them out."

"Now that we know what we're dealin' with, I'm all for squeezin' the father. He needs to step up and pay the debt," Ryder said.

"Who's to say once McMaster pays it the Castellanos don't come and wipe both Ellie and McMaster out?" Brick voiced another concern Walker had considered.

"There's no reason for bloodshed if they get their money," Walker stated, hoping that was fucking true.

"Says the sane man," Hunter grumbled under his breath.

"Okay, that's pushing it. Nobody here is completely sane."

Steel was right. None of them were a hundred percent sane. But then, that was why they could do what they did.

Walker drug a hand through his hair as he began to pace the room. Or at least in what space he could find. With the electronics and six Shadows taking up most of the room, that didn't leave much.

"McMotherfucker had to put the money he was skimming somewhere. If he had set up offshore accounts for his sketchy clients including this cartel, then I'm sure as fuck he opened at least one for himself. We need to find that account. Ellie, as his widow, should be able to access it."

"She's not his widow," Ryder reminded them. "Not unless there's a death certificate. There isn't one since the body wasn't recovered yet, right? The divorce wasn't final, which gave her the right to sell the mansion and rest. So by rights, she can legally claim anything the man owned."

"And get stuck with the debt he owed, too," Mercy added.

Which was why they were even having this whole discussion. "If he was skimming from the cartel, who's to say he wasn't skimming from other large accounts, legit or not? We know he skimmed at least a couple million from the cartel. But it could be more than that. We don't know unless we find this offshore account and see the balance."

"And what if he was? Say he has ten million stashed somewhere. Why?" Brick asked. "It would help to know the motivation unless it's just plain greed."

Walker answered him, "His business was being run into the ground. He was using it to make bank with these real estate transactions for the cartel and by skimming. He takes that bank and sends it overseas. Then he disappears and, easy-motherfucking-peasy, he can live high off the hog for the rest of his life. No responsibilities."

"So then, why would he be scrambling to sell off his shit to pay his debt to the cartel once he was caught?" Steel asked.

That was a good question. One Walker put a lot of thought into the possible answer. "His fingers got caught in the cookie jar before he planned on ghosting. So, maybe he wasn't ready for some reason. By selling his shit and draining his accounts, maybe he could pay the cartel something? To show good faith and to buy him time, possibly? It would make it appear as if he was struggling to pay them, he could beg for more time, even skim money off other accounts right before he ghosts. I don't know. Again, we won't know how successful he was until we find his account or accounts, if they exist, to see the balance."

"We only have the account number for the cartel that was provided to Ellie. She didn't have any other account numbers, right?" Steel asked.

"I didn't ask. At first, I figured he was just trying to cover his ass financially for all the bad deals he got involved in."

"Well, maybe that's where it started but that's not where it ended," Mercy grumbled.

"No, his greed became a monster," Hunter said.

"A monster that killed him," Steel reminded them needlessly.

Brick clapped his hands sharply together. "Okay, we now know we have to abandon any thought of handling the cartel ourselves. That would just be suicide. And it would put everybody at risk that we know. You don't fuck with a cartel unless you can win that war. Their army is just too fucking big."

"Agreed," rose up around the room.

Walker ran a hand down his jaw. "Which means we're down to two options. Ghosting Ellie or paying the debt and making a deal with one of Castellano's lieutenants to let her go."

"Or getting McMaster to pay the debt," Hunter added.

"I talked to the asshole, he refuses. He's a stubborn old fuck. So if the cartel takes him out because he won't pay, it lands on Ellie's shoulders again and we're right back where we started."

"Ghosting her sounds like the simplest solution," Mercy grumbled.

"It is," Brick agreed.

"Brother, you going to be able to live with her going ghost?"

Walker glanced up and met Hunter's dark, troubled eyes.

No, they needed to find a way. He wouldn't lose her again.

———

THE DOORBELL SOUNDING down the hall had Ellie jumping out of her skin as she stared at the text on her phone.

Time's up.

She thought she had at least another day. Were they calling in the debt early? Fuck, that wasn't fair.

She closed her eyes. She was dealing with a ruthless drug lord, why would she think they'd be fair.

She turned her head toward the sound as the doorbell rang again.

A cartel wouldn't just show up at the front door and ring the bell, would they?

She hurried down the hallway and stuck her eye to the peephole. Her head jerked back at the sight of the man standing on the other side.

She never saw him before, but by the way he was dressed, he looked like one of the bikers Trace had mentioned. His black leather vest was a good indicator.

But that's not what surprised her about the big, burly man standing on the front stoop.

She punched in the alarm code, unlocked the door and swung it open only enough to stand in it.

And then blinked at the sight before her.

Normally, this man would be scary looking. His thick beard, his longer hair, his huge body, every inch of skin she could see covered in tattoos.

But the anomaly was he was holding a toddler, maybe around two years old. A girl dressed in a cute pink jumper, darker pink shoes and had a little pink bow in her blonde hair.

She had one fist gripping the biker's beard. While that had to be painful, the biker didn't even flinch.

"Um, hi?"

The girl in his arms yelled, "Hi!" back and jerked the handful of beard she held onto.

Ellie winced for him.

"Fu—fudge!" The man looked down at what could only be his daughter. "It's okay, baby. You can let Daddy's beard go now, yeah?"

"Sowee, Daddy."

He lifted his green eyes, which matched his daughter's exactly, and said, "Hey. Assumin' you're," the man glanced down again, this time at an overnight envelope in his other hand, "Ellie McMaster."

"Uh... yes."

"Figured you were Walker's woman."

Ellie opened her mouth to correct him, but snapped it shut instead.

"Just to let you know, delivery services can't get into the compound. Happened to catch this one waitin' outside the gate or you wouldn't have gotten it."

"Okay... I should've realized."

"You're new. To be expected." He held out the envelope

and she took it from him, noticing the sender's address belonged to her attorney.

"Okay, well... Thank you..." She hesitated and lifted an eyebrow.

"Dawg."

Yep, that's exactly what the patch said on the front of his vest. "Thank you, Dawg."

He dipped his bushy chin toward the little girl he held. "This is Emmalee. She's named after her momma, Emma. We call her Lee-lee."

Ellie smiled at her. "Hi, Lee-lee, it's nice to meet you. I'm Ellie."

Lee-lee finally released her father's beard to wave at her. "Hi, El... El..."

"El is fine."

The little girl laughed, then screamed "El!" in her father's ear.

Dawg sighed. "'Kay, gotta go. Someone needs a nap."

"No, *Daddeee*! No nap!" She followed up her complaint with an exaggerated pouty face. Ellie could guess that expression wasn't as cute to Dawg as it was to her.

Dawg rolled his eyes up toward the sky. "Got four fudgin' females in my household. I need the motherfudgin' nap."

Lee-lee laughed loudly again. "Daddy nap. Me no nap."

"Yeah, well, will let you fight that one out with your momma."

As he turned and strode away on long legs, Ellie lifted a hand and called out, "Thanks again!"

Dawg threw a hand up over his shoulder and headed down the sidewalk.

Ellie glanced down at the envelope again, then went back in the house, locking the door and setting the alarm. She headed into the kitchen, ripping it open and peering inside.

One plain white envelope.

Her divorce attorney had called her yesterday morning before Walker had gotten back and said a sealed letter had arrived from George's attorney. They said the envelope was marked "private," so they didn't want to open it without her consent.

Ellie told them to overnight it to her instead.

And now it was here. She pulled the inner envelope out and saw it indeed was marked as they said. Not only with "private" but with her first name.

And it was in George's handwriting.

A shiver slid down her spine. Receiving something from her husband after his death was akin to seeing a ghost.

Her knees wobbled and she reached out to catch herself on a chair at the kitchen table. She jerked it out and sank into it. Ripping the white envelope open, she pulled out a single piece of lined paper that had been folded in thirds.

Her heart began to pound as she slowly unfolded it, her mind spinning with what the letter could reveal. It was written in perfectly neat script, which was so George, unlike her own messy scribble.

The message was short.

Darling,

If you're reading this, there's a good reason. Or, in truth, a bad one. I'm sorry. I'm sorry I drove you away. I thought I was doing what was best for us.

Same as she did to Trace all those years ago. So damn ironic.

I made a grave mistake by getting involved with an organization I shouldn't have. Now I need you to protect yourself because I'm sure at this point, I'm not around to protect you.

Get out of the U.S. and go to Grand Cayman. There's enough

money in an account for you to set yourself up somewhere far away.
If you budget properly, you'll be set for the rest of your life.

Again, I can't say it enough... I'm sorry, Ellie. I truly loved you
and hope you find it in your heart to forgive me.

All my love,
George

She had held her breath the whole time she was reading
it. She blew it out and then read it from the top again.

At the bottom of the letter he'd written the name of a
bank and an address in the Cayman Islands, along with an
account number.

George created this mess, was it possible he was going to
be the one to clean it up, too? Even after his death?

Could this letter be her solution to the problem he
made?

She jumped out of the chair and, leaving the letter
there, she raced into the spare bedroom where her two suitcases remained. Throwing one open she grabbed her laptop
and ran back to the table, opening it up and turning it on.

Her knee bounced impatiently as she waited for it to
boot up.

"Come on!" she urged it. "Come on!"

Finally, she could log in with the Wi-Fi password
Walker had given her the other day and pull up Google.
Glancing quickly at the bottom of the letter, she typed the
bank's name into the search engine and found the bank's
website.

Her fingers were shaking as she typed in the username
George had noted and the password. But it took her two
times to type it correctly. One more time and she would
have been locked out for twenty-four hours and she didn't
have twenty-four hours. Tomorrow was the deadline.

She either paid up or Walker would have to "ghost" her.

She'd never be able to come back to the States. She'd

never see her elderly mother again. And she'd never see Trace.

Those two people, the two people she loved the most in life, were the only reasons she wanted to avoid that second option if she could.

She yelled, "Yes!" into the quiet room once she successfully logged in.

She moved the cursor to the link that said "account balances," and double clicked.

And she waited.

The seconds it took for the page to load felt like minutes.

Finally... Finally, a screen popped up with a long list of amounts.

She scrolled down to the ending balance...

And cried out, a pain shooting through her chest.

Her heart squeezed and she ground the heels of her palms into her eyes for a second, then dropped her hands.

What she saw the first time was correct.

The account was empty. The balance zero. One big fucking goose egg.

Maybe this was a cruel joke.

But no matter what George had been, he hadn't been cruel. So what she was seeing made no sense.

She scrolled through the transactions in the account, looking at all the deposits, but noticing there were no withdrawals. Not until recently.

The highest balance was a week ago.

Five million dollars.

Five. Million. Dollars.

He had more than enough money to pay off the cartel.

George had the money and didn't do so.

Why?

The two recent withdrawals—the *only* withdrawals made on the account—were for two and a half million dollars each a day apart. And they were transferred to the same account both times.

Ellie double clicked on the "account details" link and scrolled down through the information. Her heart stopped. Her blood ran cold.

Three people were listed on the account.

George McMaster.

Ellie McMaster.

Gerald McMaster.

Gerald.

Fucking Gerald!

Son of a bitch, did George's father get a letter from him, too? Did Gerald drain the account first before Ellie could pay off the debt?

Maybe George hadn't been cruel, but she couldn't say the same for his father.

His father didn't care if she lived or died. That was clear by what she was seeing before her. The proof stared her right in the face.

Trace called George "McMotherfucker." But it was Gerald who earned the title. Hands down.

She couldn't let him get away with it.

Chapter Seventeen

WALKER HIT the garage door opener with a little more force than necessary. Smashing his boot against the gas pedal, his Dodge roared as he pulled it into the garage. He was itching to climb out and take Ellie over his knee to teach her a fucking lesson she would not soon forget.

He had called and texted her at least a dozen times and instead of staying at the warehouse to finish making a plan to get *her* ass out of a jam, he had to come back home to find out why the fuck she wasn't answering him.

He shut off the engine and pushed open the driver's door, then froze.

His fucking truck was gone. Nothing but a small oil spot stained the concrete where it had been parked.

His head twisted toward the key cabinet. It hung open and the Ford key was missing.

Of course, it was. *For fuck's sake!*

He yanked his phone out of the side pocket of his cargo pants and texted: *Where the fuck R U?* before slamming the car door shut and heading into the house to see if she left a note.

She was told not to leave the house. He'd been crystal

fucking clear about that. If she needed something from the store, he'd have Jesse or one of the women grab it for her, if he couldn't.

Worse, she left without a fucking word.

Even more motherfucking worse, the deadline was only a day away and her being out and about would make her an easy target for the cartel.

He paused just outside the laundry room to drop his head back, curl his fingers into tight fists and scream. Then he blew out a breath and stalked into the kitchen to look for a note.

There it was. On the fucking kitchen table next to her purple laptop, which was open but the screen was dark. He snagged the letter and let his eyes scan it.

"Fucking motherfucker!" he yelled then crumpled it in his fist.

He texted Ellie again: *U better answer UR phone this time.*

He gave her the few seconds it took him to head back out to his Dodge. He started it, backed it out of the garage and hit the remote for the automatic door. Then called Ellie one more time.

"You better fucking answer!" he bellowed into the interior of the car. He rubbed at this chest because his heart was pounding. He swore he was going to have a heart attack *and* a damn aneurism.

His relief was short-lived when she finally answered. Because she didn't greet him with a "hello" or an "I'm sorry for worrying the fuck out of you." Fuck no.

She immediately shrieked, "He stole it!"

Her voice held the same tremor it had the first time she called him asking for help. "Yeah, El, he stole a lot of fucking money." She wasn't telling him anything he didn't already know.

"I'm not talking about George! I'm talking about Gerald."

What the fuck was she talking about? "What did he steal?"

"The money!"

Walker pressed the heel of hand into his forehead and stared at his lap. "What money?"

"The money that had been skimmed. I got a letter today from George. It included the account information where he'd deposited the money."

"I saw the letter," he said, but she kept going, talking so fast she talked right over him.

"He left it to me in case something happened to him. But Gerald's name was on the account, too. He took it all, Trace! The money I needed to pay off the cartel! It's all gone!"

"Jesus fucking Christ," he roared. Could this shit get any more fucking fucked? "Where are you?"

"In Delaware."

What the fuck! "For what?" *Jesus*, he knew for what. This was not good.

He squeezed his eyes shut and gritted his teeth when she said, "I'm going to his house. I want that man to look me in the eye and see if he can live with himself since he's signed my death warrant."

Walker already knew the answer to that. McMaster didn't give a fuck about Ellie. He was a selfish McMotherfucker just like his son.

"Ellie," he breathed. He said each word slowly and distinctly so she knew just how important every word he said was. "Turn around now and get the fuck back here. I'll handle this."

"No, Trace. I need to do this. I need to see that rotten bastard. Now I know why George was the way he was."

No shit.

He took a breath, trying to calm himself down enough

so he didn't flip the fuck out on her. Every syllable was a struggle. "Ellie, you need to listen. Pull over now."

"No, Trace. I'll call you afterward."

"Ellie," he growled.

"I'm out of time, honey. I received the final text saying time's up." The sob she released at the end was more painful than cutting off his own fucking leg. "I have nothing to lose. It may be my only chance."

"Ellie!" was the last thing he shouted before she hung up.

She might think she had nothing to lose, but he had everything to lose.

He put the Hellcat in reverse, chirping the tires as he hit the gas, then jammed it into drive, leaving two lines of rubber on the street leading out of the cul-de-sac.

Before he totally lost his fucking mind, he called Mercy.

The man's deep grumble filled his car. "Brother."

"Ellie's on her fucking way to Delaware to confront McMaster. I got good intel in hand. I'm heading back to the warehouse with it. Make sure everyone's there. ETA less than ten." At a stop sign, he took the balled letter out of his pocket and smoothed it out as best as he could, then quickly snapped a picture of the account information at the bottom and texted it to Hunter with a message that said: *Get on it.*

He made it to the warehouse in five minutes flat.

Even so, everyone else was already there waiting.

———

GERALD MCMASTER STOOD in the doorway of his house—no, *mansion*—using his arm to block Ellie's entry as he looked down his nose at her.

"He wanted me to help you. That's why he added me to the account. He must have known you were helpless to help yourself. But here's the thing, my dear, I owe you nothing.

My son owed you nothing. If anything, you owe us. He provided for you. Gave you everything you asked for, then you left him. You had zero loyalty to him. So, why should I have any for you? All that time and money he invested in you, gone. I warned him you weren't good enough and you proved me right. A well-bred woman sticks by her husband no matter what. You forget you spoke vows in front of God regarding that loyalty. So now?" He jabbed a finger at her, his cheeks flushed, his dark eyes narrowed. "Get off my property or I'll have you arrested for trespassing and harassment."

"You—" Her head jerked back as the door slammed shut in her face. She changed the rest of that sentence. "You asshole!" she screamed at the closed door.

The door didn't respond.

She sank down on the top step of the arched stone entryway and dropped her forehead to her knees. "*Omigod. Omigod. Omigod.* What the hell am I going to do?"

If only Trace had helped her disappear. *Fuck!*

It was one thing to die quickly. But to die the same way George did?

It was slow torture.

He suffered.

She was going to suffer.

She was going to pay for his stupidity and greed.

Time's up.

But was it? Did they even know where she was? Did she still have time to escape before they tracked her down?

Or had they been tracking her the whole time?

Maybe they knew where she was at that very moment.

Shit.

The hair at the nape of her neck stood as she visually scanned the McMasters' expansive front lawn. She saw nothing. But, of course, they wouldn't be standing out in the open waving "hello" at her like idiots.

Her eyes landed on Trace's Ford in the circular driveway. She needed to go. She needed to get lost somewhere, to keep moving until...

Until...

Until what?

The cartel caught up with her?

No matter what, she couldn't just sit there and give up. She rose to her feet and rushed back to the truck, climbing into the cab.

She glanced at her cell phone that was on the passenger side of the bench seat. It was flashing at her, which meant missed calls or texts. Or both.

Picking up her cell phone, she ignored the notifications and scrolled through her contacts until she got to a familiar number. She called it, hoping she picked up. She needed to hear her voice. Even if it was for one last time.

"Hey, sweetheart, how are you?"

Sweetheart.

Only two people in her life had ever called her that. Trace and her mother.

"Hi, Mom. Just checking in." For maybe the last time. "How are you feeling?"

"Today's a good day," her warm, familiar voice wrapped around her heart, giving it a squeeze. Her mother, the eternal optimist.

At least it was a good day for someone.

"That's good. How's Frank treating you?"

"Oh, you know your stepfather. He rules this household with an iron fist."

Ellie laughed to cover her sob. Fat, hot tears rolled down her cheek, getting caught in the corners of her mouth. "No, he doesn't, Mom. He's a softy."

"No, he makes me eat all those damn vegetables."

Her mother was a diabetic, so Frank was always worried about what she ate. "You love vegetables."

"Don't tell him that. I use eating them all to negotiate other things."

Her bottom lip trembled when she asked, "What other things?"

"Like two scoops of ice cream instead of one." Her mother laughed. "I miss you. When are you coming home for a visit?"

"Soon."

"Promise? You've got nothing to hold you in Denver anymore. You can come back and stay in your old room until you make a solid plan for your future. You've been floundering since you left George."

"I know, Mom. Things were a bit rough for a while. I'm sorry I haven't called you more often. I'll come home soon, at least for a visit."

"I can't wait. Frank would also love to see you."

"Me, too." She stared unseeing out of the windshield. She couldn't stay parked in the McMaster's driveway. She wouldn't put it past the man to call the cops. "Hey, Mom, I've got to go now. I just wanted to tell you I love you and I'm thinking about you."

"I love you, too, sweetheart. And I think about you every day, even with this old, addled brain of mine."

Her words made her smile through her tears, even though her mother couldn't see it and it was a bit shaky. "Give my love to Frank," she added.

"Will do. Take care of yourself, sweetheart. And call us in a couple days."

"I will."

She reluctantly ended the call, closed her eyes, and pressed the phone to her forehead. With a shaky breath, she put the truck in gear and drove away from the McMaster mansion.

As she pulled out of the long paved lane, she realized the truck's fuel gauge was on *E*.

She had no money, no credit card, nothing.

She couldn't escape anywhere.

Without gas, the truck was dead in the water.

When she pulled into the closest parking lot to regroup, an SUV with tinted windows blocked her in, and she knew her last thought was about to come true.

Not only was the truck dead in the water, so was she.

———

"JESUS FUCK!" he shouted as he read the message from Ellie that had popped up on his phone. "Jesus fuck!"

Mercy grabbed Walker's hand and tilted the phone toward him so he could read the text.

His silver eyes hit Walker's and his expression went completely blank. His face turned into a concrete wall.

Walker recognized that look. It was one no one would ever want directed at them. The smell of death usually permeated the air afterward.

However, no one in that room at the warehouse was going to die today.

No, it would be Ellie.

He finally got her back, only to turn around and lose her again.

This time forever.

Mercy read the text out loud. "Time's up."

A loud chorus of "fucks" came from the others.

Mercy dropped Walker's hand and it fell to his side. He'd lost the strength to hold it. He was about to collapse into a broken pile of flesh and bones.

"Keep your shit together," Mercy barked at him. "That's a motherfucking order."

Walker jerked his spine straight and shook himself mentally.

They all needed to think clearly and get a plan in place.

Losing his shit wasn't going to help Ellie.

So, he collected it and growled, "Whoever's holding her, we'll take them out."

"We had this fucking same convo earlier," Steel reminded him. "We kill Castellano's soldiers and we start the war we wanted to avoid."

Hunter shook his head. "We have to cave, Walker, and give them what they want. We got no other motherfucking choice. Good news is, I now have access to both McMasters' accounts and we now know that cocksucker was sitting on five million. There's more than enough to cover the debt. Since we already have the info for the cartel's account, just say the word and I can do the transfer."

"We're not doing it if she's already dead," Mercy said, avoiding Walker's eyes. "They ain't getting shit if they took her out."

It was hard to hear, but it had to be said. Walker knew that and he tried not to let the thought that they took her out already fuck with his psyche.

"We need to let them know we have access to the money ASAP," Hunter said. "It's better to let them win by getting the dough than Walker to lose Ellie."

Sounds of agreement came from all of them except Walker and Mercy.

"I fucking hate this," Mercy growled, his body as tight as a stretched rubber band.

"You're not the only one," Walker growled back. He wasn't the only one in the room who didn't like to lose.

Eyes the color of frosted ice hit his. "You got their number?"

"All their texts and calls to her phone came through blocked."

Hunter spoke up, "I can hack into her cell phone account and see if I can somehow dig it up, but it might take a bit. And I might not be successful."

"Or maybe it wasn't Ellie who texted that message. Maybe someone else has her phone," Brick suggested.

Fuck.

"Call it," Mercy barked, "and give me the fucking phone. You've got too much to lose in this deal."

Walker agreed. He might have gathered his shit, but it was only wrapped up in a string and if he got on the horn with one of the cartel members that fragile string might snap.

He scrolled through his contacts, found Ellie's and hit the Call button. As soon as he put the phone on speaker, Mercy snagged it out of his hand.

A male voice with a thick Mexican accent filled the room. "She's been crying and begging for us to let her call Trace. She keeps insisting this *Trace* has our money. Are you him?"

"I'm the fucking person you need," Mercy barked. "Getting your fucking money."

"When?"

Mercy's head twisted toward Hunter who was waiting, his fingers paused over the keyboard. "Working on it right now."

"Time has run out."

"Not if you'd rather be paid. Assuming the money is worth more than the woman's life to your *capo*."

Walker's jaw flexed at Mercy's words.

"Money's always worth more than a useless *puta*."

Walker ground his teeth so hard in an effort to keep quiet, his jaw popped at that insult.

"Right," Mercy said, the single, soft-spoken word, deadly. "Especially this amount of scratch. This ain't milk money. Gonna make a deal with you."

"No deals."

"You'll fucking like this one."

A long hesitation. "Talk and I may listen."

"You'll get what's owed, plus."

"Now you have my attention. What's the plus?"

"We're gonna round up to one and a half. Sweeten the pot a little. Consider it a bonus."

"For?"

"We want her breathing."

"She'll keep breathing if we get our money."

"Not a fucking hair on her head out of place."

"She'll be whole."

"Not a goddamn scratch," Mercy continued. "For each bruise, mark, scratch we find, one of your soldiers dies."

"I don't think you're in the position to make threats. Especially since we have what you want."

"I'm always in a position to make guarantees."

"For that extra two hundred, I can only promise to make sure she's breathing and whole. Any minor injuries made along the way aren't negotiable."

"If she's DOA, asshole, we're hacking into Castellano's fucking account and taking everything back and more. That's not negotiable, either. Deal?"

Walker held his breath and waited. The seconds ticked off in his head. Each one more deafening than the last.

One.

Fuck.

Two.

Fuck.

Three.

Fuck.

He breathed again when he heard, "Deal. When are you transferring the money?"

Everyone's eyes in the room landed on Hunter, who began typing furiously. A second later, he glanced up and nodded.

"It's in there. Check your account. Now, I want the address where you have the woman."

"I need our accountant to confirm the transaction first. Once he does, I'll text you the location where you can find her."

"Whole."

"Whole," came through the speaker.

"Don't fuck this up," Mercy warned the man.

"She was only a tool to collect our debt. Not sure she's worth one-point-five, though. Makes me curious about what she has that's so special."

"Whole. Untouched. Or Castellano and every one of his lieutenants, including you, are done. That's a non-negotiable term."

"You don't have the balls."

"Try me."

"I'll be in touch."

The call ended. No one said a word for a full minute. The tension, so thick in the room, could choke him. They were all wired.

They'd dealt with these types of situations before. Both in the military and as Shadows, so they knew how to work as a team.

They also didn't have to wait for an exact location. That was just burning daylight. They could hit the road and head toward Delaware. Follow the path Ellie did. She probably wasn't being held far off that path.

The time between when he talked to her and when he received the text wasn't enough to take her far. She was either still in Delaware or close by in a neighboring state.

Walker accepted his phone back from Mercy. "We need to hit the road. We could be halfway there when we get that text. I don't want her waiting for us any longer than she has to."

She was probably scared to death.

"We'll take my Rover," Hunter said, rising from behind the computer.

"No, we'll take my RPV since it's bulletproof." Mercy glanced around the room. "Steel, Hunter and Walker with me. Brick, you're on McMaster." He gave Brick a pointed look and his next instruction came out flat, icy and deadly. "Do what you need to do."

In contrast, Brick grinned and gave him the thumbs up.

"Ryder, you and D get everyone to the compound. *Everyone*. Get your woman to help. No excuses from anyone. Keep them there until this is over and Walker's woman is clear. I want *all* women and children with their men and in one area. No collateral damage."

"Roger that," Ryder said and rushed out of the room.

"Let's go. Hunter grab a laptop, so you have access to any accounts or whatever's needed. Let's load up the RPV with what we need to get this done." Mercy strode to the door but paused before exiting. "Brick, you want someone at your back?"

Hunter spoke up. "I can go with him since I'll have a laptop."

"Make sure your connection is secure."

Hunter grinned and saluted Mercy. "Not a problem, Sergeant Major!"

Mercy shook his head and headed out with Walker and Steel right on his heels.

Chapter Eighteen

Two torturous hours later, he got the text from a blocked number with an address, and Walker immediately plugged it into his GPS.

"Google's saying it's a family restaurant, but it's permanently closed." Walker looked up from his phone at Mercy's hard profile. "Got another two and a half to go."

"That blows," Steel said from the backseat. "We've got no guarantee she's there or even if she is, she's alive. Could be driving all this way for fucking nothing."

As much as he hated to agree with what Steel was saying, it was the hard truth. They could get to the location and the cartel could have lied or they could be walking into an ambush. Mexican drug cartels weren't the most trustworthy.

"Want the locals to go in?" Mercy asked him.

"And what if they're waiting and watching? Doubt they'd be happy if we got cops involved. That could put their lives, in addition to Ellie's, on the line," Walker murmured. "So no, we need to keep them out of it and handle this ourselves. We can handle this mission better than any doughnut-bellied uni."

"Good call," Mercy said with a sharp nod, keeping his eyes on the road since he was pushing his mini tank as fast as it could go.

"Don't want them calling in their SERT team, either, if they have one. That could create a SNAFU for us," Steel said. "Let's just get in there and get 'er done. No long hours of questioning by them, or even the FBI, afterward. Best to keep it off their radar."

Walker agreed with that, too, as long as Ellie was safe. As long as two and a half more hours wouldn't make the difference in whether she lived or died. She might be scared as fuck during that time, but at least she'd be breathing.

She'd better be at that restaurant and she'd better be fucking alive.

"Keep it together, brother," Mercy ordered quietly. "Know how you feel right now. You wanna kill everyone involved. Go on a rampage. I get it. You're also thinking life might not be worth living if they've already done what they planned on doing before we made the call."

"We should've asked for proof of life," he murmured, turning away from Mercy and staring out of the passenger side window, not seeing anything but Ellie scared, alone and with dangerous men who couldn't give a shit about her.

"Yeah, we should've. I screwed the pooch on that one. Just gotta have faith that things will go as we expect them."

"Great," he muttered, turning to look at his teammate. "We always plan for a clusterfuck, brother."

One side of Mercy's mouth, the side without the scar, pulled up. "Not this time. Plan on smooth sailing this time."

"Hope to fuck you're right."

"I'm always right."

Steel snorted loudly in the back seat.

———

THEY DIDN'T GAG HER, so she had pleaded with them to call Trace.

They didn't blindfold her. Because of that, she figured she was going to die no matter if they contacted Trace or not, since she could identify them.

She sat alone in a chair in a restaurant that appeared to have been shut down years ago. Two men stood behind her, one to her left, one to her right, while the third man, who seemed to be their leader had gone outside with her cell phone when it rang.

It wasn't long before he'd returned and began to speak Spanish to the two other men.

She cried out when each of the men abruptly grabbed one of her elbows and pulled her to her feet.

"Please, call Trace. I have the number in my phone. He'll get you the money. I swear."

The man in charge gave her a look but said nothing. Maybe he didn't speak English. Maybe she had pleaded with them for nothing that whole time because he hadn't understood a word.

Why the hell didn't she take Spanish in high school?

Fuck!

"Please. I know who has your money. It's not me. It's George's father. He has it all."

The dark-eyed, darker-skinned man jerked his chin toward the back of the restaurant and gave a sharp order in Spanish. Both men pulled her in that direction.

Why were they moving her from the chair? The chair had been set up just like in the picture of George. Why would they take her elsewhere if they were going to do the same thing?

"Where are you taking me?"

She was dragged through the swinging double doors to the kitchen and then through the kitchen itself.

The kitchen was in the same disarray as the dining area

out front. Once the restaurant closed its doors, it didn't look like anyone ever entered it again. That meant if these men left her there, no one would ever find her.

She was going to die alone.

"Please!" She didn't even know what she was pleading for anymore. They hadn't listened to even one of her requests. It was pointless. But she couldn't give up. "I'm sorry my husband did this to your boss. I didn't know. I would've told him to stop. I would have reported him. I would have—"

They stopped in front of a thick silver door. One that had an outer latch and no window.

A walk-in freezer.

Oh no.

Oh no no no no no.

One of the men unlatched the door and shoved her through the thick plastic strips that hung just inside. She stumbled and, unable to catch herself with her hands still bound, she fell to her knees, nearly smacking her head on a nearby shelf.

The thick, heavy door slammed shut and the interior went black. She heard the latch lock. Then nothing.

Fuck.

She wouldn't freeze to death because the walk-in probably hadn't worked in years. But still, there had to be a way to escape. Even with her wrists tied, she had her fingers free.

Using the shelf to help, she pushed to her feet and shuffled slowly through the dark, keeping her hands out in front of her until she figured she was near the door. There had to be a way to open it from the inside. Commercial freezers should have some sort of safety feature, right? To keep people from freezing or suffocating to death?

She needed to stay calm. Freaking out wasn't going to help.

Her fingers brushed against metal and she began to feel

all around the edge of the door. Finally, she found something that might be a release. She pulled it and stumbled back a step when it disconnected from the door.

"No! Damn it! NO!"

She ran her shaky fingers over the area where the emergency release had been. She tried to attach the metal piece back in the hole, but it was useless. It wouldn't catch and slid right back out. It was fucking broken!

She was stuck. In the dark. In a freezer. In an abandoned restaurant. In an unknown location.

She was screwed.

They might end up killing her after all. She had no idea how long the oxygen would last in the sealed walk-in.

She turned around, put her back to the door and slid down until she landed on her ass.

She only had one thing left to do.

No, two.

Wait. And hope Trace was searching for her.

Actually, three.

Hope he got there in time.

———

WALKER WAS about to not only jump out of his skin, but out of the RPV while it was still moving. He'd already released his seatbelt in anticipation of getting to Ellie as fast as he could.

As the headlights of the utility vehicle on steroids slid over the run-down, pitch-dark restaurant, he had his fingers wrapped around the door handle. A long arm reached out and snagged him before he could bail out as the RPV came to a rolling stop.

"Don't lose your head, brother," Mercy warned. "Know you wanna rush in there. Know you're worried. Been through this, know how you're feeling. But use your fucking head."

Walker stared at the building, anxiety wanting to over-take common sense, as he hoped Ellie was in there. Hoped she was alive and unharmed.

Hoped the cartel didn't go back on their word. Because a fucking cartel's word was goddamn shit.

His nostrils flared as he sucked in a deep breath, then pushed it back out of his mouth.

"No vehicles," Steel murmured as his gaze swept the empty lot.

"Doesn't mean they don't have eyes," Mercy responded back. "We're gonna approach like we always do. Using caution and our fucking heads. Stick to cover as much as we can but keep in visual contact. Hand signals until we know it's clear. Let's search the perimeter first, see if we can get some eyes inside."

Walker heard everything Mercy said, but his attention was glued to the building at least thirty meters away.

Way too fucking far for his liking.

"Ready?" Steel asked him, clapping a hand on his shoulder.

"Never more," Walker forced past his lips.

"At least we have the cover of darkness," Steel grumbled.

Mercy must have shut the overhead light off in his vehicle because the interior remained dark when the three of them opened the doors and climbed out.

They spread out, approaching with caution, heads on swivels, weapons drawn. Keeping low, they moved along the overgrown brush that circled the perimeter of the parking lot. Until Mercy held up his fist, bringing them all to a halt.

Each of them listened carefully while visually searching the area.

So far, all clear.

Mercy made the motion to approach. As a team, they circled the outer perimeter of the restaurant staying away from the glass entry doors, even though they were covered in some sort of brown Kraft paper. Glass doors didn't provide cover if someone tried to plug a few rounds into you center mass. And especially center noggin.

Again, the perimeter was all clear.

The rear steel door was rusted, and the deadbolt missing, the outer clasp and padlock broken and hanging.

Point of entry for the cartel.

Mercy and Steel had their backs pinned to the brick wall to the right of the door, Walker to the left. Mercy reached down to the old metal door knob and turned it slowly.

The door's hinges squealed eerily as he pushed it open with excruciating slowness. All three made eye contact, nodded, then Mercy gave the signal to breach the building.

As much as Walker wanted to go first that was not how they trained. Mercy always took point if he was on scene. Steel followed Mercy nut to butt, his gun pointed to the right. Walker followed Steel the same way, his gun pointed to the left.

They moved as a unit down a short dark hallway and at the end of it, they stopped, assessed, then Mercy had them continue through the unlit kitchen. Their eyes had adjusted to the dark once they had left the RPV, which helped them make out the larger equipment and objects in the kitchen, but they took care not to knock into anything smaller that would make a noise and draw attention.

Still, they heard nothing. Saw nothing.

The kitchen was clear.

And Walker wanted to scream.

He dug deep, using his training to keep his shit together. The same way he had when he'd been pinned under the Little Bird all those years ago.

That was how he survived that situation.

That was how he was going to survive this one.

They would not fail at this mission.

Because, for fuck's sake, he could not fail Ellie.

At the double doors, Mercy rose enough to peer through the dirty plastic windows into the front of the restaurant. He slowly scanned the area and crouched back down. "Clear. But too many blind spots," he said so softly it could've been a whisper on the wind.

As one, they moved through one side of the double swinging doors, wincing when it was just as noisy as the back door.

If anyone was in the restaurant they were made.

Mercy halted them and they waited, ducked down behind the main service counter.

They waited for any signs of Castellano's men. Gun shots. Voices. Footsteps. Whispers of fabric.

Nothing.

Not even the click of a scurrying rat's nails.

The place was empty.

"One at a time," Mercy ordered under his breath.

Steel stood first. And since no one took a shot at him, Walker stood next, followed by Mercy.

The restaurant was clear. The cartel gone.

But what wasn't gone was a lone chair sitting in the middle of the empty restaurant. All other tables and chairs were tossed out of the way to make room for that single chair.

Next to it on the floor were several sets of flex cuffs. And beneath the chair and flex cuffs were large sheets of thick plastic. Enough to capture blood splatter for when someone was making a mess.

Someone like Mercy.

Walker had seen the same setup at their warehouse when Mercy questioned the former DAMC prospect, Squirrel. That setup meant someone was going to die and it wasn't going to be an easy death.

It didn't matter what answers that person gave to the questions they were asked, the result would be the same.

The memory of McMaster being bound to a similar chair with flex cuffs and his blood spilled all over plastic sheeting flashed through his brain.

However, not a spot of blood dotted those sheets now. Not one.

Thank fuck.

Even so, his relief was short lived. Ellie was still nowhere to be found.

If the cartel took her with them...

He would burn every one of their grow houses to the ground and he would slice Castellano's throat himself.

What happened to him after that, he wouldn't give a fuck. If he had to die to dole out revenge, it would be worth it.

He lived without Ellie for nineteen fucking years. Nineteen fucking years were stolen from him.

And he wasn't going to ever let that happen again.

Steel spoke up, breaking the silence, as if he'd read Walker's mind. "They got their money, to take her with them would be a burden."

"Right," Mercy grunted. "Check every corner, every cabinet, every closet. Every fucking container. Anywhere a bo— Ellie could be."

"Let's start out here and work our way back toward the rear entrance," Steel suggested.

And that's what they did. They checked every inch using their tactical flashlights.

When they found nothing toward the front of the building, all three of them moved into the kitchen and, fuck him, that's when he heard it.

They all heard it.

A muffled scream that sounded like his name and a pounding.

With all three frozen in place, Walker twisted his head and listened carefully to pinpoint where the noise was coming from.

"Ellie!" he called out.

"Trace!" It was faint, but he could hear it.

They rushed to the freezer. The cartel's soldiers had jammed a block of wood in the latch and Walker knocked it out with his boot heel, almost landing on his ass.

As soon as the block was free, Mercy ripped the door practically off its hinges to get it open.

Jesus, that man was a monster.

But that thought disappeared as Ellie rushed out, coming full bore toward him, and then bounced off his chest, falling backward onto her ass into a heap on the floor.

He dropped to his knees at her hip and grabbed her face, searching it to make sure she was unharmed.

"You okay?"

She nodded, her bottom lip trembling, tears welling in her eyes.

"Talk to me!" he yelled, trying not to shake her. He needed to hear her say it.

"Yes. I'm okay." Her voice was rough. Probably from screaming for help.

His gaze raked down her body. "They didn't touch you?"

Her eyes widened and a tear tipped over, slipping down her already streaked cheeks. "Not like that."

Thank fuck.

He brushed the tear off her skin and then shoved her face into his neck, holding her close.

He had no idea how long he sat there holding her. But eventually, a hand squeezed his shoulder.

He glanced up to see Mercy standing over him, his tactical knife in his hand.

Walker reluctantly moved back just enough for Mercy to cut the plastic cuffs. As soon as her wrists were free, he lifted them. There were marks left behind in her skin, but no bleeding. He pressed his lips to each wrist and then helped her up and into his arms.

Steel pushed through the long plastic strips hanging in the doorway as he stepped out of the freezer. "Fuck. Dark and musty for sure. Air was at a premium. Glad we hit the road when we did."

What Steel didn't say out loud was if she'd been in there too long, she might have eventually run out and suffocated.

But she was alive.

She wasn't injured.

Besides the marks on her wrists, the only other evidence of her ordeal was her clothes being dirty from sitting on the floor and the tear stains on her face.

She tipped that beautiful face up to him. "Is it over? Please tell me, is it all finally over? Am I free from all of this now?"

"Cartel's got their money and a bonus. Said the debt is paid."

"How? George's father—"

"We handled it."

And Brick was about to handle McMaster, too.

Walker's phone vibrated and he dropped a hand from Ellie's back to grab it from his side pocket.

He read the text. *Any last words? Speak now or forever hold UR peace.*

Yeah, he had plenty to give that asshole.

He lifted his chin to Mercy. "Take her out. I have a call to make."

Mercy's gray eyes got even icier as his gaze slid from the

phone in Walker's hand to Ellie, then to his face. He gave Walker an answering chin lift.

"I got her," Steel said with a knowing look and wrapped an arm around Ellie's shoulders and guided her toward the rear exit.

"Be out in a minute, El," he called to her. "There's water and some protein bars in the vehicle."

As soon as Steel and Ellie got out of sight, Mercy asked, "Brick?"

"Yeah. He must be setting up."

The side of Mercy's mouth where the scar lifted the corner, curled slightly higher. "Good. Bastard's gonna get what he deserves."

"Too bad Castellano won't."

"Gotta pick our battles, brother," Mercy said as he headed toward the back door. "Gonna go check on your woman."

Walker dialed McMaster's number.

"First Ellie. Now you. Is there a reason you two are harassing me?" was the old man's first words as soon as he answered.

"Yeah. Got a good reason. Just want to tell you, no thanks to you, Ellie is alive and well. You stole five million of scratch that didn't belong to you. And by doing so, you risked Ellie's life. I see where your son learned his greedy fucking ways. You would've let her die and not paid that debt even though there was more than enough to do so."

"You're right, Walker, I wouldn't have. She wasn't worth a dime."

"Karma, old man, when you least expect it, that bitch will be coming for you."

"Is that a threat?"

"It's a guarantee."

"I'll call the FBI."

"What are you going to tell them, Jerry? That your

248

asshole son stole dirty money from a Mexican drug cartel? That he stashed it in an offshore account which you stole from in order to deposit it into another offshore account? Yeah, go ahead, I'll even look up the number for you."

He stabbed the End button on his phone. Then texted Brick: *Clear.*

Hunter had left a million in McMaster's account as an incentive for the old man to forget that Ellie ever existed. They needed to rethink that since McMaster wasn't going to need it. Not where he was going.

Ellie not only needed it, she deserved it. He'd let her decide what to do with it all. He didn't even give a shit if she gave it all to charity. They'd just needed to get it back into the States without throwing any red flags.

They'd figure it out.

Because the fuck if Ellie wasn't going to be living easy for the rest of her life after dealing with the McMother-fuckers and their bullshit.

His phone pinged and he glanced down to read the text from Brick.

Who's UR daddy?

Chapter Nineteen

HE WAS DRIVING HER CRAZY. With touches as light as a whisper over her skin. A tip of the tongue barely flicking the tips of her nipples. A fleeting brush of his fingertip across her clit.

Only enough to notice it, but he didn't linger. He kept moving. One hand planted in the mattress next to her head, the other wreaking havoc on her sanity.

His mouth hovered above hers, his warm breath washing over her lips. So close, but yet so far.

"Stop," she groaned, even though she didn't really want him to stop. She just wanted him to hurry up and take her.

But Trace was in no hurry. "Okay, I'll stop," he whispered back. His grin proof that was a lie.

He ran his lips lightly along her jawline to her ear. "You're mine." His possessive words evoked a shiver and her nipples beaded even harder. "Forever this time, El."

Forever.

She was okay with that.

In truth, more than okay.

Things happened for a reason, didn't they? And maybe

back then they weren't meant to be. Hopefully now they were.

They hadn't talked about the future since arriving back at Trace's house in the middle of the night. Both of them quickly showered and fell into bed, exhausted.

But now they were awake, and Trace was skimming his mouth down her neck, over her shoulder, around the outer curve of her breast, down her belly.

She couldn't stop smiling at the ceiling.

The feeling of being free of that debt...

Being free to live her life as she wanted...

Being free to be with Trace...

Made her heart swell. Made her somewhat giddy.

Closing her eyes, her fingers found his short hair, hanging on as best as she could as he moved lower.

And lower.

She opened her eyes and glanced down her body at him. "You like to eat pussy." That was definitely not a complaint, more of an observation.

He murmured against her skin, his eyes catching hers. "No, baby. I love to eat *your* pussy."

She was okay with that, too.

Again, more than okay.

Her clit was already throbbing as his warm breath brushed it. Once again, he teased her with just the tip of his tongue.

"Stop," she whispered once more because she wasn't sure how much more she could take before she screamed.

He stopped, lifted his head and waited.

"*Please.*"

He smiled, then went back to teasing her.

"Trace," she groaned, digging her nails into his scalp.

"Tell me what you want, El."

"Make me come."

"I'm going to make you come."

"Now."

"When I'm ready."

"Trace..." she moaned. "Now."

"When I'm ready to give you that."

"Stop talking and just do it."

He chuckled. "Someone's impatient."

She lifted her head and glared at him. "You think? I know you enjoy doing this..."

"Doing what?"

He was purposely playing dumb. He knew exactly what he was doing. "Delaying... *Ooooh. Yesssss.*" Her head dropped back into the pillow and her back arched when she drove her hips up, wanting him to give her more.

She couldn't get enough of his mouth toying with her clit. His lips sucking, his tongue circling. The light scrape of his teeth against her sensitive nub.

"Trace," she groaned, her fingers flexing as she got closer and closer to the ledge. But she needed more. Just a little bit more.

He dragged a finger down through her wetness, then back up. He slipped one finger, two, inside her and...

Yes, that's what she needed. Him inside of her.

But as she reached the precipice, he was gone. His breath, his lips, his fingers, just a memory.

Then he was back, his knees separating hers, the head of his cock taking the place of his fingers as it separated her slick folds, opening her up to him.

He slid his chest along hers, his skin brushing over the hard points of her nipples. And then he took her mouth and her breath all at once.

He inhaled his own whispered name when he surged forward and took her completely.

. . .

WALKER FORCED his eyes to remain open. To watch Ellie's face as he sank deep inside her.

Liquid heat. Sleek, hot velvet gripped him.

No other feeling in the world was like this. He could only describe it as coming home.

After years of having different women, he no longer remembered a single one of them.

Not now. Not ever again.

Ellie was where she belonged. In his house. In his bed. In his life.

He was going to do his best to work on the future he once promised her.

Their dream could finally be a reality.

Gliding his fingers along her ribs, he then trapped a nipple between them and rolled it as his mouth tracked her pulse along her throat before moving down to suck the puckered nipple deep within it.

Her nails scraped along into his back, took purchase and he was sure they were leaving marks behind as the two of them moved together as one.

Their hips came together and moved apart like a surf surging along the shore.

This wasn't just sex. This was a deeper connection. A healing of everything that had been broken between them.

The climax would be explosive. Satisfying. Bone-melting.

But he didn't want to come yet. When he came, it was over. He wasn't ready for it to end.

Not now. Not today. Not ever.

When he said forever, he meant it. He only needed Ellie to be sure.

They needed to discuss their future, to ensure they were on the same page this time.

No misunderstandings. Not fucking one.

They needed a solid base to build that future.

He ground his hips against her, driving as deep as he could, the small scratches on his back now turning to long welts as she dragged her nails deeper along his flesh, drove her hips higher. Cried his name over and over.

He'd never tire of hearing her say his name.

He hoped it was the last thing he heard before he took his last breath on this Earth. Her not only saying his name, but telling him she loved him...

He froze and bit off a curse when he heard his phone ring next to the bed.

Fucking motherfucker.

Normally, he'd ignore it since the most important person in his life was currently in his bed. No one on the other end of the phone would ever be as important.

Unless it was Mercy. Diesel. Or one of the other Shadows.

They were his team. He owed him as much loyalty as they gave him.

They had his six. He had theirs. And that would never change.

He groaned in frustration, and muttered a searing, "Fuck."

"What..." Ellie asked, picking her head up and knitting her eyebrows together as she turned her head to give an exasperated look at the offending item on his nightstand.

She wasn't the only one annoyed.

"Sorry, sweetheart. Might be important." It better be fucking important or he was hanging up on the man.

Not breaking their connection, he leaned over slightly and stretched out his hand enough to snag his phone. As soon as he swiped the screen with this thumb and stuck it to his ear, he heard a loud growled, "Close your fucking windows."

"What?" Walker turned his head, glancing over at them. The ones facing Mercy's house were wide open. *Fuck.*

"Fuck," he muttered again but out loud this time.

"Yeah," was the answering grunt.

There was no way he was pulling out before he was done to close the fucking windows. The big man would just have to wait. "You close yours."

"Mine are fucking closed!" Mercy barked into his ear.

Walker glanced down at Ellie who bugged out her eyes at him in impatience. Had she been that loud? "Huh." Maybe. He grinned.

"Yeah... *huh.*"

Walker heard Rissa in the background saying something, but he couldn't make out what. But whatever she said made Mercy blow out a breath and a muttered curse, before telling him, "Fuck it. Keep them open." He hung up.

Walker grinned at his phone, then tossed it back onto the nightstand.

"Problem?" Ellie asked, her eyebrows raised.

"Apparently you're lighting up the neighborhood."

Her lips parted, her eyes went wide, and color rushed into her cheeks.

His soft, sweet Ellie. There she was. He hoped she'd always be there.

"Should you close the windows?"

"Fuck no. Think I've never heard Mercy and Rissa going at it? Or Ryder doing Kelsea so hard, I can hear the headboard banging against the wall all the way over here?"

"Your houses aren't even that close."

"Exactly," he muttered. "'Bout time I get some fucking revenge." He looked down into her face and grinned even wider. Revenge could be so fucking sweet. "Now, where was I?"

"About to make me come."

"Oh yeah." Tilting his hips sharply once, her eyelids immediately got heavy. "How loud can you get?"

"Depends on you."

"Sounds like a challenge."

She shook with her smothered laughter. "I shouldn't be laughing; I should be embarrassed."

"Never. Nothing wrong with being passionate as fuck and not hiding it."

"Now I'll be self-conscious."

Walker tilted his head as he heard noises he recognized in the distance. "Sounds like someone opened their own windows."

"Damn," Ellie whispered, her cheeks turning red again. "But that's kind of hot."

"Unless you're in bed alone."

"Then what?" she teased.

"Then... I, uh... put in ear plugs."

"Liar."

"Enough talking."

Her lips twitched. "I agree."

It wasn't long before the blood was pounding in his veins again, his heartbeat in his throat as he took her to that edge once more. But, again, kept her from falling.

He let her teeter, but he wouldn't let her go.

Not yet.

Not until he was ready. Not until he was standing next to her on that very cliff.

And then he was there... Ready to fall and take her with him.

"Now, baby," he murmured in her ear as he thrust harder, faster, deeper.

When her body bowed beneath him, her neck arched back, her eyes opened wide and her mouth parted, he was right there with her. She was taking everything he gave her and giving it right back.

As the ripples of her orgasm began, he went with them, powering forward one more time and staying there. He came deep inside her as she squeezed him tight like a hot fist.

And, fuck him, he didn't want it to stop.

After a few moments, when he gathered his brain cells back into his head and he finally stopped breathing like he just ran a 5k, he slid his nose along her jawline before capturing her lips.

He kissed her slowly, gently, tasting her.

He didn't want to move. He wanted to stay right there, buried inside her for the rest of his life.

In reality, a lifetime wasn't going to be long enough.

He eventually slipped from her and he had no choice but to slide to her side. He kissed her one more time before he said, "I need to clean up."

"Stay. I'll get you a washcloth."

He didn't like her waiting on him, but his crutches weren't nearby, so he just nodded. She rolled from the bed and he watched her walk totally naked into the master bathroom and a few minutes later walk back out, damp washcloth in hand.

When he held out his hand for it, she shook her head. "I'll do it."

"I'm capable of cleaning myself up, El."

She gave him a look. "I know, but I want to do it. Just let me."

"Fine," he huffed, pretending to not be happy about it, when he would enjoy every fucking second of her doing it.

He tucked his arms behind his head and watched her gently wipe him clean, then take the washcloth back to the bathroom.

When she came back out the second time, he ordered, "Stop."

She froze between the bathroom and the bed, giving him a questioning look.

"Just stay there for a second. I want to look at you."

His gaze roamed her from top to toe. And he noticed when her nipples beaded tightly again.

"With you looking at me like that, like you're the hunter and I'm the prey, makes me want to jump your bones, just so you know," she warned him.

"Back then I would've been hard again in five seconds flat. Being thirty-nine, I'd be lucky if it takes five minutes. Even as much as you turn me the fuck on, I'm still going to need a lot longer than five. Sorry, sweetheart."

She lifted one shoulder in a half-shrug. "I'm in no rush."

"Thank fuck for that," he murmured. He patted the bed. "C'mere, El. We need to have a talk while we wait."

Her easy expression turned not-so-easy at his words. "Trace... I know we have a lot of things to talk about, but can it wait?"

"We need to have this discussion." He patted the bed next to him again, more firmly this time.

"You told me you wanted me to leave when the job was over..."

"That's not what it's about."

Her green eyes hit his and held. "It's not?"

"No."

"Can you give me a hint?"

Her resistance was putting him on edge. "Can you come over here? You're too far away." It pissed him off that he couldn't just get off the bed, grab her and throw her on it. He hated that he had that limitation.

It was times like this that frustrated him the most about being an amputee.

"I'm just a few feet away."

"Ellie," he growled.

She rolled her eyes and slowly approached the bed.

When she was within arm's length, he snagged her wrist and pulled her onto the bed. Before she could settle next to him, he rolled over her, pinning her onto her back.

"This seems serious," she whispered, her face holding worry.

He cupped her face. "It's not life or death, but it's important."

"Okay."

His lips pinned together with her submissive answer. "Don't ever feel that you can't speak out against me, El. It might turn into a disagreement, like I'm sure we're about to have, but we'll work it out."

"Okay."

"El..." He shook his head.

"Just tell me!" she snapped, her eyes narrowed on him.

He smiled. That was better. "I want to discuss the money."

She groaned. "I don't want it, it's not mine."

"It's yours. All of it. Or at least, what remains."

"Trace—"

She was interrupted by Mercy's ringtone again.

"What the fuck!" he growled, grabbing his phone and answering it. "Did you blow your load already?"

"Funny," Mercy growled back, not sounding amused at all. "But I fucking know you did. It wasn't hard to miss it since you yelped like a fucking injured coyote."

"Glad to be of some fucking service to you and Rissa, though. And you should be thanking us for making her want to ignore that ugly-assed puss of yours and jump your bones instead. You can buy me a beer."

"Not calling to thank you for getting my woman warmed up."

"Then why are you fucking interrupting us *again*?"

"Jewelee's in labor."

"You act like that's surprising."

Mercy actually snorted. "We're all going."

"All?" *Fuck.*

"Everyone who's available."

"We're in the middle of—"

"See you there." Mercy hung up.

"Fuck," Walker muttered and rolled off Ellie. "D's baby's coming. Gotta go to the hospital. Not sure why since Jewel's a pro at squirting out kids by now. I doubt she needs us to rally around her while coaching her to breathe."

Ellie sat up. "Do you want me to go with you?"

He hesitated on the edge of the bed, turning his head to look at her in surprise. "Do you want to?"

"Yes. If you're going there for support, then I want to be there with you."

"It might be boring and long."

"Maybe I'll get to meet some of the DAMC sisterhood there."

Oh, fuck. He wanted to keep his Ellie soft and sweet to a point. He wasn't sure if the sisterhood would change that. They were all very outspoken, independent women. And some of them could be bad influences when it came to listening to their men. He snorted, then warned her, "You might meet more than some."

"Do we have time for a shower?"

"I want to say yes, but being baby number three, I'm going to say no. While I said this might be long and boring, I'm hoping this kid slides out in five minutes. Then we can come back here and take our time while conserving water by showering together."

"I'll wash your back," she promised, climbing out of bed with a smirk. She grabbed his crutches out of the corner of the room and brought them to him.

"That's not what I had in mind, but it'll be a good start." He took the crutches from her. "By the way, this interruption doesn't mean that conversation is over."

"O—"

He cocked a brow at her.

She stuck her tongue out at him and headed to the spare bedroom where her luggage still was.

That needed to change and was another conversation they'd need to have when they got back. If not sooner.

Chapter Twenty

"It's dirty money," Ellie whispered. Though she wasn't sure why she did, besides the fact they were sitting in a room full of strangers—most of them she only met briefly—talking about a subject which they shouldn't be talking about. At least not right now.

"After all that shit, it's yours, Ellie."

"Let Gerald have it all."

"Sweetheart, McMaster doesn't need any more money. He's got plenty. You sold everything you had to try to pay off that asshole's debt. It's paid and then some. There's more."

"It should go back to the people he stole it from."

"El, he stole from people like him. Crooks. If you think I'm tracking down..." Walker blew out a breath and shook his head. "Think about your future."

"I *am* thinking about my future."

"Are you?"

"Yes."

"Am I in it?"

She twisted her head to glance at him sitting in the chair

next to her only to find him staring intently at her. "Do you want to be?"

"Kinda figured that was a given."

She figured that, too, that's why she was surprised he asked. Again, this wasn't a conversation they should be having in a packed hospital waiting room. She glanced around. "Is this normal?"

Trace barked out a laugh. "Yeah. And there's more waiting down in the lobby since there's no more room in here."

"Are we going to wait the whole time? Births usually take a while."

Yes, he had warned her, but she figured Jewel would be close to the end before everyone gathered. She found it impressive that this many people would want to be at the hospital for the whole birth.

"Unless you've already pushed out two massive watermelons. Then babies just start falling out when you cough."

Her lips twitched. It was hard to believe that only a day ago she thought she was going to die. And here she was, sitting next to the man she loved, ready to welcome new life into the world. What a crazy last couple of days. Actually month, since it all started with those texts of George the cartel sent. "I'm sure Diesel's wife would disagree."

"Ol' lady."

She twisted her head back toward him. "What?"

"Jewel is D's ol' lady, not his wife."

Her brow scrunched low. "Isn't this their third child?"

"Yeah."

"And he hasn't even married her?" she hissed, trying to keep her voice low. Last thing she needed right now was pissing off a bunch of bikers and their ol' ladies because they thought she was judging them.

She wasn't. That fact just caught her off guard.

"Sometimes that official shit isn't important. He claimed her years ago at the club's table."

"I'm sorry, what?" A man claimed a woman? Like property? "What does that mean?"

"He officially claimed her as his ol' lady in front of their executive committee, the committee voted, and the vote passed."

"That's just..." Archaic. "Weird."

Trace shrugged. "Cheaper than a wedding."

"But it's not the same." A wedding was two people professing their love and loyalty to each other. This "claiming" didn't sound anything similar.

"Same enough for them."

"But legally..."

"Right. Third kid about to be born. D needs to make it legal just for that reason."

"This ol' lady of his... Jewel... doesn't bug him about it?"

"No. And if she did, we'd hear it since she works with us. And she has no problem making her opinions known." Trace lifted a finger. "And loudly."

"Well, as long as they're happy, I guess." To each his own.

"They're happy."

"Not so sure she's happy at the moment."

He jerked his chin over to another stretch of occupied chairs lining one wall. Trace had introduced them as Diesel's parents, Ace and Janice. They waited with their two adorable granddaughters, Violet and Indigo. Vi was asleep in her grandfather's arms. Indie was out cold against her grandmother's shoulder. "See those girls?"

"Yes."

"They make Jewel happy."

"And Diesel?"

"Hard to believe he's a great father, but he's one of the best I've ever met."

Ellie agreed. The little she'd dealt with Diesel; it *was* hard to believe. "You had a great dad," she reminded him.

"Yeah," Trace said softly, his blue eyes met hers. "And even though you lost your father when you were young, Frank turned out to be a great stepfather."

That was true. She thought back on the conversation she had with her mother yesterday. "I need to visit them." Nothing like the threat of dying to make you appreciate the people who love you even more.

"Now you can. You're rich, sweetheart. You can take them on a vacation. Buy them a new house. Or set them up in an expensive assisted living facility where people will be at their beck and call. Whatever they need, you can provide it for them. If you don't want to think about yourself, think about them."

"There's nothing nice up there." She had already searched when she thought she and George could afford it since her stepfather hadn't wanted to move away from where he grew up himself.

"There's a nice one down here."

"Trace..."

"You still want kids?"

Okay, that was a sudden switch of topic. But then they *were* in a hospital waiting for a child to be born. "You told me my clock was ticking."

Trace smirked. "It is."

Ellie rolled her eyes at him. "Need to find a great man before I make him a great father."

"There's one of them down here, too."

"Give me his name, I'll look him up."

"Smart ass."

Ellie smiled. It was strange, even though they were sitting in a hospital she again realized how free she finally felt. She hadn't felt that way in a long time.

She should be exhausted from the last couple of days

she had. But coming to the hospital and seeing all the people cramming into the small room and even more in the hallways and lobby energized her.

It gave her a sense how tight this community of bikers, their women, their kids and even the Shadows were.

She'd never seen anything like it.

She hoped to be a part of it as well.

She also wondered if the waiting room would be just as busy if she was in the delivery room having Trace's son or daughter.

Trace was thirty-nine. She was almost thirty-seven.

Did she even want to consider having children at that age? She had put that dream aside over sixteen years ago because she didn't think having children with George would be smart.

Plus, she and Trace already had their children planned and their names picked out way before he enlisted. Having children with someone else wouldn't have felt right. Every time she had even considered having a baby, she could only picture the infant in Trace's arms, not George's. Was it wrong? Yes, and it had made her feel guilty. But she never could shake that feeling.

"Do you still want that?" she asked.

"Only with you."

She'd been good. She hadn't cried once after being released from the freezer. But now...

She rubbed away the sting in her eyes until Trace's deep voice whispered in her ear, "Tyler and Taylor."

A sob-hiccup came from nowhere and she covered her face, so she didn't start blubbering like an idiot. The birth of a baby was supposed to be a happy occasion and here she was sitting in the middle of strangers about to fall to pieces.

All because Trace mentioned the two names they had picked out for their own babies long before they had even had sex together for the first time.

Trace had said that Tyler, their son, would be their first born, so he could protect his baby sister, Taylor.

She and Trace had been such dreamers.

Her thoughts were interrupted when the big man named Diesel came lumbering down the hall wearing an ill-fitted gown over his clothes. All heads turned that way.

The man didn't smile. Nothing. He was totally expressionless. His eyes dark, the circles under them almost as dark. Not the normal look of a father with a healthy newborn, which made Ellie wonder if everything was okay with the mother and baby.

Her heart skipped a beat at how quiet everyone had become. As if the whole room held their collective breaths.

But as soon as he hit the room, his eyes slid through it and landed on his parents and his two girls. He immediately went over to them and picked his daughters up. They sleepily wrapped their arms around his thick neck and tucked their faces into it, too. Then, without a word, he headed back toward the hallway.

"D! Jesus. Don't leave us hanging," a deep male voice yelled out. Possibly Diesel's brother.

He stopped with his broad back to the room.

"Is Jewelee all right?" Janice asked, rushing up to him and grabbing a fistful of his paper gown.

He turned and glanced down at his much shorter mother. "Ended up doin' a C-section an' now workin' on tyin' her tubes."

She gave that handful of gown a shake. "She's good?"

"Yeah," he grunted.

"Baby's good?"

He only nodded. His face, which had been blank, began to twist. "Gotta go. Girls gotta see their sister."

At least now Ellie had a good excuse to be caught crying.

Then just like that, Diesel simply lumbered off with Janice quickly following on his heels.

The whole waiting room was quiet for another beat, then two. Until it seemed everyone finally took a breath before laughter started quietly and quickly moved through the room, becoming louder as it went.

"Another girl!" a male voice howled.

Ace pulled a large bag out from under his seat and began to hand out cigars, yelling, "'Nother fuckin' granddaughter. Ain't gonna complain about that!" He stopped in front of a larger man, who Trace had introduced as Hawk. "Guess it's up to you an' Keeks to have the boys."

Hawk took the cigar from his father and glanced down at the tall, voluptuous woman standing next to him. "Hear that, baby? Time to go home an' make another son. Looks like we need two more to even things out."

The woman named Kiki, a lawyer Trace had told her, made a face and smacked his arm. "Dream on, honey. I'm getting way too old to pop out more babies."

"Ain't never too old to work on makin' babies."

"Working on them and having them are—"

Kiki was interrupted as all eyes turned back to the hallway. Janice came barreling back into the room, her eyes alit and a big smile on her face. "First of all, since D didn't mention it, she's perfectly healthy and just... *hell*... perfect! And," she took a deep breath, and announced with a huge smile, "Jewel named her Scarlet."

A hoot went up in the corner as one of the men crowed, "Fuck yeah! I won the pool."

The bikers were taking bets on the baby? She shook her head but thought that was a hoot.

"Trace," she whispered, and she caught his gaze.

His blue eyes dropped to hers and her heart squeezed at the warm look in them. "Yeah, sweetheart?"

She pursed her lips as she studied his face. He was so

damn handsome. So smart. He'd grown into a great man. And he was so lucky to be a part of the huge family that surrounded them. "I want this."

"Want what?"

"All of it."

His eyes crinkled at the corners. "I'll talk to Z about claiming you as my ol' lady."

She rolled her eyes. "Not that!"

"Then what do you want?"

"You."

His expression turned serious. "You have me."

"Tyler and Taylor."

His throat worked for a moment, before he said, "I'll give you them."

"This, too."

"This?"

Her gaze circled the room and then came back to him. "All of this."

"I'll give you all of this, too. Whatever you want, El. Whatever you need, I'll give it to you." He tilted his head down as he studied her face. "Just saying, though. You're going to be filthy rich; you might not need me to give you anything. You'll be able to buy whatever you want."

"I don't want that blood money."

"And that's why you need to do something with it, El. McMaster's blood spilled for it, so don't let it go to waste. Put it to good use. And if you want to buy me a Lambo, I'm not going to say no."

Her eyebrows knitted together. "A Lambo?"

His eyes widened in feigned shock. "The car."

"Is it faster than your Dodge?" Because there was no way he was getting anything faster than the car he already had. No matter who was paying for it.

He needed to be around to be that great father for their future kids.

"Not really. Maybe a tad."

"Are you lying?" She must be overly tired. It took a few moments before it finally dawned on her what a "Lambo" was. A Lamborghini. She knew exactly how fast one of those went.

"Maybe a tad."

More than a tad. "Can you fit a car seat in it?"

"I can sure as hell try."

She shook her head. Her second wind was leaving her quickly. "Can we go home now that we know Jewel and the baby are good?"

"Yeah. I'll see the baby at the warehouse once D has her strapped to his chest as he's barking out orders." He captured her chin and locked his gaze with hers. "Need a promise from you first."

"What?"

"We always discuss any major decisions before we make them. We don't do anything crazy without the other knowing."

"I'd agree with that, but what about your job?"

"Job? I thought I was going to be a kept man," he teased, then said, "My job will be an exception, most assignments we do I won't be able to discuss with you before, during or after. That's just something you'll have to trust me on. And none of them should affect us."

"Us," she repeated softly.

"Us, Ellie. Took fucking forever, but we're finally an 'us.'"

"I'm sorry."

"We're done with sorries, too. Remember what I said? You can lie down and give up, or you can rise and keep going. We both gave up and were down for a long time. Now it's time to rise and not only face our future but create it."

"I like the sound of that."

"I also like the sound of 'let's go home.'"

He wrapped an arm around her shoulders and kept it there as they said their goodbyes.

And they went home to begin the future they'd always planned. They just didn't realize it would happen later than sooner.

But she was sure Trace would agree, they would make it worth the wait.

She couldn't wait to see what the future held for them both.

Epilogue

Three years later

If Walker could be any more fucking content, he didn't know how.

The summer heat had been chased away by the night and the sky was so clear that the stars seemed endless. As they lay there in the back of his Ford pickup on a pile of blankets, they'd even spotted a shooting star.

It was like they'd stepped over twenty-two years back in time with the way the crickets chirped, owls hooted in the distance and how the big moon reflected off the still lake.

The dark cloud that had hung over Ellie's head was now a distant memory and the sun was shining on their future. The future they were building together.

They were back north in their hometown to move her mother and stepfather down to Shadow Valley. It took her a while to convince them to move closer and they finally admitted they were getting to the point they shouldn't live on their own. Though her mom's excuse was, not that they were getting too old, but they'd be close by when their second grandchild was born.

Ellie was only starting to show but was definitely filling out. Enough that he noticed it even if no one else did. Enough for her to complain that her clothes were getting tight. Which he didn't mind one fucking bit.

He loved when she carried their first child. In fact, he couldn't stop touching her. And not just her belly, either. Luckily, she also couldn't stop touching him. Pregnancy seemed to make her even hornier than usual. Seeing her pregnant did it for him, too. Not that he needed any fucking help in that department.

He grinned up at the night sky. If they hadn't already agreed to stop after two, he'd plan on knocking her up again as soon as it was possible. Someone had to give Diesel a run for his money when it came to a family brood. Though, he wouldn't be surprised if Hunter and Frankie had a third soon. Especially since number two for them was a boy and Frankie had been hoping for a girl.

He hoped this time the baby Ellie was carrying was a boy. His plan to have a son first didn't work out. Instead Taylor Adelaide Walker was the first one to come screaming at the top of her lungs into the world, looking just like her daddy with blonde hair and blue eyes. She was already a handful which didn't bode well for them in the future.

Since she insisted on being born first, Walker guessed he'd have to teach her how to protect her little brother when he joined them.

It better be a boy. Otherwise, they were trying again. And he hoped like hell, not to be in Diesel's shoes with four females in his household. Walker swore D's hair was getting thin from him pulling it out.

That was because the boss man's little Angels were anything but. Between their momma and daddy's genes, they were outspoken, sassy-mouthed rebels. He pitied the men who tried to tame them.

Hell, he also pitied the boys who tried to date them.

Diesel might not have any of that. No man wanted a taste of those sledgehammer-like fists that had DIRTY tattooed on the fingers of one hand, ANGEL tattooed on the fingers of the other.

But then Walker was sure he'd have a lot to say when Taylor was ready to start dating, too.

If he allowed her to date at all.

He wrapped his arm tighter around Ellie's shoulder and pulled her closer against his side. She rolled her cheek along his shoulder and kissed his bare skin.

"Cold?" he asked her, dipping his chin to check out her naked body bathed in the moonlight.

"No. It's perfect."

She was the one who was fucking perfect.

And to know his son was in her belly at that moment made him want to fucking fall to his knees and thank his lucky stars. He sucked in a breath of night air to keep his emotions under control.

Life had gone full circle. It took them a while to complete that circle, but they finally did.

Ellie was always telling him that things happened for a reason. He hoped to fuck there was a good reason why they were forced to wait to find their happiness.

But they'd made the best out of their situation. Especially Ellie. He'd finally convinced her to take the money, especially after she found out about Gerald McMaster's untimely death. She had insisted if she did take it, she'd do something good with it.

She damn well did. And he was so fucking proud of her.

After losing a huge chunk of it in taxes, she took the remainder and started a charitable foundation for amputees, which provided prosthetic care for those who couldn't afford it. It was growing like crazy because the need was high, and she was hiring disabled vets to help her. It not only kept her busy, but Frankie, too.

The two women who originally wanted to go to culinary school found a new calling. Though, they did spend plenty of time with Sophie and Bella at Sophie's Sweet Treats learning to bake a lot of fattening baked goods for the charity's fundraisers.

Even the DAMC got involved in doing poker runs and other club events to help raise money.

Everyone, between the MC and the Shadows, continued to do their part to help out. Even Axel, now the president of the Blue Avengers MC, got his club of law enforcement officers involved.

It was a great cause that, of course, hit home for Walker. He was lucky he could afford what he needed as an amputee; whether it be care, prostheses, or the rest, because there were so many people out there who couldn't. Vets or otherwise.

And the most heartbreaking were the children in need. Ellie bent over backwards to help them. Even his fellow Shadows and the DAMC members had dug deep into their own pockets to help a child get what he or she needed. Crutches, a wheelchair or even a prosthetic limb.

So, fuck yes, he couldn't be prouder of Ellie and her mission. As well as her skills and determination to make the foundation a success.

He pressed his lips to her forehead, his other hand sliding over the curve of her belly and settling there. "You were put on this Earth for me, El. The day you were born, our path was set. It might not have been direct, but we still made our final destination." Her hand covered his on her belly and he intertwined their fingers, giving them a squeeze. "I waited almost three years for you to be born. I waited sixteen years to meet you. I waited eighteen until I made you mine. It took over twenty-two years to return to our spot in this truck, which I always considered our little slice of heaven. Every time we lay in the back of this truck, looking up at the night sky, I got a peek of our future. And now it's here. Our dream is finally our reality."

"Trace," she whispered, her voice thick. "You're going to make me cry."

"Sweetheart, you cry constantly."

"I know, so don't make it worse."

He sighed loudly, pretending to be annoyed. "I figured you'd want to hear what I had to say."

She giggle-snorted. "I do, but I won't be able to hear you if I start blubbering out of control. I'll scare away the wildlife. Possibly even that lion."

He chuckled. "You'll never scare your lion away. And at least you'll be crying because you're happy."

"Right now I cry over a spilled drop of water, remember?"

"Isn't that the damned truth," he grumbled.

She huffed. "Well, there went *that* romantic moment."

"It wasn't meant to be romantic; it was meant to be real."

"Honey, I have no doubt this is all real." She was quiet for a long moment. "I can't believe you kept this truck."

"I kept it for this exact moment. Though, for what seemed like a lifetime, I never thought it would come."

She gripped his fingers tighter. "Took a while, but it did."

"Thank fuck it did," he murmured.

"By the way, I found that great man who became a great father."

Walker pressed his lips to her temple, closed his eyes and just let those words sweep through him. "You only make me better, El."

"Isn't that what a lioness is supposed to do for her mate?" she teased.

He growled low and rolled over her, straddling her hips

and playfully biting her lower lip. "This lion is hungry again."

"Then you better hurry up before our ferocious cub wakes up for her nightly feeding."

"Do you really want me to hurry?"

"No, we've got the rest of our lives."

He brushed his lips over Ellie's. "That we do."

———

**Turn the page to read a sneak peek of
Guts & Glory: Steel (In the Shadows Security,
Book 5)**

———

**Sign up for Jeanne's newsletter to keep up with
book news and upcoming releases:
http://www.jeannestjames.com/newslettersignup**

Guts & Glory: Steel

**Turn the page for a sneak peek of
Guts & Glory: Steel
(In the Shadows Security, Book 5)**

Sneak peak of Guts & Glory: Steel

Strength is what we gain from the madness we survive.

Chapter One

STEEL PULLED the toothpick out of his mouth and flicked it across the bar at Moose to get his attention. "Who's the new girl?"

Moose straightened up from behind the bar and narrowed his eyes on Steel. "Why?"

"Because maybe I want a motherfucking lap dance, that's why."

The manager of Heaven's Angels Gentlemen's Club barked out a laugh. "You're too motherfuckin' cheap to pay for a lap dance."

Steel twisted his neck to look at the woman on the stage who was working the pole like a fucking pro gymnast. And looked like one, too. A lot of guys didn't like a muscular woman, but that just left more for him. Because it no fucking doubt did it for him.

He wasn't like his veteran brothers and fellow Shadows, who went for the softer, curvy, cuddly type. Fuck no.

Though he had to admit, their women had some great tits.

But then, so did the woman who worked the men who sat along the stage, encouraging them to tuck their last dollar into her G-string. Though, Steel doubted her tits were real.

Didn't matter. He'd still let her crush his cock with those thighs. Or those implants.

He liked when women had enough muscles to crack a walnut. Or his balls. And with strength came endurance, meaning they could ride him for a long time, while he just sat back and enjoyed the show.

He grinned. "Give me another fucking toothpick."

Steel could hear Moose's sigh, even over the loud music which was rocking the joint. The big biker threw a box of toothpicks onto the bar in front of Steel. "That box has your fuckin' name on it. No one in this decade, except assholes, chews on fuckin' toothpicks."

Steel gave Moose the finger, while saying, "Chew on this." He tucked a fresh pick into his mouth and slid the box across the bar top toward the Dirty Angels MC member. Moose didn't need to know the reason for his habit.

One of the servers stopped in front of him, blocking his view of Moose. That didn't matter, either, since Tawny was much prettier than Moose. And she wore a tight leather corset, not a leather cut. *And* had a bottle opener tucked between her generous cleavage.

"Hey, honey. Haven't seen you around in a while."

"Been busy." He leaned over the bar, so she was sure to hear him. "Hey, who's the new girl?"

Tawny's eyes slid over to the stage and back to Steel. "Why?"

Steel sat back, shaking his head. "Really?"

Tawny raised her tawny eyebrows at him. "Yeah, really."

Steel swore he heard Moose laughing behind her. He

frowned. "Get me a beer."

"Please," Tawny added.

"Last I checked, Tawny, you're a fucking server. Your customer shouldn't have to say please for you to *serve* them."

"You might not have been here in a while, Steel, but I see you haven't changed. You're still an asshole."

"Can't expect miracles."

Tawny leaned over the bar giving him a good view of her tits. "Her name is Cherry. And I hope she makes you swallow your own fucking dick. Get your own goddamn beer." She stomped away on her four-inch heels.

"You hear that?" he asked Moose, who was now leaning back against the counter, his thick, tattooed arms crossed over his chest, a huge smile on his bearded face. The man was a big boy. Not only tall, but almost half as wide.

"Heard it."

"Well?"

"Well what? I agree with everything she fuckin' said."

"Great customer service," Steel grumbled.

"You get a pass here, Steel, only 'cause of who you are. That's the *only* fuckin' reason. Now, if you really wanna pay for a lap dance, Cherry ain't cheap. She's got skills that're worth every fuckin' penny. Got me?"

"Got you. How much?"

"Fifty for fifteen. But that fifteen will be good enough to make you blow your load."

Steel whistled low, yanked his wallet out of his back pocket and threw the money at Moose. The biker grabbed it, jerked his chin up at one of the DAMC prospects working as a bouncer and then pointed at Cherry.

The prospect did an answering chin lift and moved off.

"VIP Red Room. Fifteen minutes. Make sure you tip her well."

Steel grinned and slid off the stool.

But Moose wasn't done yet. "You know the rules. No

fucking touchin', Steel. Or will have one of the prospects toss you the fuck out an' then all you did was blow your fifty."

One of those young prospects wouldn't be enough. "Just want to inquire about her workout routine," he tossed over his shoulder with a wink as he headed toward the private rooms at the back of the strip club.

Ten minutes later, he was staring at Cherry's bullet proof ass as it was bent over in front of him and she was shaking it. It hardly wiggled.

No surprise his cock was as hard as her ass.

But it was the way her muscles flexed that got him off the most. And when she turned and climbed onto his lap...

Yeah.

Maybe he wasn't allowed to touch her, but nothing stopped the *ladies* from touching their customers. It was their choice and apparently Cherry saw something she liked.

The only thing she still wore was a thong, which was no more than a string up her ass and over her hips, and obscenely high heels.

As she ground down against his cock, he groaned, then was surprised when she shoved his face into her tits with a hand to the back of his head.

Yeah, maybe this was worth fifty bucks. She was definitely getting a tip.

"You want the extra special?" she asked, her voice husky.

The extra special?

He pulled his head away from her tits, dropped his gaze to her crotch and then closed his eyes, his heart racing.

For fuck's sake, don't tell me she has a dick.

Don't have a dick.

Don't have a fucking dick.

"Are you tucking?"

Cherry stopped grinding against him. "What?"

284

"Are you tucking your dick?" His voice might have cracked when he asked that.

"My dick?" she repeated with her eyebrows now dropped low and pinned together.

"Is that the extra special? You having a dick?"

Cherry jumped off his lap and before he could stop her, slammed both palms into his shoulders, knocking both him and the chair backward. He hit the ground hard, his head bouncing off the floor with a grunt.

"You asshole!" she screeched, picked up her scraps of clothing and flung open the door. "He's an asshole!" she screamed at the prospect who had been standing outside the door.

"Fuck," Steel muttered, untangling himself from the chair.

He heard a snicker and saw the prospect's head quickly disappear from the open doorway.

Just as he got to his feet, his cell phone buzzed in his back pocket. He pulled it out and saw it was a text from Diesel. Did Moose call the big man already about what just happened? There was no way.

Fuck.

He opened the text. It was typical D. Short and to the point.

Here. Now.

He assumed "here" was the warehouse and "now" was non-negotiable.

It was close to nine o'clock. It was late for the boss man to be working, so it had to be important.

———

"Moose ain't happy with you, asshole."

"That's why I'm here?"

"Fuck no."

"So, does Cherry have a dick?"

"How the fuck do I know if the fuckin' bitch has a dick? Got three kids an' an ol' lady, you think I got fuckin' time to watch snatch swing around a goddamn pole? Then I got you six to deal with. Always tryin' to fuckin' take work on for fuckin' free. Like we're a fuckin' charity. Well, we ain't."

"Okay then, why am I here?"

"'Cause a payin' job fell into my fuckin' lap an' I'm assignin' it to you."

Steel sat up straighter in the chair in front of D's desk. Or what should be D's desk. It was covered in loose crayons, rag dolls and a couple stray pacifiers. "What kind of job?" Steel hesitated and wrinkled his nose at the sudden stink. "Did you shit yourself?"

"Fuck," D muttered and lifted a month-old sleeping Scarlet up to his nose. "Fuck."

"There's got to be a clean diaper in this mess somewhere," Steel said, glancing around the office that was jam-packed with baby and toddler shit.

"You wanna change her?"

Steel's eyes snapped back to Diesel's. "No fucking way."

When Violet was born, D wouldn't let anyone touch her. Now at kid number three, he wasn't so worried. In fact, he might even hand her over to a stranger just for a diaper change.

He didn't blame the big man. The moment changing shitty diapers was added to his job duties, Steel was out. "Where's Jewelee?"

"Home. Tryin' to get some fuckin' sleep."

"Well, now what?"

"Fuck," D muttered again, hauling his big body out of his office chair and handing a stinky Scarlet off to Steel.

"I don't want her!"

"Just hold her 'til I find a fuckin' diaper."

Steel held the baby as far away from him as possible.

"Like ya, kid. But not when you've crapped your pants."

Diesel looked like The Hulk smashing up a city as he dug through shit on the floor searching for a diaper.

"Didn't you bring a diaper bag along?" Steel bit back his laugh at picturing D with a pink diaper bag hanging over his bulky tattooed arm.

"Fuckin' forgot."

Steel smirked. "That'll teach you."

D grunted and kept digging. Finally, he found an open box of diapers, snagged one and after pushing shit off his desk—Steel had to turn away, so he didn't gag—D cleaned up his girl and changed her, all while muttering curses.

When he was done and after he settled himself and Scarlet back into his chair, he got back to business like the big badass behind the desk hadn't just wiped a baby's ass.

"Got a call from a guy—"

"A guy?"

Diesel cocked a brow at him.

"I'll shut up."

"Don't think you fuckin' can," Diesel grumbled. "Got a call from a guy 'bout doin' some personal security for a girl."

"A girl?"

Diesel gave him a look and Steel raised his palms. "Go on."

"Girl's got a stalker. Can't shake 'im. Guy doesn't know who it is. Got the pigs involved an' nothin' so far. Worried she's gonna get hurt or takin' out. Guy's her manager."

"For what?"

"She's an athlete or some such shit. Who fuckin' cares? Payin' good. Will put a nice chunk of scratch in your fuckin' pocket for more lap dances by chicks with dicks."

"So, she does have a dick?"

D closed his eyes and shook his head like he was trying not to go into beast-mode.

Steel thought it was smart to let that subject drop. "Do I

need to find the stalker?"

"No. Just protect 'er 'til the pigs do their job."

"Which means, we don't know how long this will take," he muttered.

"Fuck no. That's why I'm sendin' you instead of any of the others. Got no ball an' chain. Can stay until it's over or they run out of scratch."

"Brick," Steel suggested. *Fuck*, him and Brick were the only single ones left out of the crew.

"You turnin' down the job? Don't even answer that. You ain't turnin' down the job 'cause you're assigned to the fuckin' job. Don't like it? There's the fuckin' door."

Steel sat back and grinned, knowing D was just blowing smoke up his ass. His team was good and worked well together, he wasn't going to break it up just because someone turned down a job.

"Lucky for you, she's a fuckin' gym rat. You'll be able to work out while you watch her."

Steel's ears perked up.

"Figured you'd like that," D grumbled.

"Where's this job at?"

"Where you want it to be?"

Steel tilted his head. "Hawaii would be good."

"Well, fuck then, it's your lucky fuckin' day."

Steel's head popped up. "The job's in Hawaii?"

Diesel gave him a look. "Yeah. On the tropical island of Las Vegas. Lots of fuckin' sand for you out there. Can work on your fuckin' tan."

Steel lifted a shoulder, thinking about the possibilities. "Vegas ain't bad."

"I say Vegas? Sorry to get your fuckin' dick hard. Meant twenty-somethin' miles outside of it. Boulder City."

"So, what you're saying is, I'm gonna be sweating my balls off."

"You got balls?"

"Of steel," Steel reminded him. "Hence, my name."

Diesel grunted and shook his head.

"Is it twenty-four-seven? Or am I getting help?"

"You're it. Unless you don't think you can handle babysittin' one girl."

"I can handle it."

"Show up at a place called The Strike Zone an' ask for Peter Berger. He's her manager. He'll give you more details when you get there."

"And when am I getting there?"

D grunted, "Yesterday."

"Fuck."

"Goin' the fuck home now. Soon as Jewelee's up to feed Scarlet, gonna have her get you on the next available flight an' email you that shit, got me?"

Steel nodded. "Got you. Least I'll be close to the Strip."

"Don't be draggin' the girl to your underground fights, asshole. You'll leave her scarred for life. This is a payin' job, not a vacation. Need to stay on her twenty-four-seven."

The boss man knew him too well. "Twenty-four-seven. Roger that."

D shook his head and stood up from the chair, careful not to wake the sleeping baby. "Now, get gone. Gotta get home before she starts cryin' for Jewelee's tit."

Steel opened his mouth to make a joke, thought better of it and closed it instead. Beside Slade, he was one of the best fighters in the area. But he was sure fucking glad he never had to go against D in the ring. The man might not float like a butterfly, but he could sting like a fucking sledgehammer.

And joking about the boss man's ol' lady's tits might warrant a not-so-gentle *boop* from D's fist.

**Get Steel and Kat's story here:
mybook.to/Shadows-Steel**

289

If You Enjoyed This Book

Thank you for reading Guts & Glory: Walker. If you enjoyed Walker and Ellie's story, please consider leaving a review at your favorite retailer and/or Goodreads to let other readers know. Reviews are always appreciated and just a few words can help an independent author like me tremendously!

Want to read a sample of my work? Download a sampler book here: BookHip.com/MTQQKK

Also by Jeanne St. James

Find my complete reading order here:
https://www.jeannestjames.com/reading-order

* Available in Audiobook

Stand-alone Books:

Made Maleen: A Modern Twist on a Fairy Tale *

Damaged *

Rip Cord: The Complete Trilogy *

Everything About You (A Second Chance Gay Romance) *

Reigniting Chase (An M/M Standalone)

Brothers in Blue Series:

Brothers in Blue: Max *

Brothers in Blue: Marc *

Brothers in Blue: Matt *

Teddy: A Brothers in Blue Novelette *

Brothers in Blue: A Bryson Family Christmas *

The Dare Ménage Series:

Double Dare *

Daring Proposal *

Dare to Be Three *

A Daring Desire *

Dare to Surrender *

A Daring Journey *

The Obsessed Novellas:

Forever Him *

Only Him *

Needing Him *

Loving Her *

Tempting Him *

Down & Dirty: Dirty Angels MC Series®:

Down & Dirty: Zak *

Down & Dirty: Jag *

Down & Dirty: Hawk *

Down & Dirty: Diesel *

Down & Dirty: Axel *

Down & Dirty: Slade *

Down & Dirty: Dawg *

Down & Dirty: Dex *

Down & Dirty: Linc *

Down & Dirty: Crow *

Crossing the Line (A DAMC/Blue Avengers MC Crossover) *

Magnum: A Dark Knights MC/Dirty Angels MC Crossover *

Crash: A Dirty Angels MC/Blood Fury MC Crossover *

Guts & Glory Series:

(In the Shadows Security)

Guts & Glory: Mercy *

Guts & Glory: Ryder *

Guts & Glory: Hunter *

Guts & Glory: Walker *

Guts & Glory: Steel *

Guts & Glory: Brick *

Blood & Bones: Blood Fury MC®:

Blood & Bones: Trip *

Blood & Bones: Sig *

Blood & Bones: Judge *

Blood & Bones: Deacon *

Blood & Bones: Cage *

Blood & Bones: Shade *

Blood & Bones: Rook *

Blood & Bones: Rev *

Blood & Bones: Ozzy

Blood & Bones: Dodge

Blood & Bones: Whip

Blood & Bones: Easy

Beyond the Badge: Blue Avengers MC™:

Beyond the Badge: Fletch

Beyond the Badge: Finn

Beyond the Badge: Decker

Beyond the Badge: Rez

Beyond the Badge: Crew

Beyond the Badge: Nox

COMING SOON!

Double D Ranch (An MMF Ménage Series)

Dirty Angels MC: The Next Generation

About the Author

JEANNE ST. JAMES is a USA Today bestselling romance author who loves an alpha male (or two). She was only thirteen when she started writing and her first paid published piece was an erotic story in Playgirl magazine. Her first romance novel, Banged Up, was published in 2009. She is happily owned by farting French bulldogs. She writes M/F, M/M, and M/M/F ménages.

Want to read a sample of her work? Download a sampler book here: BookHip.com/MTQQKK

To keep up with her busy release schedule check her website at www.jeannestjames.com or sign up for her newsletter: http://www.jeannestjames.com/newslettersignup

www.jeannestjames.com
jeanne@jeannestjames.com

Newsletter: http://www.jeannestjames.com/newslettersignup
Jeanne's Down & Dirty Book Crew: https://www.facebook.com/groups/JeannesReviewCrew/
TikTok: https://www.tiktok.com/@jeannestjames

facebook.com/JeanneStJamesAuthor

amazon.com/author/jeannestjames

instagram.com/JeanneStJames

bookbub.com/authors/jeanne-st-james

goodreads.com/JeanneStJames

pinterest.com/JeanneStJames

Get a FREE Erotic Romance Sampler Book

This book contains the first chapter of a variety of my books. This will give you a taste of the type of books I write and if you enjoy the first chapter, I hope you'll be interested in reading the rest of the book.

Each book I list in the sampler will include the description of the book, the genre, and the first chapter, along with links to find out more. I hope you find a book you will enjoy curling up with!

Get it here: BookHip.com/MTQQKK

Printed in Great Britain
by Amazon

17329335R00176